THE SUBSTITUTE COUNTESS

Lyn Stone

First published in Great Britain 2013
by Mills & Boon, an imprint of Harlequin (UK) Limited.
Harlequin (UK) Limited, Eton House, 18-24 Paradise Road,
Richmond, Surrey TW9 1SR

© Lynda Stone 2013

ISBN: 978 0 263 89831 6

Harlequin (UK) policy is to use papers that are natural, renewable and recyclable products and made from wood grown in sustainable forests. The logging and manufacturing process conform to the legal environmental regulations of the country of origin.

Printed and bound in Spain
by Blackprint CPI, Barcelona

A painter of historical events, **Lyn Stone** decided to write about them. A canvas, however detailed, limits characters to only one moment in time. 'If a picture's worth a thousand words, the other ninety thousand have to show up somewhere!' An avid reader, she admits, 'At thirteen, I fell in love with Emily Brontë's Heathcliff and became Catherine. Next year I fell for Rhett and became Scarlett. Then I fell for the hero I'd known most of my life and finally became myself.'

After living for four years in Europe, Lyn and her husband, Allen, settled into a log house in north Alabama that is crammed to the rafters with antiques, artefacts and the stuff of future tales.

A previous novel by the same author:

THE CAPTAIN AND THE WALLFLOWER

And in Mills & Boon® Historical *Undone!* eBooks:

THE WIDOW AND THE RAKE

Did you know that some of these novels are also available as eBooks? Visit www.millsandboon.co.uk

This book is for my brother and sister by marriage,
Irene and Charles Stone.
You two are great inspiration for writing love stories
because yours is so enduring.
I treasure the love, humour and camaraderie
we have shared over the years.

Chapter One

London
September, 1818

Jackson Worth tugged at his new neckcloth with an impatient finger. The damned thing choked him, its starch irritating his recently shaved throat. His newly acquired title chafed even more. He stood and began to pace.

What was he to do with an earldom that came with nothing but ominous responsibilities and no wealth to support them? Damn it all, he liked his life the way it was, with only himself to manage. Most of the time, that went rather well, and when it didn't, only *he* suffered the consequences.

Jack winced when he realized that was too

much like his father's outlook had been. Frustrated by the very thought, he sat down again and began tapping on the smooth wooden arms of the chair.

"You're certain there's no one else in line for it?" he asked Mr. Hobson, who sat behind the solicitor's desk. "I cannot afford this, you know. Every penny I owned, other than what is in my pocket at present, was tied up in my last shipping venture." A disaster, as he had just explained. He'd had a few of those, but one lived and learned. Nothing risked, nothing gained—that was his motto. Rather, it *had been* his motto.

His only ship was lost, the insurance gone to pay survivors of the crew and his investors. Devil take it, he should have captained the damn thing himself. He would recoup, of course. He had done it before, but it would take time, travel and energy. Those were three things an earl would not be able to spare while keeping a sizable estate running and its people in check and well fed.

The solicitor smiled as he laid a page of the document on the desk and turned it so that Jack could see the content. "Rest assured, there has been a thorough investigation, sir. The former Earl of Elderidge instigated the search for a male heir before he died. Your lineage is well documented through church records, proof that your father and the late earl shared a great-great-grandfather who was fourth Earl of Elderidge."

"No one ever informed *me* of this," Jack grumbled.

"The connection was rather remote. Perhaps your father thought it of no significance. You were abroad when I finally located your mother's lodgings in Plymouth—hence the message left there for you to contact me as soon as you arrived in England."

"Had I known, I might have stayed in Amsterdam," Jack muttered.

"A petition was offered on your behalf and the lords have already met. Letters of patent have been issued. You should be gazetted soon. The title and all that it entails are yours without question."

"Mine, eh?" Jack sighed with resignation as he shifted in his chair. "With no funds to run the estate. So what did Elderidge do with his fortune? Gamble it away?"

"No," the solicitor answered. "He willed it to his daughter." A sly grin lifted the old man's prodigious mustache. "Your very distant cousin, Lady Laurel, the earl's only child."

Hobson sat back in his chair and fingered his mustache thoughtfully. "If I might suggest it, you should retrieve the girl from the convent where his lordship placed her, woo and wed her, and thereby solve your problem as well as hers."

"A convent? The earl was Catholic? Is that not impossible?" Not that he cared. Jack asked only to delay long enough to consider the idea just proposed.

He had not thought to marry, especially not for money. Or even love, for that matter. He enjoyed the freedom to travel, do what he liked, whenever he liked, with whomever he liked, without any permanent ties. However, push had come to shove in a most disconcerting way. He might have to entertain the thought.

Mr. Hobson shook his head. "The earl was Church of England, of course. But his first wife was Catholic."

His voice dropped to a near whisper. "She was a cyprian, as well, and his first mistress."

Well, that brought Jack's eyebrows up. "You don't say!"

Hobson nodded. "One of the fashionably impure he got with child. He eloped with her. An outrage it was, too! She died giving birth and the earl remarried within the year. His new wife, a choice more suitable, wanted nothing to do with the baby born of his misalliance, so he placed it with the Sisters at Our Lady of Cambre, near the coast of Spain."

"Why Spain, of all places?" Jack was intrigued. He, born of a naval officer and a merchant's daughter, could hardly imagine life as a noble. Yet he simply could not understand how a man of any station could simply give up his firstborn and relegate her to a foreign country to be brought up by strangers. And leave her there while war raged around her.

Hobson continued, explaining the situation. "Lord Elderidge had visited Spain as a young man on his grand tour, I believe. There are a number of English convents there, set up after they were disbanded here centuries ago. English Catholics often send their daughters away to convent schools. In any event, she was sent to the Sisters of Cambre as an infant and they were provided generous contributions for her care. No doubt the earl believed the girl would take vows when she reached the proper age."

"So he died, the money stopped and the nuns gave her the boot?" Jack asked, interested in spite of himself.

Hobson shrugged. "She could have remained as a novitiate but I was informed on her last progress report that the young lady had elected to take a position as governess instead," Hobson explained.

"I'm surprised they would allow a lady to accept work, given who she is."

"The nuns never knew his lordship's station in life."

"Her father didn't visit her?"

"She and the earl never met, save when she was a babe in arms, too young to know him. You must understand the circumstances then, sir. Elderidge had not yet inherited. He was highly pressured by his father, the earl, his new wife and his peers. Everyone wanted the entire fiasco forgotten. The child would have been a constant reminder."

Jack rubbed his forehead and gave a huff of disbelief. "Still, it was an unconscionable thing to do, depriving her of all privileges she would have enjoyed as his daughter."

Hobson agreed with a slow nod. "Just so, but he also spared her the disdain she would have endured because of her mother's reputation. And he did bequeath every farthing he inherited and later amassed to her and her alone."

"What of his second wife?" Jack asked.

"The dowager countess has her widow's portion, of course, which was basically what she brought to the marriage. But the daughter's inheritance is considerable, more than sufficient to see that the estate *you* have inherited will prosper. In fact, more than you and she together could ever spend."

The solicitor folded his hands on the desktop as he leaned forward. "It is up to you to make things right for the young lady."

"By marrying her and stealing the only compensation afforded her by the old blackguard who gave her away? That should earn me a proper place in hell."

Hobson pressed his lips together in a grimace before replying, "Better you should dread hell than for her to endure it presently, sir. Your only alternative is to leave her introduction to England to the mercy of the woman who ordered her evacuation from the earl's life when she was but a helpless infant. Make the girl a countess, as is her due, and manage her funds to best advantage. You both will benefit. It's the right thing to do. Surely you see that."

He pushed a leather folder across the desk. "Here is the location of the estate, the house here in town and travel funds. Two hundred pounds from her account should be sufficient to see you there and back with the heiress."

"Me? Why must *I* fetch her home?"

"Who better?" Hobson smiled. "You should go there, court and wed her before she reaches England." He added, "She will surely prove reluctant to marry you if you wait until she learns of her worth and realizes that your design is upon her fortune instead of her person. I doubt she would agree then that the marriage would be for her own good."

Jack stood, squaring his shoulders. "What if I decline all? The earldom, estate and the marriage of convenience?"

Hobson stood as well, his face grave now. "By law, you cannot refuse the title. I strongly suggest you make the best of it, serve your country and meet your obligations. Those employed at Elderidge House and on its lands, as well as the staff here in Town, are now dependent upon you for their living...*my lord*." He reached down and pushed the leather folder closer to Jack. "And so is our young Lady Laurel."

Jack accepted the money, hefting the flat purse in his hand before tucking it away in his breast pocket.

Most men would leap at the chance. Why shouldn't he? He had the impoverished earldom, and marriage to the heiress would ensure a secure future. No more risky ventures.

No further scrabbling about for investors. Jack was no fool. "Her direction?"

"Written down for you in the folder."

Jack shrugged. "The least I can do is release the poor girl from service and bring her home to England."

Mr. Hobson smiled with satisfaction. "You might keep foremost in your mind, sir, that she is not a *poor* girl, but a ready means to your salvation."

All right, maybe he needed saving. He would go and take a look, see if this rich little lady and her wealth could do the impossible.

"Take your hands off me!" Laurel shouted. She raised her sturdy walking shoe and stomped on the lecher's foot. He cursed roundly and hopped backward while Laurel swept around to the far side of his writing desk. Now he stood crouched between her and the door, clenching his beefy hands, his piggy black eyes narrowed, daring her to try to escape.

She shook her fist at him. "You are no better than your sons! They don't need a governess, sir. They could use a strict minder with a stout cane and so could you!"

He straightened and grinned his oily grin.

"Usted sabe que usted esta en mi misericordia!"

"I am at no man's mercy, sir! Certainly not yours!"

The door opened and the housekeeper stood there wide-eyed, looking from one to the other. "Señor Orencio?"

A large man pushed past the woman before she could announce him and approached Orencio, towering over him. "I have come for Miss Laurel Worth." He turned to Laurel. "Are you she?"

She nodded once, astounded. The man knew her name.

"Pack your things and make haste. Your presence in England is required."

"England?" she asked in a whisper.

"Aye, as soon as may be. The ship's waiting," he replied, his piercing gaze returning to Orencio, who must have understood some unspoken command. Her employer backed away enough to allow Laurel to pass between him and the stranger and leave the room.

She ran upstairs and quickly stuffed her few belongings into the small carpetbag she had brought with her. Her hair was mussed and her sleeve torn, but she took no time to repair either, lest her one chance at getting away should change his mind and leave without her. In minutes, she was back in the foyer, just outside the door of Orencio's library. She clutched her bag and shifted nervously from one foot to the other.

Who in the world was this new arrival and who had sent him? He knew who she was and that she came from England. At the moment she would accept help from the devil himself to get away from Orencio's hacienda.

The man was obviously English, disturbingly handsome and well dressed. Also very, very angry. She hoped that his anger was on her behalf because he had overheard her exchange with Orencio. She shuddered to think that was his usual demeanor. Even were that so, she was going with him.

The gentleman in question stormed out of the library just then. "Come," he snapped as he marched to the front door, opened it and threw it wide. He didn't wait to see whether she followed, but strode right out. Laurel ran to catch up.

"Where are you taking me?" she asked breathlessly as he yanked the bag from her grasp, caught her up by the waist and deposited her upon the seat of the open carriage.

"I told you. To the coast. Then on to England."

He tossed in her bag and climbed up to sit beside her. With a click of his tongue and slap of the reins, they were off.

"Please explain!" Laurel demanded, almost as frightened of him as of Orencio, whom she had been fending off successfully for over a week. "How do you know me?"

He passed the reins to one hand and with the other took a letter from inside his coat. "Read it."

She broke open the seal and read the contents. It was from Mr. Hobson, the solicitor in London who had been sending money on behalf of her father all these years. He had visited her twice to ascertain her health and progress at school. Never once had he mentioned her returning to England. Until now.

"This says you are Jackson Worth, Earl of Elderidge!" She stared at him. "An *earl?*"

"Aye." He visibly drew in a deep breath and released it slowly. "I apologize for my gruffness. In fact, I apologize for the entire male gender. You must be horribly overset and I've only added to your misery."

Laurel refolded the letter and held it crumpled in both hands. "At the moment, more stunned than overset, sir...my lord."

"*Jack* will do," he replied, calmer now but still terse.

"Mr. Hobson writes that you are my father's heir. No one ever told me that he was a noble!" So she was baseborn, after all. A bastard and a mistake. For years, she had suspected as much. Why else would a father want his child so completely out of sight and out of mind. Well, not completely out of mind, she supposed. At least he had provided support until she was grown. That was something.

"Why did you come for me? I mean, you in particular. The task is a bit above your station, I should think." She tucked an errant strand of hair behind her ear and brushed another off her brow as she spoke, suddenly embarrassed for anyone to see her in such disarray.

He glanced at her then, a quick taking of her measure, she thought. Then he looked back at the road they traveled.

"I came because we are kin," he explained. "I am your cousin. Had I known of you earlier, I would have come sooner. It was almost not soon enough, was it? I should have shot that wretch like I threatened." He snapped the reins again.

Her cousin. She simply stared, fully taking in his sun-browned visage, wide-shouldered frame and the fine cut of his clothes. Travel dust did nothing to detract from his roguish appeal, and doubtless he knew it well.

He looked down at her travel bag and back at her. "You packed fast or perhaps had already packed before I arrived. So you were planning to leave. Where were you going?"

She didn't bother to correct his assumption. "To the convent, where else?"

"You didn't mean to take vows or you'd never have left in the first place."

His presumption irritated her, as did the flutter in her stomach that his very appearance caused. She pressed a hand over her middle and inhaled to steady her nerves. "I had very little choice of destinations."

"No matter, a different life awaits you now," he said with a smile in his voice if not yet on his face. "I know you were not aware your father was of the nobility," he stated. "No one at the convent was apprised of the fact, so I'm told. A shock for you, I daresay."

She nodded and took another deep breath that caught in her throat. There were too many questions flying through her mind to get them in order.

"We need to reach the coast before dark," he declared. With that, he snapped the reins more harshly, urging the sturdy roan to an even faster gait.

They were well down the road before her wits returned enough to realize that a total stranger, this incredibly handsome rogue, had her at his mercy. What if that letter were false? She had never met an earl, of course, but always imagined nobles having a more stately look and pleasant attitude.

Yet she had only three choices as she saw it. She could demand to be let down or returned to Orencio's house, beg this fellow to take her straight to the convent or go with him and see what happened next. The convent would be the safest choice, but she could not bring herself to ask for it after going to such lengths to escape it. Going back to Orencio was out of the question.

"This is good of you, but I still do not understand why you would go to so much bother for a bastard cousin."

"Bastard?" he asked with a short, mirthless laugh. "My lady, you are as legitimate as I. Whatever gave you the idea you aren't?"

"Perhaps the fact that I was sent to a foreign country to spend my life with nuns?"

He shrugged. "Oh, well, there is that." And he offered no explanation for it. Perhaps he did not know why, either. But wouldn't he have had the truth of it from her father if he was the heir? This made very little sense and did nothing to ease her mind about him.

If this Jackson "Jack" Worth, supposed earl, had designs on her person, then so did Señor Orencio. If she was to be ruined by one or the other, she found she preferred the stranger. Maybe she would even prefer that fate to being immured in a nunnery for the remainder of her life. That required a divine calling and ought not to be undertaken simply for the sake of security.

As if he read her very thoughts, he turned to her, his stern and angry expression softened, now sympathetic and very serious. "You needn't fear, my lady. I swear you will come to no harm, and I will see you safe to London, to your new home."

Caught by the steady blue gaze and held like a rabbit in a snare, Laurel could only nod. Why not trust him? She had nothing to lose if he was lying, aside from her virtue. That had done her little good thus far. And she had much to gain if he was telling the truth.

My lady, he had called her. Daughter of an earl. Legitimate, he had said. Could it really be true that she was born of nobility? If so, why was she never told of her circumstance before today?

"Have I other family?" she finally asked.

"Of course you do." He grinned at her then, a singularly merry expression she had not seen thus far. "There is me. I told you we are cousins."

Could she trust him? She supposed she might as well do that, since her other two options held no appeal. "We are truly kin?"

"We are. Why else would I be here?"

"I'm sure I don't know. This is all so…"

"Sudden, I understand. But there's nothing at all to worry about." His smile looked sincere. "I'll take care of everything for you, little cousin, and you will love England and your new life there."

"If you say so, I suppose I must believe you."

"I promise I will explain the details after we are settled for the voyage home. Your worries are over."

Laurel disagreed. She had worries aplenty at the moment, and there was absolutely nothing she could do to alleviate them.

Chapter Two

Jack worried about their introduction. He had planned to charm Laurel from the outset, not appear as a threat. Unfortunately, Orencio had left him no choice.

Though the girl was doubtful Jack was who he claimed, she hadn't refused to come with him. Her relief at leaving Orencio's might be short-lived when she had time to reflect on it. He wished he knew what more he could say to put her fears to rest.

He had reserved his final decision until he met her, but he now thought she would do well enough as a wife. Her looks certainly were greater than passable, but more important than that was the spirit she had shown in that confrontation with her employer.

The way Jack had first seen her—face red with anger, eyes flashing, tight little chignon askew and one sleeve torn at the shoulder seam—had roused his protective instinct to the maximum. She needed him on a level that no woman ever had before.

He knew he would miss Saskia in Amsterdam, Maria in Portugal, Joanna in Jamaica and a few others who welcomed him with open arms and merry laughter. This girl was not of their kind, however. Attaining regard from her would require more than he had offered the others. This time he would need to make irrevocable promises. Vows.

He only hoped he was up to the challenge. Given the fire he had seen in her, he figured she would be anything but boring.

Jack rarely met a woman he didn't like, even the guileful ones with nefarious schemes to trap him. Now the shoe was on the other foot, but he knew well all the means of avoiding the nuptial noose should this girl try to use them. He meant to marry her even should it require employing a bit of guile himself. She needed charming and he could do that.

"Aside from your employer's unwelcome attention, how did you like being a governess? Was the work more difficult than expected?"

he asked, assuming his most genial tone. He knew women liked questions about themselves.

"Impossible," she replied. "The boys were too old for it. What they needed was a male tutor."

"Or a lion tamer with a whip and chair?"

She laughed and Jack joined her, releasing some of the tension between them. He continued. "Like their father, eh? They had no discipline from that quarter, I'd wager."

She sobered immediately. "None. He lacked even *self*-discipline. This was not the first time he behaved so abominably, but I'm certainly glad it is the last. I might have managed by myself, but you certainly were a great help. Thank you for the rescue."

Jack was not all that surprised Orencio had made advances. Laurel was a fetching little thing, even in that dowdy garb of a governess.

She had handled the issue more than once, so she said. While that was admirable for an innocent with no worldly experience, it might not have turned out so well this time if he hadn't interfered. It gave him a good feeling to know he had saved her from ruin and she seemed properly grateful for it.

Jack didn't think it would be much of a sacrifice to marry her, assume her fortune and secure his future. And hers, too, of course. She deserved to be treated decently, especially after being dealt with in such a cavalier manner all her life. There was no reason whatsoever that they shouldn't both profit from such an alliance.

He might not become the best husband she could have chosen, given his rough upbringing and checkered past, but she would be a countess. That had to appeal to her more than scrubbing floors in a nunnery the rest of her life or herding a passel of spoiled Spanish brats while fending off their lecherous father.

He admitted feeling a certain affinity for her already, probably because they really were cousins. Very distant cousins, he reminded himself. The girl had grit and he really admired that in anyone.

They should get on rather well unless she somehow discovered his motive. He had to make sure she did not. At least not until after the marriage. Even then, he would not want her to know. A trifle dishonest, perhaps, but he would not like to see the accusation in her eyes or the death of trust.

They spoke little more until they reached the coastal town of La Coruña where he had reserved rooms.

"Here we are, Coz," he told her. It couldn't hurt, reminding her of their familial relationship as often as possible in order to further her trust in him.

He helped her down, careful to offer no suggestion of interest in her body while his hands were on her waist. A tiny waist, cinched rather firmly, he noted. His hands ached to explore more of her, but he knew self-control and gentlemanly behavior were the keys to this prize.

She clutched her bag with both arms and glanced wide-eyed around the dooryard of the inn.

"We'll stay the night here and board the ship first thing in the morning. That way we can have a good meal, a hot bath and sleep in beds that don't rock with the waves. We'll be at sea for days and will surely miss those comforts."

"I know nothing about ships or sailing," she declared.

"Then I'll see you never take the wheel," he quipped. He handed the horse off to a scruffy young ostler who stood waiting. "Is something amiss?" he asked her.

She bit her bottom lip as she looked up at him. "Shouldn't I have a chaperone if we're to stay the night here?"

"Have you the money to hire someone?" he asked.

"I have never had money of my own. Could you...?"

He feigned a sheepish expression. "I have enough for our rooms and our passage," he admitted. Quite enough, in fact. "But my funds are limited until I return and assume the title." Limited to what Hobson had given him, which was an ample amount indeed.

He didn't exactly lie, he reasoned. Not his fault if she assumed he was nearly broke. He took her bag from her and escorted her inside. "Not to worry, little Coz. We'll make do, just the two of us."

He could seduce her tonight to ensure she would agree to marry, but that would define him as an opportunist. He certainly was that, but did not want her to see him in that light. Better to act as honorably as he knew how.

When they entered the inn, he ordered a substantial meal, and they retired to the one private area set aside for dining. Jack lifted his tankard and wondered how to begin conversing with the sheltered heiress about her future.

She didn't wait for him to start. "Tell me of our family, Cousin Worth. Oh, I forget what's proper." She winced prettily at her faux pas. "I should address you as Lord Elderidge."

"I told you that *Jack* will do," he said with a short laugh. "I'm so unused to the title and it sounds so strange, I might not answer to it."

"Then you may call me Laurel if you like. Now tell me, how are we related through our fathers?"

"We share a great-great-grandfather." He set the tankard down carefully and smoothed out the tablecloth with the flat of his hand. "Apparently our great-grandfathers were brothers, yours the elder. Their sire was the fourth Earl of Elderidge. Since your father's passing, I am the only living male descendent, hence the heir."

She shook her head. "I still can hardly believe it. Who would have thought? And what of my mother? I have been told nothing of her except that she passed away before I was sent to Spain." Laurel smiled sadly, staring off into the distance. "Yet it seems I remember her. Small things, you know? The scent of her, her voice…"

"Wishful dreams, no doubt, and perfectly understandable. Unfortunately, she died when you were born. The story is not a happy one, I fear." He drew in a deep breath and began to repeat all that Hobson had told him about her parents.

When he had finished, he drank the remainder of his ale, avoiding her eyes, allowing her time to digest what he had related. She obviously trusted him now, and there was no doubt left in her eyes. The girl was an open book, there for the reading. Her naïveté troubled him, even if it did work to his advantage.

Jack had more to say and needed to get it said. He had only days to accomplish what he must. Might as well be blunt, he reasoned, so he simply stated it without preamble. "We should marry, Laurel."

She almost choked on her wine. "What?"

Jack wondered what devil urged him to shock her out of that overly tranquil demeanor of hers and stoke the hidden fire he knew was there.

He cleared his throat and looked away, staring unseeing, at the doorway. "Look, I should have waited, made better arrangements beforehand, but when I learned of you, I felt this great need to come and bring you home, to offer you my protection." He shook his head. "Familial duty seemed paramount at the time, above sensible preparation."

"Preparation?" Though she appeared a bit

rattled, he watched her draw on some inner calm and reserve that he almost envied. And somehow craved to dispel.

"Yes, well, we are to travel together now. As you pointed out, the two of us alone, with no female to accompany you, either here or onboard the ship. I have realized that once we reach England, your reputation will be in tatters unless we are wed."

"That's absurd!" Now her color was high, her spirit almost showing itself again. "I hardly know you! You cannot expect me to—"

"Don't you see? It's for your own good, Laurel. Aside from keeping your good name, there are other very important considerations."

"Such as?" she asked, frowning.

He looked into her eyes, holding her gaze with his as he reached for her hand. "You know no one in England. Every female must be under some man's protection all the while, for that is the law. You could not find employment without proper references. You cannot live alone."

She remained silent, taking in his explanation and assessing it, probably trying to think of alternatives.

He added the clinching argument. "And if your reputation is sullied in any way, as it would already be if we arrived together unmarried, you can never hope to make a decent match or be accepted in society, even at a lower order. So you see, this is the best way, the only way, really."

He plowed right ahead. "As for me, I would not be much affected. Some might term me the despoiler of an innocent, but men are seldom ostracized for that. Even so, I would hate the accusation. But you would be considered beyond the pale, quite unsuitable for any man of decent birth, even though nothing inappropriate had ever happened between us."

"You said yourself we are cousins. There are laws…"

"The king himself wed his *first* cousin. The Regent did likewise. Ours is not a close kinship at all, regardless of the fact that we share a surname. Perfectly legal, I promise you. We won't even need dispensation."

She studied him for long moments before speaking. "And yet your eyes tell me you do not like what you view as the necessity of wedding me, Jack. Is that due to my mother's… unfortunate past?"

"No! Absolutely not," he rushed to assure her. "And I'm fine with a marriage of convenience. Really." He shrugged and smiled. "One must marry, after all. This sort of union is quite the thing in English society, done all the time."

She inclined her head and paused as if considering that. Finally she spoke again. "That's true in Spain, as well. I've led a sheltered life, Jack, however reading materials were never in short supply at the convent and the nuns are a great deal more worldly than one might imagine. Few of the girls schooled there would stay on, so they had to be made aware of what to expect. The ways of the outside world are not completely foreign to me."

"Then you must admit, though we aren't well acquainted yet, this is our best solution."

She worried her bottom lip with small white teeth as she frowned. "I never expected to marry for love. In fact, I never expected to marry." She added after a short hesitation, "Now I suppose I shall wed, after all."

"So you do not object?" he asked, almost wishing that she would. He had more arguments prepared. How could she simply accept his suggestion with such calmness and practicality? There should be some fiery debate over the matter, surely.

"I have no objection on the face of it." She withdrew her hand and sat back in her chair. "All my life I have dreamed of family, given the absence of one. A husband, children, a home of my own were simply an impossible fantasy I seldom entertained. It seemed so far-fetched, I never even bothered to pray for it. Now here you are, offering all of it on a silver plate."

"There's no need to decide on the instant," he said as the innkeeper approached with a tray. "And here is our food. For now, let's get you fed." He watched as she closed her eyes, moved her lips in a silent grace and crossed herself.

Would religious differences cause a problem with what he had planned? Perhaps he was borrowing stumbling blocks. Or searching for some. Damn, but he hadn't expected it to be this easy.

Instead of pursuing his thoughts on that, he watched her eat. She tucked into the meal like a sailor on shore leave after a long voyage. "Didn't Orencio feed you?" he asked before thinking how it sounded, that she might think he was criticizing her manners.

She pulled a wry face. "I had little time to eat in peace while I was there. The lads I tended were prone to food fights."

"A handful, eh? Tell me about them." Women loved to talk about themselves, he knew, so he deliberately provided the opportunity. Calculating, the way he had been doing since they met, seemed unnatural to him, but also necessary.

She talked between bites, alternately grimacing and laughing softly, pointing for emphasis with her fork. He was glad she felt more at ease in his company, but wondered at it. Perhaps it was only an act, he reasoned, a defense to cover her inner fears.

When they had finished eating, he escorted her upstairs to the chamber adjacent to his own. "Sleep well, little cousin," he said and raised her hand to kiss the back of it. "I will call you early come morning."

"I probably won't sleep a wink," she said, withdrawing her hand and staring down at it as if it were a strange object. Her next words were a near whisper. "No matter what we choose to do next, I am glad you came for me. Thank you, Jack. You are truly a godsend."

Well, he had never been called *that* before. He answered with a brief nod and bade her goodnight. He wondered if he would sleep. Her calm and trusting nature was making it far too effortless for him to take advantage of her, and guilt was nudging him. Not strongly enough to make him cry off the proposal, though. As he saw it, neither of them had another viable choice. Perhaps she simply recognized that, as well.

The next morning, Jack noted that her mood had not changed overnight. She smiled up at him as if he were the Second Coming. Her quiet acceptance of the impending voyage made him wonder again if she were pretending away any trepidation.

At any rate, he was glad to see color in her cheeks and a barely subdued sparkle in those pretty brown eyes. Her features were not that remarkable, rather commonplace when taken individually. Her hair was the color of pale honey, her eyebrows and lashes several shades darker. She had an oval face, pert little nose, bright brown heavily lashed eyes and a sweetly curved and quite mobile mouth. All nice-enough attributes, but it was their combination and her ever-changing expression that lent her beauty.

Though there was nothing static about those expressions, they generally ranged from sweetly accepting to thoughtfully questioning. She obviously avoided excitement, outright anger or anything approaching hysteria. Why that bothered him, he could not say, except that he had seen the fire in her once and wondered how she kept it banked. He should ask her for lessons.

He had, of course, noted her lithe figure, too.

What man would not do that if in the company of a woman he might marry.

She was small of stature, a head shorter than he, and not greatly endowed at the top, though her tiny waist made her seem so at first glance.

He could not seem to dismiss his wonder at her composure. It had to be a natural acquisition from the contemplative sisters who had raised her. Yet underneath that calm, he knew there lurked a more passionate streak in her nature. Hadn't he glimpsed that at Orencio's? Righteous anger, that had been, and not what Jack wished to stoke. It was the passion in her that he was looking for, of course.

Pretense or not, she treated him like her liberator now, so perhaps he really was. It gave him a sense of satisfaction to think so. And it almost justified in his mind what he definitely meant to do.

Chapter Three

The next afternoon, they stood at the rail of the *Minotaur,* a trade vessel on which he had purchased their passage to England, and watched the port of La Coruña grow distant.

Jack appreciated the way Laurel adapted to sea travel, as if it were some great undertaking to be quietly savored. He only hoped mal de mer didn't claim her if the seas grew rough. At the moment she genuinely seemed to be embracing all that was new to her with an equanimity that amazed him.

"You love the sea," she guessed, staring out at the waves.

"Grew up next to it and then on it," he said truthfully. "As a child I dreamed of traveling to distant shores, having adventures, sailing my own ship."

"Did you?" she asked. "And have you seen the world already?"

He inclined his head as he slapped his hands lightly against the rail. "Aye, I've seen most of it."

"Then you must tell me about your travels. Have you had adventures enough?" she asked with a knowing smile. "Ready to settle now?"

"Ready as I will ever be," he answered ruefully, unwilling to delve too deeply into what life might be like as a land-bound lord stuck with tallying rents and arguing with stuffy peers. Restricting himself to one woman.

His father had never done that, he recalled with shame. While his mother remained in Plymouth producing candles to sell and essentially supporting them with the profits from the family business she had inherited, his father sailed off constantly. He enjoyed adventures and, as Jack had learned when he went to sea with him, cavorted with other women whenever they docked in foreign ports.

Jack was no saint and had taken to bedsport as soon as he was of an age to do so, but he resented his father's excuse for infidelity. It was an *excuse,* he had realized early on, not a valid reason to stray, if there existed such a reason. Marriage required fidelity.

Could he remain faithful? Well, he would have to if he was to keep his honor, Jack decided. Though he might have lied a little to attain what he must in this case, he would never cheat. A man had to draw the line somewhere.

He quickly dismissed the thought and changed the topic. "Were they kind to you at the convent?"

"Of course. Our Lady of Cambre is not only a convent, but a convent *school* and it afforded me an enviable education. Not all of the pupils there came as infants, nor did most of the nuns. While they probably wished for all of us to enter the order, they were aware that most would leave, return to their homes and marry."

"But you did not expect to do so."

She shook her head. "Never. But my point is that the sisters took us as individuals, respected and enhanced whatever natural gifts they saw in each and prepared us accordingly. I was given to understand that females are not supposed to have intellect enough to master many of the studies offered there." She glanced up at him with a grin. "Not to boast, but I excelled at Maths. Numbers fascinate me."

Jack pressed the heels of his hands against the rail and resisted the urge to push away and pace. He needed to curb his impatience with all of this conversation. A man of action, he would much rather live in the moment than delve into the past as they were doing. "Maths, eh? Well, I suppose you will need that knowledge when counting linens and silver."

"Not only that. I can help you with accounts as I did Sister Josephina," she offered with a decisive nod.

Jack felt a stab of foreboding. It would not do for her to examine their finances and discover that he had assumed her fortune. "I'm sure I can manage that on my own."

He quickly turned from the subject of accounts. "I'll wager your Spanish is also enviable. You have the barest trace of an accent, did you know? It's quite charming."

She smiled sweetly at the compliment. "How nice of you to say so. English was always prevalent, though the nuns and students were a good mix of nationalities. Languages were spoken interchangeably at times, so we received a working knowledge, if not fluency, in several tongues," she explained. "My French is atrocious, I'm told, and my Italian, little better. What of you?"

"I know enough to get by. Trading required that." He looked out across the sea, arms folded on the rail, the tense muscles of his legs working against the motion of the waves. How could she simply stand there, unmoving, untrammeled, perfectly tranquil in the face of such an uncertain future? Was that ability inborn or learned, he wondered again. No doubt it came with schoolroom discipline.

Her formal education certainly surpassed his. "I never went to school," he admitted. "Mother taught me until I was seven, reading, writing, numbers and so forth. Then my father took me to sea with him as soon as he left the navy and sailed with a sea merchant."

"Well, you had the basics everyone needs," she said.

"Just so, and my father tutored me on board as did others with learning who had nothing better to do. I had a practical education rather than classic."

She smoothed back a strand of hair that had come loose in the wind. The gesture was practiced, not out of any coyness, but because those errant golden curls constantly escaped the severe chignon she wore. Jack thought there might be other rebellious attributes in Laurel waiting to slip their carefully schooled containment.

She sighed as she looked out over the seas. "Practicality is a good thing, isn't it? I never became proficient at those useful things one needs to know. For instance, I loathe sewing. We embroidered innumerable altar cloths and my stitches were always uneven. My fingers are only now recovering."

Jack turned and lifted both of her hands to examine her fingertips. They were red from the cold so he enclosed them within his to warm them. "You need never sew another stitch. What of music? Can you play and do you dance?"

She wore a faraway expression. "No. Are those accomplishments necessary for a lady? I've always thought I should like to dance if I could be taught."

"Of course you can. We will arrange for lessons," Jack promised.

"After we are married?" she asked.

"So you are still of a mind to marry me, Laurel?" he asked, determined to keep his tone light and conversational.

She turned and cocked her head to one side. "I think so, yes. We get on well enough, don't you think?"

He nodded. "Do you worry that your soul's mate is out there somewhere waiting to meet you? Most women hold that hope, so I'm led to believe."

"I told you that is only the stuff of girlish dreams," she replied with a soft little laugh. "I will be content with a good match."

Content and also rich and at my mercy, Jack's conscience reminded him. Would to God, she never found out his real reason for this marriage. He did not want her feeling betrayed. She might even demand a separation if she ever learned of it. That would free him to pursue his own desires and live as he wished, of course, but at what great cost to her feelings and his honor?

"Shall we marry immediately when we arrive in England before anyone knows we're there?" she asked.

He dared not wait that long. "The wedding itself could pose a problem," he informed her in case she had not thought of it. He had. "You are Catholic and I am not."

"Oh." She looked crestfallen. Then she brightened. "Perhaps the captain could marry us before we get there. I read of that in a novel once. Is it true captains of ships can perform weddings?"

"Well, that would be a romantic tale to tell, wouldn't it? But considering our stations, our marriage must be recognized by the Church of England and duly recorded in other than a ship's log. What I meant to ask is if you will mind if there's no priest, no Catholic service?"

She shot him a wry look. "Did I not suggest a ship's captain? So if not the captain and not a priest, what shall we do?"

"There is a vicar on board." He had seen to that, as well as to obtaining a special license and a ring, before leaving England, in the event things progressed this far. It paid to plan ahead for every contingency.

"Very well, shall we apply to the vicar?" she asked.

Jack looked out across the waves again to avoid her gaze. It could not be this uncomplicated. He was so used to fighting hard, struggling for everything he got, it was hard to accept.

Despite what looked to be trouble-free success, he kept thinking how this would impact his own life. There would be no more nights of delight in foreign ports, no further risk-taking adventures and no indulging in wild investment schemes to increase his fortune. He would be a married man, honor bound to exclusivity, tied to one woman and an estate for which he would be solely responsible. Sobering thoughts indeed, but he had already decided that's what must be. There were others to think of now besides himself.

Though he often wished to, he could not bring himself to ignore the needs of others as his father had always done. Though Jack had loved the man, he recognized the shortcomings at a very early age.

Now the welfare of many rested with Jack, just as it had aboard his own ship. Delegating that task for the last venture had proved disastrous. Responsibility was a weighty thing, but something he had to embrace. However, embracing Laurel would be no sacrifice at all. Perhaps it would prove to be the reward for his diligence.

Still, he should give her one last opportunity to assert herself or question the sanity of the plan. "I would like you to be certain, Laurel. As you said at first, you hardly know me."

She shrugged. "Better than I know anyone else. So do *you* really want to?"

"Yes, of course," he replied and did not elaborate any further for fear he would talk her out of the notion. And whyever should he do that? Their marriage would solve everyone's needs. Hobson would be satisfied with the fairness of it, and Laurel would have the family she wanted. His mother would be delighted he was to give up the sea. As for himself, he would…well, he would live a changed life, one of wealth and privilege.

"If you will excuse me, I'll go and speak with the vicar and to the captain for his permission to use the deck. We might as well have done with it as soon as may be."

She frowned up at him and he immediately realized how dreadful that had sounded. He forced a hearty laugh. "You know how grooms cavil at wedding formalities." When she shook her head slightly, he added, "No, I don't suppose you do. I'm quaking in my boots, wondering if I'll be able to live up to your trust in me. That's all. Sheer nerves."

She nodded, smiling as she smoothed the lapel of his coat and gave it a pat. "Then we must keep the ceremony simple with no fuss and bother."

"Aye, that's best," he said, raising her hand to his lips and pressing a long kiss on her cold fingertips. "Until later, then."

He strode quickly away, every fiber of his being screaming for release of tension. If only he could shed his boots and climb the rigging, haul rope or shift barrels. Any activity to dispel the feeling of confinement in his own body. He was on an edge that a bridegroom's nerves did not explain. He suffered it almost constantly and never found an explanation.

The very next morning Laurel shook out her white muslin and spread it over the bunk in her cabin. She had only two gowns, the gray she wore every day and this one she and Sister Mary Anne had sewn for her confirmation years ago and recently altered for any dressier occasions that might occur at the Orencio household. Not that there had been any of those occasions.

There were ribbons, too, that she had already threaded through the braids that crowned her head. She might not be the most fashionably dressed of brides, but at least she wouldn't look like the gray mouse her groom would be expecting.

Doubts about her decision had kept her awake most of the night. None she would admit to Jack, however. The way he had explained things, this truly did seem her only chance at a normal life.

He was very considerate, gallant, handsome, even titled. What more could she hope for in a husband? The very thought of having to meet numerous candidates and choose another terrified her.

According to him, any chance for such a choice would not be possible anyway, because everyone in England would believe her compromised after their trip together.

Even if she and Jack turned out to be mismatched in future, she would somehow make things work between them. He was a good man to do this for her.

She donned the crinkled muslin and smoothed it out as best she could. Her white slippers were a bit tight, having been constructed when she was but thirteen. Still, her feet had not grown much since that age. Laurel took a deep breath, pinched her cheeks, raked her teeth over her lips to induce a little color and went out to join Jack on the deck.

She smiled at his reaction. He looked rather shocked for a moment to see her wearing something different from the gray. And then pleased. His appreciative smile warmed her heart.

He looked wonderful in a coat of dark blue with gray breeches, black boots that reached his knees and incredibly white linen at his neck and wrists. Well dressed and well formed was this cousin and soon-to-be husband. The wind tossed his light brown hair about his brow, affording him a boyish charm that delighted her.

How tall and imposing he looked despite that

small disarray, every inch a nobleman, every ounce a strong, capable man of the world. When she stood next to him, he made her feel small, yet in no way insignificant. Her wishes and opinions seemed to matter to him. He had been nothing but forthright, kind and considerate.

Laurel hoped this would prove to be the best decision for both of them. Jack was giving up his bachelor status, which he must surely have enjoyed enormously, to save her reputation.

Marriage would not become a total sacrifice on his part, she would see to that. She was good at organizing and very economical, both attributes that would be handy for managing a large household. After all, the convent was no more than that, and she had become adept at helping the sisters in almost every area. She would know precisely what to do.

Even more important was the fact that as a new earl, Jack would be thinking of setting up his nursery. The novels she had read indicated that every man of rank needed to wed and produce an heir. She promised herself she would, in every way possible, make this marriage as good for him as it would be for her. She would make it perfect.

The captain and the minister stood before

them at the bow, flanked by a number of the crew and the half dozen other passengers. Strangers all, for there had been no time yet to form friendships or even to acquire acquaintances.

Jack held out his hand and she took it. How gallant of him to do this for her, to come for her and then to save her from scandal. What a good heart he had.

The rise and fall of the ship seemed to set the cadence for the minister's words as he read from his book.

Hers was the first wedding she had ever attended, so Laurel hung on every word, committed to memory each promise Jack made, amazed that this outrageously handsome man, this earl, this treasured new friend and cousin, vowed so sincerely to become her husband forever. Her heart was so full of gratitude, she could scarcely breathe.

"I, Jackson Templeton Worth, take thee, Laurel Winspear Worth, to my wedded wife. To have and to hold from this day forward, for better, for worse, for richer, for poorer, in sickness and in health, to love and to cherish, till death us do part, according to God's holy ordinance, and thereto I plight thee my troth."

Laurel repeated the same vows with the

word *obey* added to her litany. She slipped *cherish* into her part, as well, for she meant to truly cherish this wonderfully selfless man.

"With this ring, I thee wed," Jack said, looking down at her hand as he slid a plain gold band on her finger. "And with all my worldly goods, I thee endow."

A brief hint of doubt intruded. How was it that he had a ring? And, so conveniently, a minister? But he could not have planned this wedding in advance. He'd had no reason to marry her before it became necessary to save her reputation, had he? No, he was a resourceful man. He'd probably bought a ring from someone, and the minister being onboard must simply be a happy coincidence.

"By the power vested in me by the Church of England and His Majesty, King George," the minister intoned, "I now pronounce you husband and wife. What God hath joined together, let no man put asunder."

The ceremony was over and she was a wife. Jack's wife. His *countess,* though he had not made their station known as yet on board the ship. She wondered about that, but he had said he was still unused to the title.

Perhaps he merely wanted to be treated equally by their fellow travelers. Laurel admitted that not being either avoided or bowed to at every turn would make for a much more pleasant journey. Jack was wise and obviously thought ahead.

"Kiss 'er, mister!" one of the crewmen shouted as the vicar closed his book. Laughter ensued as Jack leaned to touch his lips to hers. Everyone applauded and a few added whistles.

Laurel savored the sweet feel of his mouth as it lightly caressed hers. He smelled of bay rum, starch and the sea. His closeness felt lovely, though unsettling, and caused a quickening of her heartbeat as it always did. She experienced a small pang of regret when he drew away.

Moments later, after a spate of cursory congratulations, the onlookers scattered and the ship was back to business as usual.

Jack still held her hand and turned to her then. "Well, my lady. I wish I could offer you more festivities, but there is a wedding breakfast for the two of us in my cabin. I bribed the ship's cook."

"How wonderful," she said, growing nervous at last. One could only dismiss thoughts of the consummation for so long. She knew vaguely what was to happen. His kiss had stirred all sorts of imaginings. Would he wait for night? Did couples even do such intimate things in the light of day? "I should have read more novels," she muttered to herself.

"So you had novels in the convent," he said. "Those are fairly new. How did you get them?"

"Smuggled in by the girls who came late to us. The books were few, well dog-eared and treasured."

She stopped on the stairs. "Jack? I feel I should warn you I know very little about becoming a wife. Are you…experienced at all?"

He bit his lip and looked away. "Ah…well, somewhat. That won't be a problem. If you like, we will wait until we land and find more comfortable accommodations. To make things official, that is. To, you know…" He actually blushed, delighting Laurel, dismissing her own qualms.

"That would be best I think. Yes, we should wait." She hesitated before asking the next question, lest he think her too eager. "How many days will we be at sea, do you think?"

"Three or four at best. Longer if the winds aren't with us."

"Then we shall arrive in London?"

"We're to put in at Plymouth, then go on to London by coach," he explained. "Well then, shall we breakfast? A good English repast seems a proper way to begin, doesn't it?"

"Indeed. How thoughtful you are. Women all over the world will probably wish me dead when they hear you're leg-shackled."

He laughed out loud, banishing some of the tension between them. "Where did you hear such a term? Aha, those infamous *novels*."

To her great relief, he took her hand again and led her through the common room into his cabin. The space was minuscule, quite intimate and not conducive to any sort of formality.

There was a bunk fastened to the wall on which they would sit side by side. His small travel trunk served as a table. It had been set very simply with two plates of eggs, bread and ham, assuredly cold by this time. She didn't mind in the least. It was his effort to please her that mattered.

Laurel could scarcely believe the events of the past three days or credit her good fortune at Jack's coming to Spain for her and taking her to wife.

She was almost afraid to celebrate. Where had she heard that when something seemed too good to be true, it usually was?

Chapter Four

Early next morning, Jack leaned against the rail again, looking out to sea, wondering if he would ever sail again after this short yet momentous voyage.

How strange it seemed to be aboard a ship and have nothing to do. Even so, the restlessness that constantly plagued him seemed somehow less today.

He knew what he would like to be doing, but accepted the wait as his punishment for tricking Laurel into a hasty marriage. She was no lightskirt to tumble in a narrow bunk and laugh with at the inconvenience. She was his wife, an untried, convent-bred young lady with tender sensibilities.

He had not slept. Of all the men he knew, he

was the last he would have figured to spend his wedding night alone. His friends would have a great laugh over that if they ever learned of it.

Especially Neville Morleigh. He smiled recalling the joint venture that had reaped such a grand profit for both. They had met aboard the *Emelia* when Jack served as navigator for Captain Holt, the privateer. Neville had been about some havey-cavey government business.

The two had formed an instant friendship. Later on, by combining funds, refitting an old merchantman, gaining his license to captain and a letter of marque, their privateering had gone smashingly well.

The *Siren* had given Neville a means to travel to almost any port so he could do whatever intelligencing he had been set to do. When they captured French ships, England had acquired the vessels while he, Neville and their crew shared the booty. Neville eventually bought out and continued his furtive work elsewhere.

He had not seen Neville since, but had read in a London paper of his friend's marriage to a baron's widow shortly after the war ended. Perhaps Neville had lost his profits on another venture, too, and decided to marry for money.

"Lost in thought or watching for whales?"

Laurel's cheerful question dragged him back to the present.

"Just thinking of a friend of mine with whom I sailed in times past," he admitted, turning to smile a greeting. "Good morning. Did you pass a comfortable night?"

"Not very. Did you?"

He shook his head, laughing a little. "Not at all, but then I seldom sleep well. Shall we take a turn around deck?" Jack took her arm and they strolled, avoiding the coils of ropes and a sailor who was busy swabbing the planks. He noted that their walk seemed almost restful to him instead of being merely a thing he must do to keep her in good spirits.

The wind picked up considerably in the next quarter hour and a bank of clouds moved closer, obliterating the horizon. "We're in for a blow," he muttered, squinting to the east. "Best you go to your cabin."

Her fingers dug into his arm as she looked up at him. "Please, no. I would rather face it on deck if there's a storm."

"Don't be a goose," he said. "If it's only rain, you'll be soaked through, and if it does get rough, you could be injured. At best, you'd be in the way."

"You'll come, too?"

"No, I'll give a hand up here," he said, speaking more calmly than the situation warranted. The ship had begun to pitch appreciably even as they spoke. The sky grew dark and drops began to pelt them.

He shrugged off his coat, slung it around her shoulders, then plopped down on a coil of rope to quickly remove his boots and stockings. He handed them to her. "Go, Laurel. *Now!*" he ordered as he looked up at the billowed sails and whipping flag.

"You will be careful!" she cried, hugging his boots to her chest, struggling to keep her balance as the pitch and roll grew worse. She glanced up at the crewmen who had hopped the rigging. The first mate was shouting orders.

"Hurry! Go!" Jack gave her a gentle shove in the direction of their quarters, watching for only a moment to be sure she minded.

The captain stood at the wheel, issuing orders to the first mate, who then bellowed them to pilot and crew. Jack made his way toward them to offer his services.

By the time he traversed the distance, waves were visible, rising higher than the rails, sloshing over the deck.

Laurel must be terrified. He hoped she had made it inside before getting soaked. Sharp needles of rain increased in density, nearly blinding him. He was wet to the skin. And back within his element.

They were in for it all right. He put Laurel out of mind and leaped into the fray against his oldest enemy, the weather at sea.

The mate had him helping to secure cannon when Jack heard the shout of *man overboard* not ten feet away. His first thought was Laurel. What if she had come back on deck and a wave had swept her over?

He grasped the end of a coil, deftly securing it around his waist with the proper knot. Already halfway over the rail, he shouted to the two men working beside him to man the rope. He saw something white bob in the water, then disappear when a heavy swell rocked the ship.

"There! I'm going in!" he shouted and dived.

Under the surface, he saw a column of white flutter and made for it. All he could think was of Laurel in her white frock, sinking without a struggle. He fought the tow, kicked until he thought his legs would break and lungs burst.

Finally, when nearly there, he pushed to the surface, dragged in a deep breath and went under again. When he reached the small body, he grabbed it with one arm and lifted, scissoring his legs, pulling upward with his free hand until he felt the welcome pelt of rain on his face.

Immediately, the rope jerked taut and he was being hauled backward. Salt stung his eyes and his hair plastered to his face like seaweed.

As he touched wood, fingers grappled at his shirt, caught and hauled him to the rope ladder. "Here, man! Let me put 'im in the net. Can ye climb?"

"Aye," Jack rasped as he released his burden to strong hands and reached for the ladder hanging over the side. With tremendous effort and heaving for breath, he gained one flexible rung at a time until he was at the rail.

Seamen dragged him up and over and laid him on the wet deck. Jack rolled to his side and sat up. "Where—?"

"Just there, sir, pukin' up enough brine to fill a bucket, but he'll do," someone said with a hearty laugh. "We'd ha' lost pore Timmy, weren't for you!"

Jack fell back onto the wildly rocking deck and closed his eyes. *Not Laurel.* He began to laugh. Would he have gone in after the boy had he known? Probably, he thought, but he would have kept his bloody head while doing it.

This preoccupation with a wife might be the

death of him. He laughed harder as the rain pounded and the wind raged.

"You all right, sir?" One of the crew who pulled him in began untying the rope from around his waist.

"Aye," Jack said, rolling over, sitting up again and slicking his hair back with both hands. He had a job to do yet. Moments later he was busy again, tying down the brights while dodging the monstrous wheels with his bare feet.

The storm abated at last and the damage proved minimal. No one had been lost and only a few sustained injuries. Weary to the bone, Jack headed for his cabin to dry off and rest. He encountered the captain on the way.

"Join me for dinner, you and your wife," Captain Pollack said. The invitation sounded like an order, but Jack knew it for an honor.

"Very well, Captain. Thank you." He clenched his eyes shut for a moment to clear them and proceeded to his quarters.

Laurel waited for him in the common room to which each of their cabins opened. She rose when he came inside. "It's over," she said, stating the obvious. The ship's motion had grown relatively calm.

"We're asked to dine with the captain," he told her. "Are you well enough?"

"Very well," she said, frowning at him. "You look done in. Was it very bad?"

"I've seen worse," he admitted, passing her to reach his cabin door. "At least it blew us in the right direction." He noted how pale she was. "Were you afraid we would die?"

She shook her head. "It wasn't death I feared. We were taught not to fear it."

He gave a snort of disbelief. "Well I was taught not to welcome it. So you just thought to meet it face-to-face in the gale instead of taking precaution?" He felt unreasonably angry that she hadn't been afraid at all and he had been scared out of his bloody mind for her.

She ducked her head as she shook it. "I didn't want to leave you out there."

Oh. He blew out the pent-up breath he'd been holding lest he say something else that was mean and uncalled-for. "I'd better change," he muttered and left her there in the common room.

God, he had wanted to grab her and hold her close, kiss her like a madman and declare how profoundly glad he was that it had not been her bobbing up and down in the sea.

Damn, but being married was a maddening thing, especially to a virgin you couldn't have yet and to a girl who hadn't sense enough to get in out of the rain.

The captain's table was a great deal more formal than the one in the common room they had passed through to go there. Laurel marveled at the china and crystal, even finer than that of the Orencio household. The table linen was spotless and every man there was dressed formally, except Jack and a young lad clad in white.

Everyone stood when they entered. "Welcome, Mr. and Mrs. Worth," the captain said with a warm smile. He proceeded to introduce them to each of the five men present, all officers of the ship. And then he gestured to the young boy whom she guessed to be about thirteen. "Timothy Bromfield, my godson and cabin lad to Mr. Tomlinson, my second in command. Say your piece, Tim."

The dark-haired boy turned wide brown eyes to her, bowed and said, "Ma'am." Then he spoke to Jack. "Sir, I owe you my life and I thank you for your heroic deed. If ever I can repay you in any way, you must call upon me." He smiled the sweetest smile. "They say in the Orient that if you save a life, it belongs to you." He shrugged. "Or something equivalent to that."

Everyone laughed, including the captain. "Well, you can't take it with you, Mr. Worth, because we should miss this fellow aboard. And may I add my eternal gratitude. He is my brother's only son. Should I have lost him at sea his first time out, I would have been persona non grata in my family home forever."

Mr. Tomlinson piped in, "The way you leaped over the side and performed the rescue, one would think you'd had years at sea yourself!"

Jack smiled self-consciously. "Almost twenty years of it, sir. I began as a cabin lad myself aboard the *Mosquitobit*."

Laurel paid only half attention. She still couldn't process the fact that Jack had jumped overboard to save the boy. He had said *nothing* about it!

All sorts of feelings rushed through her, from hot anger that he would take such a mortal risk to abject pride in the champion he turned out to be.

But she had known already how unselfish he was, hadn't she? Everything he had done for her proved he was heroic and this feat only seconded that. The men were raising a toast to

Jack at that moment. Laurel quickly reached for her glass and joined them.

Later when they were returning to their cabins, she requested that they take a stroll about the deck rather than retire immediately. "I want to see the ocean calm or I shan't sleep," she said.

"A good idea," he agreed, and led her down the gangway and up the steps.

"That was a very brave thing you did, saving young Tim," she said.

"An impulse, I assure you. Had I stopped to think, I probably would have tossed him a buoy instead."

Laurel knew better. She smiled up at the stars that were abundant in the clear night sky. Canvas had been unfurled and they were sailing along as if nothing had happened. Several of the other guests were out on deck, ostensibly for the same reason she had wanted to be there.

Suddenly she stopped and looked up at the wooden pole they were passing by. "The spar," she remarked.

"I beg your pardon?"

"That is a spar, isn't it?" she asked as she reached over to touch it lightly.

"It is. Have you read of ships then?"

She shook her head and placed her fingertips to her temple as an image occurred. "I remember it from when I sailed before. The word sounded like *star* to me. I thought a star was falling until someone told me differently."

She met his puzzled gaze. "There was a flash, of lightning, I think. I suppose that was what I saw. The thing snapped, you see. Someone shouted, "Spar's falling!" There was a huge crash and everyone began dashing about. I was knocked down."

Jack frowned and stared at her. "How could you remember that incident if you were only—? How old were you?" he asked.

"I have no idea," she said with a shake of her head. "Odd that I've never thought of it since, isn't it?"

He nodded. "Strange indeed. Tell me, do you recall entering the convent?"

"Not at all," she replied truthfully.

"Probably another dream," Jack said. "You know, such as the ones you mentioned having of your mother. It stands to reason a child brought up in a ritualistic environment like a convent would exercise imagination in such a way."

"You make the convent sound like prison and it wasn't that at all," she informed him. "But perhaps you are right about the dreams."

"I wonder how you knew of the *spar,* though."

Laurel wondered, too. The dream seemed so real.

"Shall I point out other parts of the ship?" Jack asked. "I've been a seaman for most of my life, so this is a second home to me."

She took his arm and they continued their stroll around the deck of the brigantine. Laurel found herself searching in memory for other nautical words she might have dreamed of or learned as a child, but nothing else they passed by seemed familiar.

Only the spar and the storm.

Chapter Five

They sailed into Plymouth Harbor four days later on a gray afternoon. Laurel found the town fascinating when they disembarked, so different from the buildings in La Coruña or any others she had seen in Spain. When she began to ask about the differences, Jack did not patronize her. He answered with alacrity and encouraged her to question.

"This Plymouth is the harbor where, two hundred years ago, the famous *Mayflower* set sail for the new world, isn't it?" she asked, turning to look back out to sea.

"The very place. You studied about that, eh? A group of dissidents spurned Church of England ways." He smiled as he hefted his travel trunk onto his shoulder. "They thought the rituals too Catholic."

She lifted her bag and set off beside him down the cobbled street. "Not all aboard left England due to that," she said, glad she could show him that she knew a little something of the world. "*Saints and strangers,* they were called. Whatever their reasons for leaving, weren't they courageous to set out on such a venture, facing the unknown in a strange land?"

"Precisely what you are doing yourself," he said with a grin. "Aren't you the brave one!"

She smiled. "Am I? I hadn't thought of that. The natives here are welcoming and civilized, I trust."

"Most of them are, but it pays to watch your purse," he advised. "In regard to scoundrels, may I offer you a bit of advice?"

"Of course," she replied.

"Here, and especially in London, there will be very many men everywhere you go, something that will be new to you, having been reared with the sisters. If I'm not by to provide you protection, have a care around them, Laurel, even those who appear to be gentlemen."

"For they do not always mean well," she said, mimicking his low, serious tone of voice. "Especially beware of those from *Spain* with roving eyes and hands," she added, pointedly reminding him that she had already learned that particular lesson.

He laughed. "Well then, now you know of the pickpockets, as well."

Laurel felt safe enough since she owned no purse or anything to put into one. The only two things she treasured were within her travel bag. She held it closer, uncertain whether he had been jesting about thieves everywhere.

"Plymouth seems a lovely town from what I see."

"I like it. My early years were spent several streets from this very spot."

"May I see where you lived?" she asked, hoping for a better picture of the boy he had been.

"Aye, and you must meet my mother. She has a larger place now that she's remarried, but it's very close to our old home."

"You have a *mother!*" Laurel exclaimed.

"Well, I wasn't hatched," Jack said with a twist of his lips.

She laughed. "You know what I meant. Never once have you mentioned she was alive. I assumed you were an orphan like me."

"Sorry, but you never asked. So I am telling you now, you have a mother-in-law. Come, we'll go and see if she will let me keep you."

Laurel knew he was joking now, but worry set in nonetheless. Would his mother tolerate a Catholic daughter-in-law, one who had very little real knowledge of the world and barely looked presentable?

She hurried to keep up with Jack as he strode the smooth stones of the streets, winding through the alleyways, a beatific smile on his face.

"Just there," he said as he stopped and pointed to a row of small shops. "We lived above the chandler's. See the sign? Mother's family were candle makers. She did right well during the war but sold out when she married the chemist."

"When did your father die?" Laurel asked, wishing they had dwelt more on his family's history. They were her kin, too, after all.

"Ten years ago. I was eighteen and sailing on my own then. All those years Da survived at sea, could climb rigging like a monkey and battle pirates and privateers better than anyone. Then he fell off a ladder while hanging a new sign over the shop when he was home on a visit. Broke his neck." He shook his head. "An ignominious end for a born sailor."

"That's so sad. But your mother is happy in her new marriage?"

"Mr. Ives does right well by her, so she says.

I sailed out of here on my way to fetch you, so she'll probably be expecting me back sooner or later."

"But not me," Laurel guessed.

He laughed. "No, not as my wife. She'll be shocked to silence to find me married. And glad of it, too, when she recovers."

They walked on down the street to the chemist shop and Jack entered first, holding the door open for Laurel. He set down his trunk just inside.

A statuesque, fair-haired woman in her mid-fifties threw up her hands and cried, "Jackie Boy!"

Laurel noted the resemblance in their features. The mother had the same strong nose and chin. The indentations in her cheeks that could almost be deemed dimples softened her countenance just as Jack's did. Her mother-in-law was a tall, handsome woman with a proud carriage and a capable air about her.

Mrs. Ives rounded the counter and grasped her son in a hearty hug. "Seeing you twice in a month almost never happens!" Then she noticed Laurel and stepped a little apart from Jack, though she seemed not at all embarrassed by her open display of affection.

"Excuse me, miss. I didn't mean to ignore you. What is it I can do for you today?"

Jack hugged his mother with one arm and gestured to Laurel. "You can welcome a daughter, Mum. This is my wife, Laurel. Laurel, my mother, Hester Ives."

The woman's mouth dropped open and she gaped, first at Laurel, then up at her son.

"See? I told you. She's speechless. Not a condition we shall see again right soon." He seemed delighted.

"Mrs. Ives, so nice to meet you," Laurel said, hoping to break the woman's spell. She dropped a curtsy and ducked her head.

"Wife?" his mother gasped. "Is it true? You're not having me on, Jack?"

"Not at all. We were wed aboard ship. Isn't she lovely, Mum?" He winked at Laurel.

"Who is she?"

Jack cleared his throat. "Daughter of the former earl. Of Elderidge. Remember I told you I was going to fetch her home from Spain?"

Mrs. Ives reached behind her to grasp the countertop with both hands. "Then you were not jesting, Jack? Do not play with me," she warned. Her voice dropped to a whisper. "Did you inherit that title or no?"

"Indeed I did, Mum. I told you there was no other male heir."

"You jackanapes, I never took you *seriously!*"

"Well, you may this time. I am the earl and Laurel is my countess. She has no more experience with the nobles than I do, you see, so we decided to muddle through it all together."

"My God. I think I might faint," the woman declared, clenching her eyes shut and pressing a hand to her chest.

"Steady on, old girl!" Jack said, laughing. "Here. Let me close shop for you and we'll go up and have a chat. Where's Mr. Ives today?"

"Gone for the week to purchase stock," she murmured, taking Jack's arm as he led her to the stairs. "Will you stay the night, dear? Please?"

Jack looked over his shoulder at Laurel with apology in his eyes and a plea for understanding. She nodded emphatically.

"Of course, Mum, we'll stay if you like," he replied.

Laurel realized right away why Jack had looked a bit crestfallen at having to stay with his mother. There was only the one bedroom and a small parlor above stairs.

Mrs. Ives had declared on the way up that

she and Laurel would occupy the bedroom and Jack would be relegated to the sitting room couch.

Laurel was a bit disconcerted by that herself. The longer they put off making their marriage real, the more she worried about it.

Mrs. Ives regained full voice in good time, and over tea, Laurel learned much about Jack's early life through tales of his derring-do as a lad. She laughed even as her heart melted, seeing the lovely relationship that still existed between mother and son.

When she and the woman retired for the night, Mrs. Ives insisted that Laurel call her Mum as Jack did.

"He won't be an easy one to live with," she warned Laurel in a near whisper. "Jack has trouble being still, you see. Never a quiet moment around him, I swear. How he ever managed all his energy aboard ship for weeks and months at a time, I can't imagine."

Laurel could well imagine it. He probably had spent the time diving in after errant lads who fell overboard or climbing to the top of the mast. If there had been battles, he would have thought so much the better, but she said none of that to his mother. Instead, she tried to ease the woman's mind about Jack's future.

"Perhaps he has done with the sea, ma'am. He will have lands to manage now."

The mother looked doubtful. "His da was a born seaman and did his best to make one of Jack. It's probably in the blood anyway, so I daren't hope you're right."

Laurel dared. "He is your son, too, you know."

Mrs. Ives smiled and turned down the bed covers. "So he is and I do so wish him happy, above anything. You as well, child."

"You have missed him, haven't you, all these years he's been away? Please say you'll come and visit us often once we're settled. You and Mr. Ives will be most welcome at any time."

"What a dear little thing you are and so thoughtful. Jack's chosen well, I think."

Laurel certainly hoped so. Thus far, they got along well. And she admitted there had been a mighty attraction on her part right from the beginning.

The next morning Laurel donned her gray gown again in preparation for their journey to London. Jack's mother had other ideas. As they drank their tea in the shop, she pleaded with Jack to stay one more day.

He hesitated and Laurel knew why. It was high time they consummated their marriage and could hardly do so in the confines of his mother's living quarters. Laurel smiled at him and gave a small shrug to say she didn't mind if he wanted to visit longer.

"I hate to impose longer," he said, but finally acquiesced when Mrs. Ives insisted they stay. "Very well, one more day," he agreed. "But then we really must go on."

His mother beamed. "All right, but as penance for rushing your visit, you must come with me this evening. It will be the perfect practice for you, Laurel, before you get to London!" she exclaimed. "And I confess, I would enjoy showing off my new daughter."

Laurel could tell that he didn't want to disappoint his mother in any way, perhaps because he had spent so much time away from her. "Where are we going that's so important?"

"To the Theatre Royal! I had planned to go one evening this week anyway. The Olander Company is doing *Hamlet* and our own Rose Madson is to play Ophelia! Tonight is opening night and the entire town should turn out."

"Who is Rose Madson?" Jack asked.

"My good friend Emma Madson's daughter, of course." She flapped a hand. "You wouldn't remember her, I suppose. I think she was born about the time you went to sea with your father.

She was such a lovely girl. Her parents were so upset when she ran off to London to become an actress, but you can imagine how proud they are now she's performing in her own town!"

Laurel couldn't imagine it at all. It must be a parent's worst nightmare. She had heard about actresses. Perhaps her information was a bit skewed, however, considering where she had gotten it. Her curiosity was piqued. "I do love Shakespeare," she said, hoping Jack would allow them to go. "I've never seen a play before, but I've read *Hamlet* so many times."

He looked speculatively at her as she waited for his answer. "I suppose we could. It might be better for you to begin with an outing more modest than some London event." He nodded. "We shall go then."

Mrs. Ives clapped her hands. "Wonderful! You will love the theatre, Laurel. It opened five years ago and I've only been the once. The building itself is so *grand,* I'll wager it's as posh as anything London has to offer."

"I look forward to it." She truly did, but wondered what it would be like with crowds of people and all the noise. Plymouth was the largest town she had ever visited and the passengers and crew of the ship, the most numerous crowd she had yet encountered.

While Jack went out to arrange their transportation to London for the following day and purchase tickets for the play, Laurel spent the hours helping his mother in the chemist shop.

Mrs. Ives proved good company, bragging on Laurel each time a customer came in. She assigned her small tasks anyone could do and then praised her efforts as if Laurel were the most amazing apprentice ever. They kept busy until the hour arrived to get ready for the evening.

Laurel donned her white frock and added the ribbons to her hair. Mrs. Ives was busy digging inside a trunk beside the wall. "Ah! Here it is!" She stood and approached Laurel. "Wear this," she said, draping a soft, blue-and-white paisley shawl around Laurel's shoulders. "Jack's father brought it to me as a gift once when he'd been away for nearly a year. If you like it, I want you to have it."

The soft, finely woven wool felt as supple as silk. "I've never felt such a wonder!" Laurel said, breathless, as she smoothed the delicate folds over her shoulder. "I'll treasure it always." She gave Mrs. Ives an impulsive hug. "Thank you so very much."

"It's only a shawl!" Mrs. Ives said, laughing and patting Laurel's back. She stood back, looked at her and tweaked one of the ribbons in her hair. "My girl needs pretty things."

It wasn't the lovely gift that warmed Laurel's heart, but the sentiment behind it. Jack's mother liked her, called her daughter and seemed so happy to have her in the family. The shawl represented a long-held dream coming true.

"The carriage is here, ladies!" Jack called up the stairs.

"Ooh, a carriage, he says!" his mother exclaimed, her eyebrows raised in mock surprise. "Mr. Fancypants is taking us out in style!"

"*Lord* Fancypants," Laurel whispered, and they laughed together like girls.

The theatre was every bit as grand as Mrs. Ives had declared, Laurel thought when they arrived. Huge columns at least thirty feet tall graced the entrance. "My word, it's so large!"

"It's also a hotel and has assembly rooms," Jack told her. "The theatre's only a part of it, but that alone can accommodate over a thousand people at once."

"I hope they all are not here tonight," she muttered.

He helped her and his mother out of the carriage. "I tried to get a box, but they were all taken, so we'll have to be in the general audience."

Laurel was nearly overcome with excitement as they threaded their way through the throngs gathered in the enormous atrium and found seats. Though the air outside had rather a chill to it, inside the theatre it proved almost stifling due to the crowded conditions.

Above them were the balconied boxes with beautifully dressed ladies and gentlemen looking down. Most held quizzing glasses, or she supposed that's what they were. She had read of those and wondered how the distant stage would look when seen through them. She took her seat on the bench between Jack and his mother and tried to settle down for the performance.

There were two acts preceding it, a soprano who sang a tragic love song and then a trio of rather inexpert acrobats who drew loud derision from the crowds. At last the curtains closed and it grew relatively quiet as the play was announced.

Laurel grew more fascinated by the moment as the play she had read so many times came to life on the stage. The girl who played Ophelia seemed truly mad, lovely as she was, and drew tears well before her character's death. Even Jack seemed entranced to the point of unusual stillness.

When it was over and the applause died down, Laurel released a heavy sigh. She wished their outing could go on and on. Jack ushered them out and hailed their carriage which he had arranged to come back for them after the performance.

"So, what do you think of theatre?" he asked as they waited.

Laurel grasped his mother's hand. "Thank you for this, ma'am. It was the most glorious thing I have ever seen!"

Jack laughed. "That's not as great a compliment as it might be if you hadn't lived all your life behind the walls of a convent!"

"Still, it was wonderful," she declared with a firm nod, "and you mustn't make light of it. We should be regular theatre-goers in London."

He winked at his mother. "You see how she stands me around, Mum? And you worried that the big city might intimidate her? Scoff at the thought. She'll take it by storm, wait and see!"

The ride back to the chemist shop proved jolly, followed by an excellent supper of purchased meat pies and very good wine. Laurel hoped this night was a portent of happy times to come.

"This truly is the best night of my life, by far," she said to his mother after they retired.

She hugged the beautiful blue-and-white shawl once more before folding it away.

The night would have been absolutely perfect if she were retiring to bed with her husband, but Laurel knew that delay only left her something else wondrous to anticipate.

"Jack seemed to enjoy it, too," Mrs. Ives said as she tucked her hair into her frilly nightcap. She was obviously pleased that she had suggested just the right entertainment. "I thought he might excuse himself and wander around impatiently until it was over. He had trouble sitting still for very long, even as a lad. Never left us once tonight, though, did he!"

"No, ma'am, not once. I don't even think he thought about it."

Mrs. Ives had put her finger on the one thing that had begun to trouble Laurel about Jack, however. He proved a most active man, not fidgety, but highly strung as if constantly poised to tackle anything that wanted doing. And if there was nothing apparent pending, he seemed to conjure something out of thin air. When he was quiet and still, it seemed somehow forced and she could sense his tension.

His very nature apparently required perpetual vigilance and a quick response to whatever happened around him, and yet, he seldom seemed exhausted. "I envy his enduring vigor. He's so capable. And quite the hero, too, your lad," Laurel said with a smile as she climbed into bed. "Everyone aboard the ship coming here greatly admired him and so do I."

"Admiration is well and good, but I hope you will *love* my son, Laurel." That was the last thing the mother said after the lamp was blown out and they were settled for the night.

Love. Obviously Jack had grown up with that, even though he must have been away for long stretches of time since he had gone to sea with his father. The closeness with his mother had remained constant.

Could she learn to love him?

Chapter Six

The next morning Jack had gone out to the bakery two doors away and brought back sticky buns. His mother heated water on the small brazier downstairs and made tea.

When they said goodbye, Mrs. Ives embraced Laurel as heartily as she did Jack. Then she grasped both their arms in an almost punishing grip. "Be happy, you two. Be good to one another. And do not let these titles of yours give you airs. Mind you, there's nothing worse than haughty swells!"

"Yes, Mum," Jack promised and nudged Laurel who answered likewise. They shared a smile.

When they were steps away from the shop, he glanced down at Laurel. "Well, my lady, what did you think of dear old Mum?"

"She's absolutely wonderful. Thank you for sharing her," Laurel said with a smile.

"I suppose you had a lecture last night on how to manage the rowdy me."

Laurel nodded. "I did get advice and I plan to follow it entirely."

"Oh? What did she suggest?"

"That would be telling," Laurel said in her most cryptic tone. "If you notice yourself behaving, then you will know it has worked."

"Women! You are such a mysterious lot I wonder why I bother with any of you."

"A great concession, I'm sure," she replied, thoroughly enjoying the moment. She felt so free and excited about the future, it was difficult to maintain her poise.

He glanced up at the sun. "We should make good time to London."

"Where will we stay when we arrive?" she asked, her mind still on that privacy that had been in such short supply.

He was silent for some time, possibly considering the same thing before he answered. "I'll decide on the way there."

Thus far he had moved everything forward with astounding speed. Now she thought he seemed uncertain. "I would think an earl could stay almost anywhere he chooses."

A smile tugged at his lips as he sighed. "I suppose we shall soon see."

The title was so new to him, he obviously had not stopped to consider the cachet it would offer. Or if he had, he simply did not know what to do with it.

It made no sense to feel as she did, but Laurel found she liked him even more after this glimpse of vulnerability. She thought that take-charge attitude of his could become quite wearing if it were the only attitude he possessed.

His mother's words, that solemn plea in the dark, kept echoing in her head every time she looked at Jack. *I hope you will love my son.*

Laurel hoped so, too.

They arrived in London exhausted by the journey from Plymouth. Jack had hired a private coach at the last stop to carry them into town. Darkness was falling when it deposited them at the address furnished by Hobson before Jack left for Spain. They might as well meet the challenge head on instead of staying the night in a hotel, Jack had decided.

He had spent the entire trip wondering how he would go on once he returned. Men destined to become nobles usually were trained for it from childhood. How was he to learn all that was expected of him?

Jack had met many noblemen before in the course of his business and in his travels, but meeting one was far removed from *becoming* one.

For once in his life, he knew he must ask for help before forging ahead. That need did not sit well at all, but it did exist.

Hobson was a possible source. The solicitor would have some ideas, but certainly no more firsthand experience at being noble than Jack had.

He thought of his good friend Neville Morleigh again and wondered if he was still in London. He had married a baron's widow, and Jack recalled that Neville's uncle was a lord. Neville would help if he could be found.

However, for the present, Jack knew he must fend for himself and try to act the part fate had foisted on him so unexpectedly.

Jack glanced up at the columned facade of the stately town house that had been left to Laurel and now, through her, belonged to him. "The knocker's not up," he muttered.

He glanced down at the trunk their driver had placed at the edge of the street. He left it where it was, took Laurel's small bag and placed it there, as well. Then he escorted her up the steps and banged on the door with the side of his fist.

"Chin up, Countess. Here we go."

Presently, it opened to reveal an aging fellow who was little more than a skeleton. Jack stood tall. "I am the new earl," he said simply.

The old man smiled. "Of course you are. Sorry, we are not hiring."

Jack wanted to laugh, but dared not. He had to begin as he meant to go. "I am not applying," he said firmly. "I already have the job. What is your name?"

"Echols. Shall I call the watch or will you decamp without a fuss?"

"Call them if you wish to seek another position at your age." Jack pushed past him into the foyer. "Mr. Hobson should have notified you I would be arriving eventually. Please summon the staff and have a footman retrieve our baggage." He turned and beckoned to Laurel. "Come in, my lady. We are home."

The butler had stepped back, glaring at them, mouth open in disbelief. He had obviously recognized the solicitor's name.

"Step lively, Echols. Her ladyship is weary and we are both in need of sustenance after our journey. Fetch the staff at once!"

"How do I know you are who you say?" Echols asked, his voice now subdued and uncertain. "Anyone might burst in and declare—"

Jack nodded once, interrupting. "Yes, and I commend your caution, Echols, but it is unnecessary in this instance. Now gather everyone so that we may introduce ourselves but once."

Echols left them, his progress still hesitant.

"Damned if I'll prove myself to a butler," Jack rasped under his breath.

Laurel nudged his side. "Airs," she said, shaking her head. "What would your mum say?"

"Don't make me laugh," Jack warned, struggling to keep his countenance stern. "I have to be earl-like."

The butler returned with five people in tow, a housekeeper, two maids and two footmen. Jack looked them over, then glared at Echols.

"His lord and her ladyship, the Earl and Countess of Elderidge," the man intoned in a sonorous voice. "Mrs. Price, housekeeper, George and Will, footmen, Betty and Meg, housemaids."

Jack nodded as they bowed and curtsied. "No cook?"

"Mr. Carson has been notified of your arrival. He and the potboy, Ned, are preparing your supper, milord," Echols announced.

"Thank you, Echols." He turned to the housekeeper. "Are our rooms ready? If so, we would like a bath and our meal sent up. After that, we should not like to be disturbed unless the house catches fire."

Echols cleared his throat. "As you wish, milord. Mrs. Price will see you up. Will there be anything else, sir?"

Jack smiled. "I'm sure you will be contacting Mr. Hobson immediately to verify my identity. While you're about it, ask him if he knows the direction of Mr. Neville Morleigh, married to the former Lady Ludmore, I believe."

Echols raised his eyebrows. "Why, Mr. Morleigh and her ladyship are just down the way, sir!"

"He resides nearby?" Jack could hardly believe the luck. But then, he understood that a great many of the Ton were concentrated here in Mayfair.

"He does for a fact, sir. Shall I send for him?"

Jack thought for a moment. "No, not this evening. That will be all, Echols, thank you."

He wondered if he should have added the thanks. Did one thank the butler for doing his job? Well, a word of thanks never hurt in any instance he could think of.

He took Laurel's arm and they followed the housekeeper up the winding stairs. Laurel had remained quiet, he noticed. If he was at a loss as to how to behave in his new station, she must be doubly so. Still, he wished she had presented herself in a more authoritative way.

Jack had no idea whether he had made a good or bad impression on the staff, or if he had followed the correct procedure for such an assumption of command, but at least he and Laurel had beds for the night.

He had heard that two bedrooms were the custom for uppercrust married folk. Well, he would have to see about that tradition and possibly change it in his own household.

That thought consoled him as nothing had since this fiasco began. He knew precisely what to do in bed with a woman. That role was certainly nothing new to him.

His only worry was that the role would be all too new to Laurel. How would a woman with no experience at all react to bedding? Perhaps this particular situation would be new to him, after all.

"Milady's chamber," Mrs. Price announced, leading them into a large chamber delicately bedecked in green and white. Jack thought it rather ostentatious, but hopefully Laurel would appreciate the frills after living in the austere environment of the convent. He imagined the nuns would have only approved bare essentials.

A graceful and elaborately carved desk displayed a fancy silver inkwell and dyed plume pen. The windows were covered in pale green damask that matched the subtly flocked wallpaper. Flowing floral silk adorned the good-sized bed's delicate canopy and complemented the heavily embroidered coverlet and bolster. A French chiffonier covered half of one wall.

For a long moment, he imagined Laurel lying there in all that splendor, waiting for him to come to her. The sharp tug of desire, held so firmly in check during their travels, refused to abate now that he knew the time for it was almost upon them.

"How lovely," Laurel said, but timidly and without much enthusiasm. He heard the tremor in her voice and wondered if her thoughts were running in the same vein as his.

"They'll be bringing up your bath in a trice, ma'am," Mrs. Price said. "If you will come this way, sir?" She gestured to a doorway at one side of the chamber.

Jack followed, entering an adjoining dressing room that contained a large copper tub, now empty, a lidded closet stool, slipper chair, a petticoat mirror and shelving. Through an opposite door lay his room.

This chamber, a bit larger in size than Laurel's, had been dressed in greens and browns with much heavier and darker furnishings, consisting of a gateleg table flanked by two upholstered chairs and a tall wardrobe. The bed, a canopied four-poster, was enormous, the largest Jack had ever seen.

He sensed Laurel hovering behind him in the doorway. She must be wondering, too, whether each needed an invitation to visit the other's room. He stood aside. "Come in, my dear, and have a look."

Then he addressed the housekeeper. "Mrs. Price, have our meal served in here if you will. The lads must be busy below, so I shall light the fires in both rooms."

The portly woman's eyes widened. "But, sir, *they* should..." Her voice trailed off and she cleared her throat before continuing, "As you wish, sir. If you will excuse me, I'll go down and send the girls up to assist my lady. George can attend you, though he's not much experience in that regard."

Her expression held the question of why an

earl and countess had arrived with no valet or maid in tow.

"Very good," Jack stated. He imagined an earl would not stoop to explain, so he said nothing more.

After a bob of a curtsy, she swept out, using the hall door, and closed it behind her.

"Well!" Jack exclaimed, turning to take Laurel's hands in his. "Here we are. What do you think of all this?"

She gave a nervous little laugh, still eyeing the bed. "It seems...sufficient to our needs, milord."

"Don't *milord* me, Laurel. I expect I'll have enough of that from now on without hearing it on your lips, too."

"It's all so, well, so *grand*, isn't it," she said in a small voice.

He shrugged. "And ours to bear. I wonder what we shall find at the country house. A much larger abode, wide expanse of property and many more servants, I expect." And tremendous responsibilities for the both of them.

She exhaled heavily and looked up at him. "I'm afraid I don't know how to go on or what to say. I thought I would. Hoped that I would. It's...overwhelming."

Jack enfolded her in his arms, wishing he

could wave some magic wand and spare her the effort of fitting into her new life. Even though he genuinely wanted to protect her, he couldn't help wishing for some of that confidence she had shown before. Or perhaps, he was really wishing for a bit of that in himself.

Jack took a deep breath and dismissed all qualms. He could do this and so could she. "We'll get used to it in short order, I daresay. I've captained a ship, after all, and this can't be so different. As for you, why not pretend you are Mother Superior and take charge of these people?"

He felt her muted laughter as she relaxed against him. "I don't believe you'd want the Mother Superior biding next door to you."

"Certainly not tonight," he agreed, and her laughter stopped.

Someone knocked just then and he released Laurel. "Come," he commanded and the door opened. One of the footmen entered with a large tray bearing silver-covered dishes, a crystal decanter, two glasses and a vase with three bedraggled roses.

Behind him, from inside the dressing room, Jack heard the slosh of pouring water and the whispers of the maids who had entered through Laurel's room to prepare the bath.

Precious little privacy even now, Jack thought, wondering if he and Laurel would ever be alone long enough to seal their marriage vows. There would be the baths, clearing away of the dishes, turning down of the beds and God only knew what else.

He glanced at the door to the hall to see if it had a lock. It did, with a large key, probably the mate to one hanging on the housekeeper's chatelaine.

The footman deposited the tray on the table and bowed to them. "I shall serve you, milady, milord." He held out a chair and looked expectantly at Laurel.

"Never mind that. You may go. George, is it?"

"Yes, sir. I'll return later and help you undress."

"Not *tonight,* George," Jack insisted with a meaningful look.

The young footman bit back a smile. "Very good, sir."

"Good night, George," Jack said with a sigh.

Their meal consisted of a simple stew, none too fresh bread, cheese and a mixture of sliced fruits. The wine proved only adequate enough to wash it all down.

Jack figured that either the staff had been forced to make do with very limited funds since the death of the old earl or they were pocketing a good portion of the household allowance.

He must ask Hobson whether there were funds to pocket or if these servants were simply hanging on, waiting for another employer who could authorize expenditures.

The meal progressed, not the intimate supper he had envisioned, but accompanied by the soft giggles of the maids in the next room and a nervous Laurel picking at her food.

He sorely wished this night over, despite any pleasures that might be had. That wish was a wonder, since there was so much to do come morning, he would scarcely know where to begin.

"I'll be visiting an old friend tomorrow," he informed Laurel. "Perhaps he can navigate us through these unfamiliar shoals." He poured another glass of wine for her as he continued, "I hope he can advise us where to shop. You need new clothes and so do I."

She reached for the glass and sipped a few times. "I have never shopped. And I have no money to do so."

Jack wanted to tell her she was among the wealthiest heiresses in England, but that would certainly rouse her suspicion as to why he had married her so hastily.

"We will have sufficient funds for you to buy whatever you like, Laurel. I'll see Hobson tomorrow, deal with the bank and bring you a generous amount to spend."

"Oh, I shan't need much," she said.

"Oh, yes, you will," he argued, keeping his voice low so as not to be overheard by the maids. "And so will I if we are to keep up appearances." He knew that sounded shallow and self-serving. "What I mean to say is that we must at least signal to our staff, here and at the country house, that we are not destitute and their positions are secure."

"How much *do* we have?" she asked as she set down her empty glass.

How much, indeed. Jack shrugged as he poured her more wine. "Quite enough, I assure you." Hobson had indicated that if Jack married Laurel, they would not need to worry about money for the duration of their lives. That the interest alone would provide whatever they would need and then some.

She stared at him, wide-eyed. "You have no idea how much, do you?"

"Of course I do!" he exclaimed, lying through his teeth. "It's simply a husband's duty to manage assets. You needn't trouble yourself on that account."

"I see," she said simply, pushing her chair back from the table. "If you will excuse me, I'll go and have my bath now."

He stood immediately as she rose. "Yes, of course."

When she opened the door to the dressing room, one of the maids, a plump little redhead with a merry smile, greeted her, then glanced through the opening to speak to Jack. "Will's brought up your trunk, sir. It's in here."

Jack went to get it. He didn't want a curious Laurel or one of the saucy maids digging through his things. His journals were in there.

He had begun keeping his daily doings on paper as a young lad aboard ship, practicing for the day when he would captain his own vessel. It was a habit he continued even after that goal had been reached because it helped him to organize his thoughts and make decisions.

Some of those decisions did not need sharing with any other person, especially those of the past few weeks.

He glanced at the large copper tub with its cloth liner draped over the sides. Inviting steam drifted up from the water, awaiting Laurel. The other maid halted in unbuttoning Laurel's gray gown.

Jack wished to take the maid's place and do that deed himself, but gallantly lifted his trunk and left the women to it. Both maids bobbed likes corks as he turned to close the door.

He poured more wine and waited for Laurel to finish her bath so he could bathe next. The water would be cooling by then. Cold, he hoped. Perhaps that would serve to banish the worst of his urgency to have her.

He couldn't approach her like some ravenous rake bent on his own quick satisfaction. No woman, virgin or not, would appreciate that. He had never tupped an untried lass, but was well aware of the protocol involved. Patience. Not his strong suit, but he would employ it.

He tried hard not to think of Laurel sliding naked into that tub, squeezing a spongeful of water over her shoulders and breasts. Soaping that lovely, fine-pored skin of hers and scrubbing softly, inhaling the scent of lavender with eyes closed and a soft smile on her face.

He shook his head to clear it of the salacious images, drew in a deep breath and released it slowly, determined to dismiss the heat now rolling through him in waves.

The fact that he did want her so fiercely surprised him a little, but he put that down to the denial he had endured this past week in which they shared adjacent quarters. And also, the knowledge that she was his wife and should have been available to him already.

Circumstances being what they were, he thought he had behaved rather well, hopefully well enough that he had calmed her fears of the consummation, if she had any.

Jack decided he was exceptionally lucky to have married Laurel. Not only was she innocent, she was also very attractive, intelligent and biddable. What more could a man want in a wife? He could never have found one more perfect.

Heaven help him if she ever discovered *why* he had married her and the lies he had told her to make it happen.

He had removed his coat and boots and was writing in his journal when the maid knocked and called out that her lady had finished.

Jack wasted no time having his own bath and donning a nightshirt from his trunk. He hated the things, much preferring to sleep as God made him, but it had seldom been practical for him to do so. Perhaps later, he thought with a smile.

Chapter Seven

Jack knocked softly on the connecting door to her room. No answer.

He opened it slowly, fully expecting to find her ensconced in the fancy bed, waiting for him with wide eyes and bated breath.

She was sound asleep, tangled in the covers, on her back and crossways on the bed, arms outstretched to either side. One bare foot peeked from beneath the coverlet. Her hair, unbraided and uncoiled, framed her head and shoulders in a shining cloud of waves and curls.

He had never seen it or the lady herself look so free. She was always so buttoned up and tightly braided, surely as she had been taught to be.

He couldn't slip into bed beside her. Though the mattress was larger than most, she claimed the better portion of it with her outflung limbs and body position. How in the world had she ever slept on a convent cot? He had never seen one of those, of course, but knew they must, of necessity, be small and narrow.

He approached the bed, loath to wake her. He noted the modest, unembellished nightdress that covered her neck to wrists, and he imagined to ankles, as well.

Oddly, seeing her in this state of total abandon proved enough to satisfy him for the moment. She slumbered on, unaware of his appraisal. Jack wondered if she would welcome him with a sleepy smile or if he would frighten the life out of her by his sudden appearance.

He watched her sigh in her sleep and realized she must have been exhausted by the long trip to London. Sharing a bed with her mother-in-law last night could not have been conducive to good rest, either.

As much as it pained him in his present state of arousal, Jack decided he should be considerate enough to leave her alone for one more night.

His mind replayed their kiss aboard ship, the remembered softness of her mouth stirring him further. He must *wait*, he thought with a huff of frustration. When they did make love for the first time, her very first time, things should be perfect for her. Guilt over the way he had tricked her into the marriage made that even more important.

Besides, he did not want to seem a demanding sort determined to claim his husbandly rights, even at her inconvenience. She should want this, not simply endure it, or else she might dread it in future. If he was to keep himself only to her, as he had vowed and fully intended to do, he did not want her reluctant in bed.

Quietly, he covered her exposed foot, returned to his own room and crawled into the gigantic bed alone. Until his body folded into the heavenly soft feather mattress, he had not realized the toll the day had taken on him. He drifted into sleep thinking of Laurel and what pleasures tomorrow night might bring.

When morning came, Jack awoke in a pensive mood. He would go to see Neville today, as well as the solicitor. Once he and Laurel acquired new wardrobes, he meant to leave for Elderidge House and assess the condition of the estate.

That was a must. The Corn Laws would have affected everyone in that borough adversely and they would probably be wanting, or at the very least anxious to see what the future held for them. Jack made a mental note to learn more about the laws in short order so that he could find a way to reassure the tenants. *His* tenants. Ah, the task of managing an estate loomed heavy on his mind.

He did not look forward to encountering the dowager countess. She would certainly resent Laurel's presence and probably his, too. He only hoped there was a dower house on the estate for the widow or that she would move elsewhere to avoid their company.

George, the footman, brought him tea and insisted on helping him to dress. Jack allowed it, then dismissed him with orders to take a message to Neville's house down the street and await an answer.

Breakfast proved a lonely affair, taken in the large dining room with no company. Apparently the lady was breakfasting in her chamber. Jack wondered if she thought she was expected to do that since they had supped above stairs last evening. She had so much to learn.

And so did he, Jack admitted. He hated feeling like a fish out of water. He really hated what he must do to correct it. No man wanted to admit he couldn't solve his own problems.

A mere half hour later, the butler announced, "Mr. Morleigh awaits you in the parlor, sir."

So Neville had returned with the messenger. Jack stood and laid down his serviette. "Thank you, Echols. Have coffee served us there."

He strode down the hallway to the parlor, wondering how different he would find Neville nowadays. "So good of you to come, Neville," he said by way of greeting.

The man had changed a bit, Jack noted as Neville turned to face him. Older, of course, and now decked out like a fashion plate, Neville's lithe build lent itself well to the current, rather understated mode of a gentleman's attire.

Neville flashed his signature grin. "Jack, old man! *You* are the Earl of Elderidge?" He strode forward and extended his hand, grasping Jack's in a firm shake. "I had no idea until your footman came with the message! Good to see you, man, and where the devil have you been? I looked for you at Plymouth when I returned to England but your mother said you were abroad."

"In Amsterdam," Jack said. "I read of your marriage in a London paper whilst I was there. Congratulations."

Neville's eyes grew soft. "Wait until you

meet her, Jack. She's been the making of me, that woman."

"A baroness, no less," Jack said. "Leave it to you to find a prize, you old pirate."

"Oh, she is a prize all right! She bought me, you see, and I surrendered without a peep."

Jack nodded. "I *do* see, but I'll bet my last groat the money wasn't her best quality, was it?"

Neville laughed. "You know me well, mate. Not that I needed her blunt. Business has been good and investments are sound enough. And you? Still privateering?"

"On this last voyage, I hired Terrell to captain. The *Siren* burned and sank over a month ago near Barbados. All hands lost but two crewmen who cobbled three barrels together and floated until the tide took them ashore."

Neville cursed. "Gad, I'm so sorry to hear that, Jack. Have you another ship yet? I'll gladly invest if need be."

"No, my seagoing days are done now."

Neville brightened after a moment of reflection. "However, you've not done badly for yourself since, grabbing an earldom! How in hell did that happen? Did you kill off all the competition?"

Jack indicated they should sit. "Hardly. Inheriting was a shock. I didn't even know the old fellow or that I was ever in line for a title."

He looked up, meeting Neville's interested gaze. "I have just married his daughter." He tapped his fingers on the arms of his chair, wishing he didn't have to do this. "Look, I hate to ask it of you, Neville, but I need your help."

"With the wife?" Neville asked with a wry twist of his lips. "Can't help you there. I have my hands full at home."

Jack rolled his eyes. "With decoding the expectations. You know, society manners, dealing with staff and tenants, that sort of thing. Hell, I don't even know where to go here in Town to buy my wife a frock. She's straight out of a Spanish convent and was working as a governess, so she knows less than I do about what's expected of us."

Neville leaned forward, listening with interest. "I sense a fascinating story behind this countess of yours."

"Indeed, and I'll share it with you later. But for now, I know your uncle is an earl and that you've married into the Ton. I was hoping perhaps you could give me a few suggestions as to how Laurel and I should get on with this new endeavor and not make complete cakes of ourselves?"

Neville was nodding already. "I will go you one better, friend. Fetch your wife and bring her to meet my Miranda. We will take you both in hand. Before the week is out, you two will be the toast of London."

"No, no, that's too much of an imposition," Jack protested. "I only want a quick lesson in protocol, a few names of shops and so forth. You needn't *adopt* us."

"Nonsense, it'll be fun for all of us! An adventure." Then Neville paused, his dark brows drawn together. "Wait. There's nothing much going on in Town until Parliament opens. So there's no point in making toast of you two when no one's around to notice. Well then, we shall have plenty of time to bronze you both, won't we!"

"Perhaps you should ask your wife if she's willing."

Neville flapped a hand to dismiss that. "Miranda will be delighted with whatever I suggest," he insisted with a sly wink. "I left her in an excellent mood this morning."

No need to ask why. Neville had always been a ladies' man. "Well, I suppose we could at least come for a chat. You'll let me know what day is convenient for us to visit?"

"No time like the present. Collect the countess and let's away! I have a suspicion our women will be most eager to divest us of a small fortune. We might as well all go shopping." He raked a wincing look over Jack's attire. "That the best kit you've got?"

"One that's better for important occasions," Jack said defensively.

Neville threw up one hand. "Fine! Go and don it then. My haberdasher will toss you out on your ear if you turn up wearing this. Unless you wave a fistful of pound notes under his nose, of course. Then you could walk in stark naked if you wished."

"Of course it takes money," Jack replied with a sigh.

"What's wrong?" Neville asked. "You haven't any?"

Jack shrugged. "Aye, plenty, but it's all hers."

"Well it's *yours* now," Neville reminded him. "C'mon, Jack. Don't second-guess yourself. If I know you at all, you arranged this marriage to bring her out of service as a governess and reinstate her in society, didn't you?"

"That, and to save the estate from falling to ruin and putting a sizable number of people out of work. The bare fact is that I married her for her money to do just that. Now I must figure out the best way to put it to good use. How does one run an estate, do you know?"

"Well, I've no experience there, but perhaps my cousin Caine could be of help with advice on that. He's had to learn the ropes himself of late since he became our uncle's heir." He slapped Jack on the back. "Let's conduct one mission at a time, shall we?"

Jack excused himself when a maid came in with a tray bearing coffee. He went upstairs, changed quickly and knocked on Laurel's door. When she answered, he was glad to see her wearing the white gown instead of that gray monstrosity of a governess's frock. Even so, he wished he could go out and buy her something more appropriate without her having to face a modiste's or shopkeeper's ridicule.

"Get your bonnet," he instructed. "We are going to visit friends."

She complied with obvious reluctance, and Jack knew she wanted to refuse. He didn't much want to go himself. "Look, we must have new clothes. Neville said his wife will assist you in choosing things and he will instruct me. We have to stow our pride and accept their help."

Laurel donned her bonnet, then turned to him. "Jack, I must apologize for falling asleep last night, but I—"

"Neville is waiting for us," he said, interrupting her, unwilling to enter into any discussion about the postponed consummation at the moment.

"Are you angry?" she asked.

"Of course I'm not angry," he snapped. "Only anxious to have done with this business of shopping. A more tiresome activity, I cannot imagine, but it can't be avoided." He took her arm. "Come, let's go."

He escorted her downstairs where Neville waited in the foyer, his hat in hand. "Laurel, Neville Morleigh, an old friend of mine. Neville, this is my wife."

"*Enchanté,* Lady Laurel." He bowed and kissed Laurel's hand. "Welcome home to England."

"Thank you, Mr. Morleigh," Laurel said in a near whisper as she ducked her head and curtsied.

"I see my old mate has done himself proud. He has always had an eye for beauty," Neville said. "May I wish you all the best in your life together?"

"Thank you again, sir." She blushed and shrank as if she wished to disappear right through the floor.

Why did she persist in this worse than humble attitude? What had happened to the spirited miss he had first encountered? Had he imagined that set down she'd been giving her employer? Come to think of it, the only time he had ever witnessed her actual fieriness was at Orencio's.

But he should be more fair about judging her. Bringing her to London first might have been a mistake. As well as accustoming herself to the newness of a large city, she would have to undergo the indignity of being taught how to dress and act by a woman of inferior rank.

Still, he couldn't resist an attempt to break her out of this dreadful meekness. "Square up, Laurel. London isn't full of devils out to get you, you know."

"It's a beautiful morning for a walk," Neville said, shooting Jack a dark look of reproof.

Now what? Was Neville disapproving of Laurel or had Jack's curtness bothered him? Whatever was the matter, Jack just knew he felt all out of patience, upset by Laurel's loss of spirit, already disliking London and worried about the future.

He hated the uncertainty of it all, the unfamiliarity he was bound to experience. This was the first time he had felt this way since boarding a ship for the first time as a lad. The feeling left him tied up in knots. Worse than usual.

They left the town house and made their way down the street to Neville's. Jack listened with half an ear to Neville's ramblings about the changes in the city these past few years, merely grunting a response now and then. Laurel remained silent.

He knew he should act more gracious since he had been the one to ask for Neville's help in the first place. And he ought to do something to put Laurel at ease. He patted her hand that clutched the inside of his elbow. That was the best he could do at the moment.

Laurel wished she had more social skills. She knew how to address her betters. That had been drilled into her when it was thought that almost everyone she would ever meet would be considered her betters. But rules had changed now, and the nuns had never thought to teach her what a countess must do.

Add that to the fact that Jack was obviously displeased with her and she was at a total loss. On that point, she was a bit displeased with him, as well. She had seen Jack's display of quick temper with Orencio the day they met, but when directed at her, Laurel did not appreciate it at all.

His friend, Mr. Morleigh, seemed a considerate sort. She only hoped his wife was of the same nature or this day might prove a terrible disaster.

The town house Mr. Morleigh ushered them into was virtually the same in structure as the one in which they had stayed last night, the one she had trouble thinking of as actually belonging to her and Jack. The furnishings at this one were newer and brighter, she noted.

"Ah, here is my girl now!" Mr. Morleigh said, his affection for his wife apparent.

Small wonder. The lady approaching looked like something out of a fairy tale, Laurel thought. How beautiful she was with her hair all done up in curls with blue ribbons to match her softly pleated gown. Even her pretty satin slippers were blue.

Her features appeared to be slightly enhanced by traces of kohl about the eyes and something shimmering and rosy on her smiling lips. Face paint had never been allowed in the convent, but Laurel had read about it. This, however, was so subtle and barely noticeable, Laurel thought it quite acceptable. Perhaps all ladies wore it. Would she?

"Miranda, here is Jack, Lord Elderidge, of course, and his countess, Lady Laurel."

The baroness dropped into a graceful curtsy, which Laurel returned in kind. Then the woman raised her gaze to meet Laurel's directly. "It is so good to meet you both. Welcome to our home."

After an uncomfortable moment of silence, Neville took charge. "Look, let's dispense with formalities, shall we? We are Neville and Miranda, you are Jack and Laurel. Titles be damned or we'll be tripping all over them. Any objections?"

Jack laughed at last. "None whatsoever. Leave it to the commoner among us to set things straight. Miranda, it is a great pleasure to meet you. This rascal is so obviously besotted, I can't think you are anything but wonderful. We appreciate his offer of help, but if you have better things to do with your time when he explains our untimely visit, we will surely understand and remain friends."

Apparently Jack had put aside whatever caused his foul mood for the benefit of their hostess. Laurel wondered if it would resume once they were alone again.

Neville slipped an arm around his wife. "My dear, we have the distinct honor of bringing out these two during the next Season." He gave her a quick hug, drawing her closer. "And today, we shop and get them up to snuff! Sartorial splendor, that's the battle plan for the day. No limits, right, Jack?"

"No," Jack replied with an emphatic shake of his head. "No limits. Laurel may have whatever suits her and she needs everything a lady requires."

Miranda clasped her hands together under her chin and her eyes fairly sparkled. "What a wonderful way to spend the day! Or perhaps the week! I love nothing better than prowling the shops!"

"And piling up purchases," Neville added with a chuckle. "She's infinitely adept at it, too!"

His wife shot him a grin, then turned a sweet smile on Laurel and reached out for her hand. "Come with me, my dear, and off with you lads! We two have serious matters to discuss before we go out."

"But we planned to go together to the shops, all of us," Neville protested. "Think how you'll miss me."

"Don't be a donkey, Nev. Laurel and I must get to know one another so we can decide what sort of image she will require. You men can all look alike in any old things, but we women have to form a colorful strategy. Go now!" she ordered, flicking her elegant fingers toward the front door. "Take the carriage and send it back for us in an hour or so. We shan't see you until evening. There's a dear."

Laurel watched Neville shrug and take Jack by the elbow, ushering him out as instructed. Jack flashed her a worried frown over his shoulder, so Laurel smiled tightly and gave him a little wave.

"There now, we're rid of the rascals," Miranda said with a merry laugh as she led Laurel to the stairs. "Come on, I have the most darling rose walking frock that will look stunning on you! Not my color, I find, but on you, it will be absolute perfection!"

"I cannot wear your clothes! Jack said I could buy my own." She bit her lip as they ascended. "Though he forgot to give me any funds for it."

Miranda gave her hand a squeeze. "Oh, you won't need money. You must charge everything to Elderidge's account and have the bills sent later. That's how it's done, you know. There's not a merchant in London who would refuse your custom. We will delight them no end."

"Frugality is much admired in a woman, so I was always told," Laurel declared.

"Where in the world did you hear such sacrilege?" Miranda asked with a happy laugh.

"In the convent," Laurel replied.

"Oh, my word, a convent," Miranda said with a sigh. "That explains the dress."

Late in the day, Laurel began to feel faint with exhaustion. She feared she would fall asleep again tonight before Jack came to her unless she rested beforehand.

She and Miranda, that gloriously wonderful new friend of hers, lounged comfortably in the parlor of the Elderidge town house, sipping tea and waiting for the menfolk to return.

"Just wait until he sees you!" Miranda exclaimed. "I cannot believe the transformation myself and I watched it happen! Even after an entire afternoon of shopping, you still look ravishing!"

Laurel felt strange rather than ravishing. Miranda had insisted on having her own maid dress Laurel's hair before they went to the shops. Then she had foisted the rose confection of a walking dress onto her, along with shoes and French bonnet to match.

After that, the entire day had progressed in a

blur of fittings and choosing furbelows. There were quick, whispered instructions that Miranda slid between conversations with the dressmakers and shopkeepers as to how Laurel should behave with them.

Miranda was a wealth of information when it came to Laurel's physical deportment as well as how to assume expressions worthy of a countess. For the most part, Laurel simply copied whatever Miranda did. She wondered how Jack was faring under Neville's tutelage.

When they first arrived at the Elderidge house, Miranda had instructed Laurel to remove her bonnet, gloves and the elegantly tucked fichu that covered the upper half of the bosom. She declared it was nearly evening so a more revealing dress was appropriate. She, however, kept her walking attire intact for when Neville would escort her home.

"Keep your white frock for a morning dress," Miranda advised. "It's not to be worn out, but you may receive guests while wearing it. The rose is for outings in the day or a casual evening at home as you wear it now. Never go out without your gloves," she reminded Laurel.

Laurel had never owned but one pair of gloves in her life and those were meant for warmth in winter. Now she had a dozen of varied lengths, all for show. It seemed such a waste.

"Your purchases should be delivered this evening or in the morning. Those frocks being sewn will take at least a week, but you should have enough of the ready-made to suffice until then."

They had shopped no less than four dressmakers to find six frocks in the proper size already done up for customers who had not claimed them. Ten more had been ordered at Miranda's insistence. Laurel wondered where in the world she would ever wear so many.

There were morning dresses, day gowns, walking dresses, two ballgowns and a riding habit. Also hats, caplets, a lovely paisley shawl, two jackets and one mantle for cold weather. Not to mention the unmentionables Miranda had insisted she purchase! The cost would be outrageous.

Laurel had worried aloud that Jack would accuse her of trying to beggar him. He would have good cause if he did, but Miranda assured her he would not.

"Have your maid press and hang the gowns as soon as they arrive."

"I haven't a maid," Laurel said. "That is to

say, not a lady's maid as such. There are two housemaids here, of course."

"Choose one and train her. It's good to promote from within if you think one of those girls will do. That gives the other staff hope of advancement. Tomorrow I shall send my Kerrick over to instruct your girl in the basic things she should know and see that she has her own proper clothing for her new station."

Miranda thought for a moment. "Oh, and you're to address your maid by her surname. That's how it's done."

"You are too good," Laurel said sincerely. "I have never had such a generous friend, Miranda. Your time must be valuable, and here, you've spent the entire day assisting me. I wish there were something I could do to repay you."

The other woman leaned forward and grasped her hand. "Being a friend is thanks enough. I have not made many of those, you know. My first husband would never allow it, and after he died, all the wives were shy of widows. Now most of my time is spent with Neville."

"He adores you," Laurel declared. "You are so fortunate."

"Jack doesn't adore you?" Miranda asked, frowning.

"Well." Laurel shrugged and pulled a face. "Not *yet*."

They laughed together and Miranda gave her hand a pat. "As I said, wait until he sees you *now!*"

Just then they heard the men coming into the hall, arguing about a hat.

"In here, you two!" Miranda called out.

The door was open and the men walked in. Neville went straight to Miranda, who rose to greet him. Laurel stood as well, her gaze seeking Jack's. He had stopped dead still in the doorway.

Chapter Eight

❧◈❧

"My God!" Jack exclaimed. "Look at you!"

Laurel could not decide whether he was pleased or merely shocked. "Well?" She offered a tentative smile.

"Well, indeed!" he replied, dragging his gaze from her to Miranda. "And well-done."

Miranda laughed. "You might wait until the bills arrive to wax too grateful, Jack. But she is lovely, isn't she?" Her next words were for her husband. "Neville, I believe it is time for us to go home."

Jack stood aside as the couple left. He murmured another word of thanks to them as they passed, his gaze still fastened upon Laurel.

She tried not to blush and tried to remember all that Miranda had told her. *Never slouch.*

Never show apprehension or lack of confidence. Hold yourself at high value and see that others do as well. If they do not, give them the cut direct.

Miranda knew well the way of things, for she had been born to be what she was, a diamond of the first water. Laurel had read that phrase in a book and thought it described her sparkling new friend exactly.

She watched as Jack strode slowly across the room. When he reached her, he took her hands in his, raising them to his mouth. His lips were warm against her skin as his eyes met hers. "You are truly beautiful," he whispered.

Why that should have made her angry, Laurel could not say. After all, that had been the objective, had it not? All she had allowed done to her this day was to reach this very conclusion.

"So now you want me," she stated without inflection.

"I do indeed," he admitted.

She jerked her hands from his and turned away from him. "I am the same person I was last week, yesterday, this morning!" she declared. "The very same as I was when dressed wrongly, without rouged lips and rice powder!"

She raked at the curls so carefully wrought

by Miranda's maid, tearing the pins away, loosening her hair even as she loosed her temper. "Do not judge me by the way I look, Jack Worth!"

"Everyone else will," he replied. "I was only reacting the way they are likely to do. As for me, I liked you very well the way you were last week, giving a set down to that Spanish snake. I liked how you weathered the voyage without complaint and how gently you dealt with my mother. Even the huge crowds at the theatre never bothered you. However, you were *not* the same last evening or this morning, and I confess I did not like you *that* way."

Laurel snapped around to face him again. "And what way would that be?"

"Subservient. Timid. Intimidated."

"Behaving as I was taught!" she exclaimed. "'The meek shall inherit the earth!'"

He scoffed. "Six by two feet of it, for certain, and probably claim that sooner than the strong! If you intend to greet every stranger you meet in that manner, you might as well have donned a habit and stayed with the nuns!"

Much to her horror, Laurel burst into tears. She dashed from the parlor, ran to the stairs, up to her room and slammed the door. She leaned against it. *Damn the man!*

No one had ever made her cry. No one, not even Orencio! The entire day had been so incredibly strange. Never had her feelings swung so rapidly from one extreme to the next, fear to elation, bright expectation to hopelessness, humility to overconfidence. And now, this unexpected and unreasonable anger had flared.

Suddenly she felt deflated and exhausted, yet her nerves were thrumming so that she could hardly be still. For once, she quite understood Jack's unnerving energy.

Betty came out of the dressing room and stopped short. "Milady, are you unwell?"

Laurel nodded and pushed away from the door. "Please go." She so wished to be alone, to further examine what was wrong with her to allow such rapid changes in her emotions. The sisters would be aghast at how she was neglecting her training.

True, it had always proved a struggle to be as they demanded, but she thought she had mastered their teachings. Well, first Orencio and now Jack certainly had sent whatever serenity she had acquired flying to the four winds.

"Chamomile tea, that's what's called for. I'll just go and bring it up," Betty announced.

"Wait. Unlace me first," Laurel ordered. "I cannot stand this corset a moment longer!"

"Oh, yes, ma'am!" The little maid scurried over and began to unbutton the back of the rose gown. "We shall have you out of this in no time at all! Will you be dressing for supper in a while?" She laid the gown aside and began undoing the laces at the back of the new, stiff undergarment.

"No supper, just the tea. Then I will go to bed for the night."

"It's not quite dark yet, ma'am! Are you ill?"

"In a manner of speaking," Laurel admitted with a heavy sigh. She rubbed her abdomen where there must be red furrows on her skin caused by the dratted corset's boning.

"Aha," said Betty in a knowing tone. "Let's get you into your nightgown then and I'll fetch you the tea and some comfits. Me mum always says that perks a lady up at the off times."

Laurel shook her head and released another deep sigh now that she could breathe normally. "Well, today certainly qualifies as one of my *off times*."

Jack returned from trying to walk off his frustration and confusion. He still couldn't figure what on earth had happened to Laurel to turn her so contentious all of a sudden.

He had never had a woman resent his calling

her beautiful before. What had she expected after going to all that trouble to change her appearance? Damn it all, she *was* a beauty. He had suspected she could be.

A nice frock and new hairstyle improved her as it would any woman, but he had never thought her plain. Rather ordinary at first, perhaps, but not later when he'd had a good look. Thank God he hadn't said *that*. But maybe he had inferred somehow that he'd thought her looks to be too ordinary before this evening.

Maybe he shouldn't have brought to attention her earlier attitude. He'd only done that to mark how he knew she could hold her own in any situation if she would but try. Things had gone awry from the start and he didn't understand why she took such offense.

Oh, well, he would go up and apologize anyway just in the event it really was his fault. Aye, an apology should turn her up sweet. A smile and a kiss should finish the trick. Then a great lot of kisses and what would follow those should banish all of her squalls by morning.

The maid was just coming out of Laurel's room when he topped the stairs. "Good evening, Betty, is it?" he asked, practicing his smile.

"Yes, sir. And a good evening it is, sir," she

said, returning his smile with a toothy grin. "I'm to be our lady's maid. She just now said so, so you may call me Thornwhistle hereafter if you like."

"Uh, excellent. Congratulations. Lady Laurel's in her room then?" he asked, with a nod toward the door.

Betty frowned as she nodded. "Yes, sir, but I'm afraid she's indisposed this evening."

"Ill?" he demanded, worried that she had come down with something caught during her outing. That could explain her attack of temper earlier. Or maybe she was just angry.

"Not exactly ill, sir. *Indisposed,*" the maid said again with emphasis, raised brows and inclined head, as if imparting a secret. Or something not to be directly discussed.

Ah. He was to glean from that, Laurel was undergoing the unspoken malady suffered monthly by all women, he supposed. Damn it all. Another week of denial. "All right then. Thank you, Betty. Uh, Thornwhistle, is it?"

"It is and you're quite welcome, sir. Shall I send George or Will up to you?" She hesitated a beat. "I would recommend George as the most likely gent's gent."

"Thank you, no, I'll ring if need be. Go along now," Jack said, his mind still on Laurel, wondering whether he should look in on her or if she'd rather be left alone.

Alone, he decided. The mystery was solved as far as he was concerned. Women were known to behave rather strangely at times like this, so he had been told. He must get used to it now that he was a husband.

The problem was that he was not really a husband yet. None of the rewards, yet all of the liabilities, he thought with a huff of resignation.

He went back down the stairs to the old earl's library. Perhaps a dull book and a snifter of Elderidge's brandy would sand away the rough edges of his thoroughly vexing day.

Jack breakfasted alone again the next day and headed for the solicitor's office. He needed to discuss the finances in more detail. Laurel's questions as to the actual amount involved in the earl's bequest underlined the need to have specifics.

There were also questions as to how the staffs were to be paid and how bills were handled at both locations. However, when he arrived at Hobson's office, he found that the man was at the bank on business and might not be returning until early afternoon.

The male secretary advised Jack that Mr.

Hobson would gladly attend him at the Mayfair residence at whatever time would be convenient. Jack suggested four o'clock and left the place.

He wandered rather aimlessly after that, walking briskly along unfamiliar streets, trying to banish some of the pent-up energy that constantly plagued him when he did not exercise to extreme.

London was not well-known to him, though he had been there a number of times. Normally he would have a specific errand there, conclude it and either go on to Plymouth or set sail. Today he paid more attention to his surroundings since he figured he would spend a good part of his life here from now on.

The smells of rubbish, dung, smoke and fumes assailed his nostrils. He had to watch his footing for horse droppings even as he side-stepped little pickpockets darting around and through crowds of pedestrians and carriages like schools of fish.

The city was not as dirty and impoverished as some he had visited on his travels, but it was nothing to boast about, either. It gave him a renewed appreciation for the cleanliness of ships at sea, despite the well-known inconveniences that must be endured onboard.

He passed some of the shops he had visited the day before and thought of the expensive articles he had purchased. Spending wealth he had not earned himself did not sit well with Jack.

When he had been flush, before losing his own small fortune, he'd had little time or opportunity to spend freely of it before reinvesting.

A brisk walk back to Mayfair helped clear his mind and restore some equanimity. Less than half an hour after handing his hat to Echols and retiring to the library, he heard the butler announce Mr. Hobson.

"You should have sent for me!" Hobson exclaimed immediately after Jack greeted him. "I regret I missed your visit at the office. How... how did things go in Spain?"

Jack smiled at the man's eagerness. "I brought her home. We were married aboard ship and she's upstairs resting as we speak."

Hobson closed his eyes and released an audible sigh of satisfaction. "Thank goodness. How is she? Is she well?"

"Quite well. We docked in Plymouth and traveled by coach, arriving here the day before yesterday." Jack offered Hobson a seat and got down to business.

Jack began asking questions about the financial matters concerning both the town house staff and upkeep and the main estate. "We are leaving for the country tomorrow or the next day, so we should settle these things as well as the bills Laurel and I have incurred when we purchased our wardrobes yesterday," he told the solicitor.

"Not to worry, I will take care of everything," Hobson said. "If you would give me leave to disperse funds now, I could go with you to Elderidge House and deal with the estate manager."

"What of your other clients here in London?" Jack asked.

"Oh, I thought you understood, sir," Hobson said with a proud smile. "Elderidge has always been my one-and-only responsibility. I was schooled as a solicitor so that I might handle all legal matters and documents as well as issues dealing with the earl's finances."

"You don't say!"

"I do. His lordship, as well as his father before him, regarded the discussion of anything to do with banking, investments or dispersing of funds with any other than his solicitor quite beneath him."

"He trusted you with *all* of it?" Jack asked, amazed at the former earl's naïveté.

Hobson laughed softly. "Not so much. In fact, he kept excellent track of every penny he ever owned or earned, believe me. But he refused to deal directly in business with anyone other than his emissary. That was my role, family solicitor, man of all business and funds manager."

"I see." Jack was not completely comfortable continuing in that particular vein. The man could steal him blind. Just because he presumably hadn't done so with the former earl did not mean he held the same loyalty to the new one. Still, Jack was at a loss as to how to deal with the estate, so he would have to exhibit a modicum of trust.

"Very well, you may come with us. Judging by Echols's reaction when we showed up here unannounced, perhaps it would be best if you could at least validate who I am once we get there." He added, "And bring the account books. I will need to evaluate precisely where we stand at the outset."

"Of course." Hobson cleared his throat. "Do you think I might see Lady Laurel this evening before I leave?"

Jack frowned. "Why? Do you not trust my

word she's well and was agreeable to the marriage?"

"No, no, that's not why at all!" Hobson rushed to explain. "It's only that I've spent the last two decades keeping track of her progress and providing for her at her father's behest. I feel…somehow responsible for her still. Personally responsible."

Jack nodded, understanding perfectly. Hobson had no family, as he had said before. The child must have stirred his sympathy at the beginning and become important to him over the years. "I'll send someone to fetch her."

He got up and tugged the bell cord. When Echols answered, Jack said, "Please notify her ladyship that we have a guest and ask if she would be so kind as to join us here."

Then he turned to Hobson. "Will you stay for a light supper?"

The man looked aghast at the very thought. "Oh, no, sir, I would never presume." He spoke in a near whisper. "It's not done, you know."

"Nonsense," Jack replied. "It's not as though you're some vagrant off the street. I owe you a great deal and so does Laurel. You'll stay. Unless you have other plans, of course."

Hobson bit his bottom lip, quite obviously wanting to accept.

Only then did Jack think that the solicitor might inadvertently mention Laurel's fortune and how it had been conveniently transferred to her new husband. "I would ask you to refrain from any discussion of finances in Laurel's presence."

Hobson nodded emphatically. "You needn't ask. But you will reassure her that she need never worry about those matters, now or in future?"

"I have done so already," Jack assured him.

Laurel entered the room and Jack immediately forgot all about money, the solicitor and supper. She wore a lovely, delicate green frock that skimmed her slender figure and flared out over her dainty emerald satin slippers. Dark green ribbons adorned her swept-up curls and cinched the gown just beneath her half-exposed breasts.

The urge to exclaim how beautiful she looked almost overwhelmed him, but he recalled his misstep of the evening before. She had not liked her looks complimented. So what could he say? As it happened, he had no need to speak.

"Mr. Hobson?" she cried and rushed across the room, both hands extended.

Hobson took them and raised them to his

lips, kissing first one, then the other. "Lady Laurel," he whispered. "My heavens, how you've grown!"

"Well, it has been *years!*" she said, laughing more freely than Jack had ever seen her do. "It is so wonderful to see you again! You haven't changed at all."

"You two have met?" Jack asked, though it was quite obvious they had.

Laurel answered, still holding on to the solicitor's hands. "Oh, yes! Mr. Hobson was kind enough to visit the convent when I was ten and again when I was sixteen."

She turned her attention to their guest again. "Remember that little poppet you brought me the first time? I still have it, one of my most treasured things. And the rosary you gave me, I use every day."

The man beamed. "I'm very glad you decided to come back to England." He glanced at Jack, then back at her. "And now you are a married lady. May I wish you every happiness?"

"Of course you may. And you will stay awhile and visit with me, won't you, sir?"

"I've already asked him to sup with us," Jack said, glad he had done something that she would approve. She gave him an open smile of gratitude.

He could hardly take his eyes off her. Hobson's visit had added an animation that Laurel seldom exhibited and it lent her even more beauty.

Supper proved a simple affair with only three courses, but was elegantly served and enjoyed. Laurel carried the conversation, eagerly relating happenings at the convent and making light of what she termed her dismal failure as a governess.

"That's because you were meant to be a countess," Hobson declared, finishing his wine with a flourish. "And this fine gentleman has seen to it that you are. Thank you for that, milord."

Jack nodded, worrying that the solicitor's imbibing might be bringing him perilously close to revealing that the marriage had been his goal at the outset.

Jack rose and went to the back of Laurel's chair to pull it out for her. "If you will excuse us, my dear, I believe we gents will enjoy port and a cigar." Ladies retired from the dining room while gentlemen remained. He had been told this was de rigueur in a proper household and hoped Laurel had learned of it, too.

She looked puzzled, but took the hint and got

up. "Then I shall say good evening, Mr. Hobson. Please do come again and often."

Hobson reached for the hand she extended and placed another fervent kiss upon the back of it. "I will see you again very soon. Thank you for a wonderful evening, and may I say again how delighted I am to see you in such fine fettle."

When Laurel had left the room, Hobson did not take his seat again for the promised port and cigar. "I should go now," he said. "You were most generous to invite me and allow me time with Lady Laurel."

"Why didn't you tell me you knew her before? I had no idea you had ever been to Spain to see her."

Hobson sighed as they walked to the door. "Because I feared you would insist that I go and get her instead, and I believed the task should fall to you for obvious reasons."

"And it has all worked out exactly as you planned," Jack said, nodding.

"So it has. Good night, milord," Hobson said with a smile. "And congratulations. You are a *very* fortunate man."

Jack thought so, too. Or at least he would be if he could bring about the happy reaction that Hobson had done with Laurel. He could almost be jealous of the solicitor if the man weren't old enough to be her father and didn't act as if he were.

As soon as Hobson departed, Jack knew he needed to get himself above stairs and offer that belated apology he had not been able to deliver last evening.

She would still be *indisposed,* he guessed, so there would be no consummation for a few more days, but he could begin to get in her good graces now in preparation for that.

Chapter Nine

Laurel tensed when she heard footsteps in the dressing room. She clutched the hairbrush in both hands, wondering whether he would enter her room and if this was to be the night. The knock on her door was muted as if he wouldn't wish to wake her. He had not before.

"Come in," she said, quickly applying the brush to the locks spread over one shoulder. She wore her new blue silk nightdress and wrapper. The smooth fabric lay soft against her skin and without the corset and underpinnings of the day, she felt quite exposed.

She wished she were sitting on the bed to greet him instead of on the stool at her dressing table. How awkward it would be to move to the bed if he had come for the reason she imagined?

"Laurel?" he said, offering a tentative smile. "Am I welcome?"

"Of course," she replied, unable to return the smile. Her face grew hotter as his gaze caressed her. Did he really know how handsome he was, how appealing? He wore a brown silk banyan over his breeches and open-necked shirt.

He stopped several feet away and looked down at the vacant slipper chair. "May I?"

She nodded. The brush seemed glued to her hair at half stroke.

"I came to apologize for last evening," he said with a wry twist of his lips. "It seems I have a few things to learn when it comes to dealing with women."

Laurel's laugh surprised her, too. "I doubt that very seriously. And I admit I overreacted to your flattery. There's no need to apologize."

"Not flattery, merely honest observation. And I should not have said what I did about your shyness with people. In fact, I admire the way you're adapting to such a new way of life. It's a wonder you haven't—" He stopped, as though her first comment had only just registered. "Why do you doubt it?"

She began brushing vigorously. "I think you must have dealt with a great many women in the past."

His shrug looked weary. "Some, yes, but none like you."

"Like me?" she demanded, the banished anger nudging her again. "Am I so odd then?"

He stood and paced, stopping at her window to stare out into the night. "Not odd in a bad way. Only incredibly different from those I have known. There's Mother, of course. She has always been an effusive sort, as you saw for yourself. A businesswoman who had to take charge of her own life as well as mine when I was little. My father was ever away at sea, and after a while, so was I."

"There were certainly other women in your life besides your mother," she declared.

"The others," he said on a sigh. "Well, as you might guess, we had precious little conversation." He turned and looked directly into her eyes. "Laurel, if we are to have a decent future together, I think we must be friends, not only lovers."

That shocked her into silence. She laid down the brush and waited for him to go on.

He sat down again, leaning forward in the low chair with his elbows resting on his knees. "Look, I want you to feel comfortable with me, not on edge, not searching for hidden meanings in everything I say. I want to be comfortable with you. Do you think that possible?"

"I suppose so," she answered, a lie if she had ever told one. How could she ever be comfortable with him when his very presence made her tremble like leaves in the wind? When the sight of that mouth of his brought the memory of their kiss onboard the ship, of his hands on her waist, his arm around her shoulders? When she wanted more, to be a lover, not just a friend, and he seemed so ignorant of that?

He stood. "Well, that was what I came to say."

"That's all?" she asked, breathless with disappointment.

"That, and to tell you we will be leaving for Elderidge House tomorrow at noon. There will be plenty of time for your maid to pack your new things for you in the morning."

"But I thought you came to..."

"No, no," he said with a sympathetic smile as he reached for the door handle to the dressing room. "I *do* know enough of women to delay when I must. Sleep well, Laurel."

She sat there staring at the door, wondering what in the world he had meant by that. *Delay when he must?* Why? She had not asked a delay, had not indicated in any way she wanted one.

Sleep well, indeed! She threw the hairbrush at the door and watched it bounce.

The next morning Laurel could barely function. She held Jack responsible for the headache she endured. Betty had packed the new gowns and accoutrements that had been delivered. Chocolate and toast had been dutifully consumed and the maid was now applying the curling tongs to Laurel's hair.

"A bit of rouge to the cheeks, ma'am?" Betty asked. The dark blue traveling costume and bonnet did little to compliment a pallid complexion. Laurel nodded.

When she went downstairs, Jack was in the foyer with Mr. Hobson. "Good morning!" she said, addressing both as she interrupted their conversation.

"Good morning, Laurel. Mr. Hobson is accompanying us," Jack told her. "This time we shall have a proper introduction when we arrive."

"I took the liberty of sending a messenger to inform the staff of our arrival."

"How kind of you, Mr. Hobson," Laurel said with a nod. She hid her disappointment that she and Jack would not be alone in the coach. Then she remembered that Betty and George would also be going, so they would not have had privacy anyway.

George rode atop with the coachman Mr. Hobson had hired, so they were four inside. Betty looked smart and very proud in a black traveling outfit Miranda's maid had given her. She offered Mr. Hobson a sidelong smile that was nearly a flirt when he joined her, opposite Jack and Laurel.

"Mr. Hobson, this is my maid, Betty," Laurel said, making the introduction. "Betty, Mr. Hobson is our solicitor."

"*Thornwhistle,* now I'm a proper lady's maid," Betty said with a succinct nod. "Nice to meet you, sir."

"Delighted, Miss Thornwhistle," Mr. Hobson replied with a grin. "Unusual name. Have you a mum at the baker's on Pierson Lane by any chance?"

Betty's eyes widened. "My auntie! I do declare, you know 'er, then?"

"Best pies in the neighborhood for the past fifteen years," he said. "I'd likely have starved without them."

Laurel listened with interest for a while until they exhausted their mutual acquaintances and lapsed into a comfortable silence.

Jack had said nothing but shifted restlessly

She figured they could hardly surpass the opulence of those at the town house anyway.

She discovered she was wrong. The countess's chamber was nearly twice the size and dressed completely in white with accents of periwinkle. Even the furniture had been painted white. The dark polished wood of the floor contrasted beautifully with the patterned rug of blue and white. The windows were nearly floor to ceiling with gorgeous toile hangings.

She raked off her bonnet and looked up at Jack to see his reaction. He wore a frown.

"This will do nicely," she said in a blatantly bored tone. His lips quirked as if he were suppressing a sudden smile.

As in the town house, a dressing room similar to the one in London separated the two bedchambers. The housekeeper led the way, opening the doors for them as she swished through. "Milord," she said as she moved aside for him to enter his own room.

Laurel followed. His room was a great deal larger, but decorated in greens and browns, much like the other in the city. She supposed those to be the former earl's favored colors.

Fires had been lit in both rooms but the warmth had not yet extended to the perimeter. It brought memories of the big chapel at the convent that was too large to warm with two fireholes blazing. She shivered just thinking of it.

"Ooh, milady, you must be freezing! Come, let us change," Betty whispered. Laurel jumped. She hadn't realized that Betty had followed. But of course she had. That was her job. Behind her stood George, waiting for them to move so that he could attend Jack.

Lord, would she and Jack ever be left alone again?

She turned and went back into her own room, where a footman was depositing her two brand-new trunks full of the dresses and things she had purchased. Laurel also noticed the old tapestry bag she had brought all this way from the convent.

Betty closed the dressing room door and shooed the footman out the other. Then she turned, fingertips to her lips as she giggled. "Have you ever?"

Laurel shook her head, unable to pretend ennui a moment longer. "No, never," she whispered as she looked in wonder around the room that was to be hers.

"You must change now, mum," Betty said, dropping to her knees beside one of Laurel's trunks. "Let me shake out a gown for you. The pale pink one, you think?"

"The sapphire," Laurel answered, thinking of the livery worn by the help. Perhaps they would appreciate a lady who had taken note of the colors of Elderidge. One must begin somewhere.

A half hour later, she entered the cavernous dining room on Jack's arm. He escorted her to one end of the thirty-foot table and seated her, then proceeded to the other. Obviously someone had given him instructions on where to sit. Neville, probably.

Laurel sighed. Mr. Hobson was not present, but then he was probably having a much more casual meal elsewhere, lucky man.

Except for their servers, she and Jack would dine alone and probably in silence unless one of them decided to shout at the other down the length of the table. She could not even see him unless she leaned to look around the massive floral centerpiece.

The London house began to seem cozy by comparison, Laurel thought as she ate methodically. She was cold in her bare-shouldered, nearly bare-breasted frock. Her head had begun to ache from holding her chin as high as possible. And her stomach roiled after eating the cold fish soup.

Before the next offering was served, she started to wonder whether she would be expected to excuse herself shortly and allow him to remain by himself to enjoy port and a cigar. She fervently wished that she and Jack could dash upstairs hand in hand, blow out the lamps, huddle together and pretend they were not here in this grand old mausoleum.

But perhaps he was enjoying all of this or felt he would come to do so. Laurel sighed when the next course was presented and it did not appear to be dessert. Her corset was too tight to allow more food anyway. She held up a hand and shook her head, refusing it.

"Madame would care for something else?" the server murmured.

She blinked hard and shook her head again. "No, madame is finished." Then she pushed back her own heavy chair and stood.

Jack rose immediately. "Laurel, are you unwell?" he asked as he quickly walked the length of the table to where she was. His brow furrowed as he reached for her hand.

"I am very tired. Please excuse me and enjoy the remainder of your supper."

"Nonsense, I will accompany you upstairs

and see that you aren't ill." He turned to the nearest server. "Send someone for Bet...Thornwhistle."

The footman looked confused.

"Lady Laurel's maid," Jack clarified impatiently.

Then he hurried her out and to the stairs. "Are you ill, Laurel?" he demanded as they ascended.

"No," she replied. "Only tired. It has been an exhausting day and the food was entirely too much for so late in the evening. We will gain two stone within the month."

He laughed softly and added in a near whisper, "I hope that was only the cook's attempt to impress us and this won't be an everyday affair. Dreadful, wasn't it?"

"Do you think we could order up a tray for every meal? I loathe that dining room," she admitted.

"Surely there is a more intimate arrangement to be had other than for formal occasions and I certainly hope there are few of those required."

"So do I!" Laurel began to enjoy their quiet conversation and the camaraderie fostered by their peculiar situation. She wished he had not sent someone to fetch Betty.

How perfect it would be if he simply took

her to her room and stayed on. The scent of him, the feeling of his warm hand linked with hers and his concern for her stirred Laurel's need for further closeness.

"I must meet with Hobson in a while," he said, as if he had read her mind. "Shall I look in on you later?"

Laurel smiled up at him and nodded, afraid to speak for fear a spoken invitation might seem too forward.

"Later then," he said as he opened her bedroom door for her and saw her inside.

Finally, she thought as she pulled the pins from her hair, he would come to her as a husband. It was high time and she felt ready to become a wife in truth. She knew it might prove awkward but he would know what to do. There had been precious little physical affection in her life thus far and she hoped to find that with Jack.

His kiss had stirred something that had lain dormant within her and his frequent touches, innocent as they had been, warmed her to near melting. The memory of his mouth on hers had not diminished at all, and he had such wonderful hands. She had been held in his arms of necessity a time or two. Now she wanted his embrace for real, not prompted by protection or comfort, but by desire.

He kept delaying for some reason, but she knew that he wanted her, at least some of the time. Perhaps she would choose one of those times and become the instigator. One thing she did know, she was heartily tired of waiting for life to sweep her along this way and that.

Her father had sent her away. The nuns had secured her employment. Jack had spirited her away and arranged their marriage. Perhaps it was time she chose a direction for herself instead of waiting for things to happen to her and trying so hard to react correctly when they did.

She smoothed her hands over her breasts as they swelled beneath the blue silk of her bodice. Would he touch her there? Laurel felt uncomfortably confined in the tightly laced corset and gown.

Jack had told her that her mother was not of good repute. She had been labeled a cyprian, one of the fashionable impure. Laurel wondered if perhaps she had inherited her mother's wanton ways. If so, at least she could satisfy those leanings within the married state, and no one but Jack need ever know.

He might not see her as wanton since he had probably never had a highborn lady in his bed.

His experience had likely been with women who earned their living by offering pleasure. She would not be adept at it, given she knew so little about such things. But then, Sister Josephina had always remarked on how quickly Laurel learned new skills.

The thought made Laurel smile. She wrapped her arms around herself, fell back onto the white silken counterpane and waited for Betty to come and undress her.

Two hours later, that was how Jack found her. He almost left her to sleep, but couldn't bring himself to do so this time. Hadn't that wordless welcome in her eyes qualified as a near demand? Well, perhaps not, but it certainly gave him a good excuse to see whether she was serious about it or simply testing her flirting skills.

She came awake slowly as he removed her slippers. "Jack?" she murmured as she rubbed her eyes. "La, I'm still dressed!"

"I didn't mean to wake you. Betty can't be found and neither can George."

She sat up. "They're *missing?*"

He nodded as he set her slippers aside and sat with her on the bed. "I suspect it's on purpose."

"An assignation?" she asked, biting her bottom lip to keep from smiling. "I hadn't noticed an attachment."

"Neither have I, but that seems to be the case."

"Whatever should we do?" she asked, and again he saw the invitation he thought he'd imagined earlier. He figured she would not have that slumberous look in her eyes if she were still indisposed and wished him to leave.

Chapter Ten

"We might have to fend for ourselves tonight," he said, pulling a fake frown. "However on earth will we manage?"

Laurel pursed her lips and shot him an inquisitive look. "Do you mean to undress me yourself?"

"Oh, very well, I'll help you out, but I'll need instructions," he said with a sigh. "And I suppose you'll have to do for me, as well."

"Only fair I should," she replied as she slid off the bed and stood with her back to him. "Laces, please."

Slowly, enjoying every small tug, he drew the blue woven cord through the four embroidered eyelets until it came completely free. With his thumbs, he slid the sleeves off her arms and the blue gown puddled on the floor around her stocking feet.

"There now," he crooned, smoothing the length of her arms with his palms. "And what is this contraption?"

"A torture device obviously invented by a man who hated all females," she informed him with a breathless little laugh.

"We should divest you of it immediately, hunt down this fellow and hang him," he said, his voice soft and deep. "Allow me."

He untied the petticoat attached to the corset, then repeated the unlacing, a bit faster this time. They stood so close, the lilac scent of her had enveloped him in some sort of erotic spell. He did not want to hurry, and yet he did want to.

She liked the teasing nature of his seduction, and Jack was glad. This could prove uncomfortable for the both of them if she turned shy and frightened. Her mood seemed almost playful. Odd, for a virgin, but he appreciated her courage.

He bowed to kiss her shoulder. She leaned to give him better access, and he trailed his lips to her neck, tasting the smooth creaminess of her skin. Her slight shiver felt more like anticipation than fear.

Jack peeled the corset from the wrinkled shift she wore underneath and tossed it aside. Her body felt warm beneath his hands as he slid his palms over her waist and ribs, soothing away the garment's constriction. "You are so slender, you need no enhancement," he whispered close to her ear. "So beautiful." He tried to bite back the word that had angered her before, but it had slipped out.

She did not seem to mind it this time, he thought with a satisfied smile. He continued to caress her, slowly moving to the underside of her breasts, then cupping them, teasing the tips. He felt her inhale sharply, so he changed direction and palmed her abdomen instead. Her body undulated slightly. "Ticklish?" he asked, his mouth against her ear, and followed with a nibble there.

"No." She turned her head, seeking his mouth, and he complied, kissing her softly as he turned her body around to meet his. Fire caught in his belly as her tongue met his in bolder exploration than expected. *Not too fast,* his reason warned, and Jack drew away from her slightly, ending the kiss.

He smiled down at her as he plucked the pins from her hair and dropped them to the floor one by one. Her pale tresses tumbled around her shoulders and he stroked that sweet scented silk with the back of his hand. "Eagerness becomes you. Have a care you aren't ravished."

Her eyes widened and she ducked her head, but he framed her face in his hands and lifted her lips to his again, varying the intensity, shifting the connection, tasting her fully, then nipping softly at each lip. She made a sound of impatience and he smiled inwardly.

He felt her hands on his shoulders, fingers plucking at his coat. "Ah, so it's my turn," he murmured against her mouth. He loved that she made no secret of her need. No coy posturing, no pretense at all.

When he released her, she placed her thumbs beneath his lapels and pushed the coat off his shoulders. He let it drop to the floor and watched her face as she examined his neckcloth, then untied it. Next she unbuttoned his waistcoat and slid her hands beneath it to embrace him again.

Her cheek brushed against his shirtfront. For a long moment, he simply enjoyed the feel of her warm breath at his chest and the way her breasts pushed against his body.

If he didn't have her soon, it would be a swift coupling when it did come about.

He took her arms and moved her away so he

could remove the waistcoat and slip the shirt over his head. Her hands immediately returned to slide over his chest and shoulders as he bared them.

It was as if she had never seen a man unclothed before, and Jack knew that must be true. Where would she have done? Again he reminded himself she was an innocent, dependent upon him to guide and instruct, protect and pamper.

By her own admission, she knew little of what this event would entail, possibly not enough to fear it. "Shall I explain what we will do?" he asked softly.

"Show me," she murmured, her attention and fingers now on the buttons of his trouser flap. Jack almost laughed at his estimation of her. She might be untried, but she definitely was not shy in this regard. However he did not want his trousers trapped around his ankles, so he removed her hands, raised them to his lips and kissed them. "Boots first," he explained.

She watched as he sat in her desk chair and tugged off his Hessians. He removed his stockings, as well, all the while keeping an eye on her reactions. Her hands were fisted in the fabric of her shift. Perhaps she was a bit apprehensive. "You aren't afraid, are you?"

She shook her head, still watching avidly every move he made.

He stood and shucked off his trousers, allowing her to look as she would. Only fair that he should let her become accustomed before she bared everything to him. Jack had never been overly modest, but he did feel a bit self-conscious at the moment. He expected she would be a little frightened since he was in a full state of readiness.

She turned away, fingertips pressed to her lips. "My. That is not at all as I envisioned." Her voice faltered a bit. Was she laughing? Gasping?

"What?" he demanded, approaching to turn her back around so he could see her face. And so that she could not view him naked again with that expression. He wasn't certain if her wide-eyed look had been one of wonder or horror. "What did you expect, then?"

She bit her bottom lip and shook her head again before answering. "I saw this statue," she said finally, brushing against him. The soft material of her shift raked his erection. "At the hacienda. It had, well…less." The back of her hand touched his member. He almost lost control. Was this teasing deliberate or a product of her innocence and curiosity? The question incited him even more.

"You play with fire," he warned, smiling as he closed his eyes, inhaling the wonderful scent of her, loving the very sound of her breath and how uneven it was at the moment. And her touch, deliberate, or so he thought. "I think you are seducing me and I had such plans...."

Her tentative laugh was as soft as her skin. "Do you still think to carry them out?" she asked.

"Indeed," he groaned.

A knock at the door jerked him out of his trance. "I will throttle whoever that is," he muttered. Then he shouted, "Go *away!*"

She jumped at his sudden exclamation and stood apart from him as she glanced at the door.

Jack strode naked to the portal and turned the key in the lock with a loud snicking sound. He marched to the dressing room door and did the same, fully aware that she was following his every move with undivided interest.

When he turned back to her, she was covering her mouth with her hand, laughter in her eyes. Minx. He returned to her and grasped the hem of her shift, divesting her of it immediately. "There now."

She covered herself with her arms and hands.

"You've seen me," he challenged. "Fair's fair."

She ducked her head, then looked up at him. "I've not even seen myself but twice."

"No mirrors in the convent? I can assure you, you are beautiful."

She curled inward a little as she shook her head. "I mean without clothes. We even bathed in our shifts. Until my baths here and in London, I had not seen what I look like."

"Like a goddess," he said softly, trailing his fingertips down her neck to her shoulder. Slowly he took her arm covering her breasts and raised her wrist to his mouth, tasting her vulnerability. He reached for the other hand and gave it the same attention, moving back a step as he did and exposing the rest of her body.

"Venus," he whispered as he raked her slowly with his gaze and then met her eyes again. They were half-closed as she tilted back her head, welcoming his attentions.

"Or a vixen in disguise." He smiled as wickedly as he knew how.

"I'm not afraid," she assured him. "Is this how it goes? No modesty between us? You teasing…"

"Bedplay. Anything is allowed," he whispered, nipping the tip of her finger. He released her hand and caressed her shoulder, sliding his palm down to one breast. "Touch anywhere," he said softly, explaining and inviting. "Kiss anywhere..." He leaned down to kiss the bud his fingers had found. He circled it with his tongue, loving the sound of pleasure that he drew from her. He raised his head. "Now, where were we?"

"Bedding, I think." Her words rushed out in a gasp. Then she pressed one hand against his chest. "So should we be on the bed?" Her back was against it.

He grasped her by the waist and tossed her onto the mattress, coming down beside her and burying his face in the curve of her neck and shoulder. "So helpful. I might have skipped over that step."

She tugged his hair, a playful gesture that brought his face to hers. He kissed her madly and without a thought to ease into it.

His hands moved with purpose, finding her breasts, squeezing her waist, sliding over her thighs and in between. How soft and sweet, so delicate. The fear was all his now, that he might hurt her, might disappoint her or destroy her future eagerness if not careful.

She writhed against him, encouraging every move he made, even when he stroked her intimately. Ready and willing, he noted absently as his brain fogged with urgency. "Now?" he rasped as he moved over her.

Her open invitation was all the answer he needed and the deed was suddenly done. He had buried himself inside her with no heed to her maidenhead.

For a second he paused. "Are you...all right?" he gasped.

She nodded. Her nails dug into his waist and her body was as tense as a bowline. "Is...is that all?"

"No, no, love. Just beginning. Relax," he advised. "Let go." Immediately her hands uncurled and left his sides.

"No, darling, not of me. I mean let yourself go. Just float for a moment. Is there pain?"

She shook her head. Her hands returned to stroke his back softly instead of leaving nail prints. "We fit," she said on a shuddering sigh.

"Then be easy. Don't think, just feel." She went all soft beneath him and Jack struggled against his need to move. "There now. See?"

Her hips undulated slightly and he managed to hold still. Only just. When she moved again, he lost all thought. The primal urge proved too strong and swept away everything but the need to thrust.

Dimly he noted she did not fight. In fact, she began to engage just as he poured all that he was into her. Too soon, he thought, groaning when absolute ecstasy mixed with guilt. He had failed to bring her pleasure.

The thought of moving so much as a muscle seemed too great an effort, but he slowly disengaged and shifted to her side. Sleep tugged at him but he fought it. He slipped a hand over her hip, threaded his fingers through her nether curls and caressed her gently, rhythmically.

She responded with a small cry of surprise, then welcomed his touch. A moment later her body rose against his hand and she shuddered. He found the moment of her coming almost as pleasurable as his own.

"There now," she murmured on a sigh, echoing his earlier words of assurance. She snuggled close, slid one arm over his chest, rested her head on his shoulder and promptly fell asleep.

Jack felt profound relief. Now the worst was over and the worst was the best ever. And he had called her timid? Shy? Intimidated? Finally he had unleashed the passion within her that he had known was there.

A sense of peace stole over him that he had rarely felt before, even after bedding other women. The plaguing devil within his body, the one that demanded perpetual activity nearly every waking moment, had retreated for the nonce. He drifted in a restful state, unwilling to surrender to sleep, because he feared the peace would dissipate before he woke.

Perhaps all his self-denial coming to a conclusion had provided a temporary surcease, a dulling of his nerves. All he knew was that he felt abnormally calm and quiet within. Even his thoughts seemed less chaotic.

Laurel was good for him—that much he did know. She must have lent him some of her stillness of soul that he had envied so.

But was he good for her? Jack wrestled with his conscience daily, hourly, knowing he should tell her and knowing he could lose her if he did.

The only way he could make up for his deception was to keep Laurel as happy and contented as he possibly could. She cared for him, and he could not bring himself to destroy that regard with the truth. Not yet, while their relationship was so new. There would be little hope of reviving it unless she knew him better and felt more deeply. Maybe if she did, she'd be more inclined to forgive.

The next morning Laurel woke alone in her bed. She reached out to find that the pillow next to her was cold. She was cold, too, and still naked, though at some point during the night Jack had moved them under the covers and held her close. He had slept with her.

No doubt he had returned to his room before light and was likely out surveying the estate already. Would he think of her today? Would he look forward to the night?

She hugged herself and snuggled deeper into the feather bed. Now she was a wife. The duty was not exactly what she had expected. It made good sense that there was great pleasure in it, or there would be no procreation. Certainly no fornication or adultery, for the penalties for both were too severe to risk unless the act itself was greatly rewarding. Even so, she had not realized how very rewarding it could be.

Would Jack be proud of her? She had shown not a whit of the timidity he hated. In fact, she had felt more curious than apprehensive when the time came. They had waited for so long, she had wanted it over and done so that she could stop worrying about how it would go.

She smiled as she replayed the memory of it in her mind. It had gone very well, she thought. She had pleased him and he had pleased her. It seemed to her that everything else in their lives would fall into place now that was settled. She hugged herself and grinned into her pillow. She was a wife for real now.

They would learn what was needed to govern the Elderidge estate, set all to rights and perhaps have children in the near future. Even if they never quite came up to the mark on social niceties, they had each other, a glorious home and the probability of an heir. Family had always been her greatest desire and she felt fulfilled.

He must have imbued her with his energy last night because she could hardly wait to hop out of bed and begin their wonderful future together. There were other wifely duties she needed to see to while Jack husbanded the estate matters.

Betty swept in with a tray. "Good morning, ma'am," she chirped. "Here's your chocolate and toast!"

Laurel sat up, holding the coverlet to cover her bare chest. She knew she was blushing, but she couldn't suppress her smile.

"Aha! Good *night,* too, I see." She set the tray on the bed and turned to the wardrobe. "Which morning gown?"

"The sprigged lavender. Is there hot water?"

"In the basin," Betty said, her back to Laurel

as she plucked the gown out of the wardrobe. "I was late last evening. Shan't happen again."

Laurel sipped her chocolate. "If that is an apology, it won't serve, Betty. Are you walking out with George?"

Betty turned, a worried look on her face. She paused as if wondering whether it would pay to lie. "It wasn't allowed at the London house, ma'am. We have feelings, you see. And—" she paused before continuing "—we thought since he's Sir's valet and I'm attending you, it might be…well, convenient for you and his lordship." Her eyes held a plea. "You won't forbid it, will you, ma'am?"

Though her first instinct urged her to allow it, Laurel saw this as a test. Was she to let the servants believe she was too softhearted to govern? Or else that she was a martinet who had no thought for the happiness of others? She sensed that Betty and George, as well as all the other servants on staff, would take advantage of her inexperience if she allowed it.

"I shall speak with his lordship and inform you later of our decision. Until then, you both are to maintain decorum and perform your duties on schedule."

Betty looked a bit confused by Laurel's firmness. She had obviously expected immediate permission. "Very well, ma'am," she muttered.

Laurel drank her chocolate and munched on the toast as Betty went back to laying out clothes for the morning. She stifled the impulse to explain to Betty that the affair with George might cause problems with the rest of the staff. The girl should know that already.

"Is George seriously taken with you?" she asked. "Has he asked for your hand?"

Betty's head bobbed up and down rather frantically. "Not asked yet, ma'am. Neither of us figured it would ever be possible for us to marry."

"Do you want to marry him?"

Betty's face was now alight with hope. "Oh, yes, ma'am, more'n anything, for near on a year now. Could we, you think? If his lordship says yes?"

Laurel sighed and set the tray aside on the bed. She was so delighted with her own marriage this morning, it pained her to think of poor Betty with no expectations of her own. And yet, she did not yet know whether it was against some hard-and-fast rule of society for servants in the same household to marry.

"Let me discuss it with him. Say nothing to

George about this until it's decided one way
or the other."

The ormolu clock on the mantel struck nine.
It was past time to rise and begin her day. "I
can dress myself this morning, Betty. Would
you go and find Mrs. Mundy and tell her I wish
a tour of the house first thing?"

"Anything you wish, ma'am. *Anything!*"

Once she learned her way about, Laurel fully
intended to take full charge of her household.
Jack had told her to pretend she was Mother
Superior here. If he could play captain of this
stationary Elderidge ship, she could surely provide order.

Jack had begun early in the day, knowing
that he must confer with Hobson yet again and
see that all monetary matters were understood
and in order. Then they were to meet with Mr.
Northram, the estate manager, and later, the
village council and some of the tenants. Oddly,
he felt no dread at any of it.

He began with a comfortable residual of the
contentment that had lulled him to sleep the
night before. Normally, he would have been
wearing a hole in whatever floor he paced upon
or firing questions faster than they could be
answered.

As planned, he and Hobson had pored over the accounts, then visited the village to meet with the vicar and town council. They also rode out to speak with a number of the tenants whose homes required repair.

All of that had taken a full morning and half the afternoon. He was frankly amazed at how neatly things were being handled. Or rather how they had not tripped into chaos since the old earl's death.

His own demeanor surprised him, as well. Only a little of his anxious need to leap at every issue had surfaced. He felt good about things with only a healthy bit of apprehension intruding.

He dusted his hat on the leg of his breeches and ran a hand through his hair. "I begin to believe I can do this, after all," he confided to Hobson as they walked from the stables to the back entrance of the house.

"Of course you can! You have good men in place to take care of the details. All that's needed is your overall direction and perhaps instituting limits now and again if anyone oversteps."

"I might go over those books again in the next few days," Jack said.

"They are in the library, still on your desk,

sir," Hobson replied. "I'm for London in the morning unless you need me here."

"You'll dine with us tonight? No, I insist," he said as Hobson began to shake his head. Jack grinned. "As captain of this unwieldy land-bound ship, I may invite whomever I wish to share my table."

"I'm honored that you ask," Hobson said finally. Jack could see that the old fellow was pleased, but he also saw apprehension in his expression. "You might not care what the staff would think of having an employee join you, but the dowager countess will most certainly not approve."

"They say she's gone to Bath while the dowager house is being readied for her."

Hobson hummed. "Yes, I sent word while you were in Spain that you were expected here and she should be preparing to move."

"It's settled then. You will join us." Jack nodded and they started to part ways as they entered the house. Jack realized then that he had neglected a most obvious necessity. The atrium, office, dining room, stairs and the master suite were all he had seen thus far.

"I shouldn't risk being lost in my own home. Show me where everything is?" he asked Hobson.

"Certainly. I quite forgot you've never been

here." He gestured to his right. "This way. We'll begin with the gallery so you may become acquainted with the former occupants. Some are rather forbidding characters. You'll be adding your own portrait one of these days. May I suggest you smile for it, sir?"

Jack laughed. "So as to break tradition?"

On the way there, they passed the door to the office, which stood open. Jack's breath caught in his throat as he halted. Hobson almost collided with him.

Laurel sat at the huge mahogany desk, staring down at a page in one of the account books he had examined earlier.

Chapter Eleven

"What are you doing in here?" Jack demanded, realizing too late how he had snapped at her.

She stood, slowly closing the book. "Good afternoon, gentlemen. A lovely day, isn't it?" She placed a palm on the cover of the book. "I've been studying the account books, and I must say, I'm thoroughly stunned!"

"How so?" Jack asked, trying not to reveal how concerned he was that she might have discovered whose funds she had been perusing. Obviously, something had surprised her.

"You are *disgustingly* wealthy," she said to Jack in a laughing whisper.

He approached and took her arm, leading her from behind the desk and escorting her to the door where Hobson waited and watched, nervously crimping the edge of his hat brim.

"Come away now. I've told you that you needn't bother with financials," Jack said. "Mr. Hobson and I will see to all of that."

"Oh, it's no bother. I told you I'm exceedingly good with numbers."

Jack fought for patience. "You'll have a household allowance to deal with, of course. There will be another book for those records."

She patted his arm, smiling up at him. "That's as it should be, I'm sure. So how has your day been, sir?"

"Productive thus far. I was just about to take a tour of the house if you'd care to join us," he said, hoping to distract her completely away from all talk of accounts.

"Thank you, but I've already made the rounds with Mrs. Mundy this morning. If you two will excuse me, I'd best meet with her about the week's menus as I promised."

Jack huffed out a breath of relief even though the old and familiar tension within had now returned full force. He wondered if maybe Laurel could dispel it again if he held her for a moment and absorbed some of that inner peace. No, he'd definitely need longer than a moment and probably more than a mere embrace.

He was thinking nonsense, of course, and giving Laurel entirely too much credit. Peace came from within a person, and was not something one could borrow or steal.

He said nothing until he was certain she was out of earshot. "Perhaps you'd better take the account books back to London with you in the morning, Mr. Hobson," he said quietly as they continued down the corridor to the gallery.

What a narrow escape. All morning, he had felt so much more contented than usual, even with the dreaded assumption of the new tasks and responsibilities of the earldom. Now he sorely missed the calm. He knew last night's event, if not Laurel herself, was the reason for his contentment, of course. But when he had seen her with the books, his heart had jumped to his throat and even now, he couldn't shake off the jangling of nerves.

"You haven't finished with the books and there's nothing in them about the will or the former earl's intentions," Hobson assured him. "She need never know."

But Jack knew. The lie of omission continued to bother him, not to mention the dread of being caught in it. When he had grown such a delicate conscience, he couldn't say. That conscience would simply have to suffer in silence, however. A confession was out of the question.

"She seems quite happy. I had so hoped she would be," Hobson said as they walked.

"I plan to keep her that way," Jack declared, as much to himself as to Hobson. Laurel was truly good for him and not only in the physical sense. He could not afford to lose her and the threat was always there.

Laurel reveled in her first attempt at entertaining even though Mr. Hobson was their only guest. She was happy to start out with a modest supper.

Jack had showered her with compliments when he had come to her room to collect her. How appreciated he made her feel. She wore her new ruby sarcenet, and Betty had done wonders with the hairstyle, assuring her it was the latest thing.

Mr. Hobson had flattered her sweetly, too. He was such a dear and her only real link to the father she had never known. He did what he could to fill that role for her when she was younger, gently turning aside her eager inquiries and replacing them with stories of England and his own experiences there. He had encouraged and applauded her efforts and exhibited pride in her accomplishments.

One day soon, she would question him as

an adult about what sort of man had sired her and then sent her away. Not tonight, however. The mood was too pleasant to mar with unhappy history.

Instead, they spoke of his and Jack's outing, their visit to the village and tenants. "I look forward to exploring beyond the main house myself," she added after Jack expressed how well everything had progressed.

Mr. Hobson excelled at holding up his part of the conversation, and she could not imagine anyone of more exalted rank doing any better.

"Must you return to London so soon?" she asked as they sat watching their main course being served.

"Yes, I am afraid I must. I need to see about contracting someone for repairs on some of the cottages and begin negotiations for next spring's wool sales."

Laurel nodded her understanding. The man had duties. "Well then, you should return for the harvest festival. Mrs. Mundy says the tenants—"

A sudden commotion in the doorway interrupted her words as a woman shoved the butler aside, marched in and halted near the head of the table.

"Lady Portia!" Mr. Hobson jumped up from the table and his chair tipped backward, slamming to the floor, its loud report echoing in the silence that followed.

Laurel watched as Jack laid his fork on his plate and stood. She followed suit, knowing who the woman in unrelieved black must be. The dowager.

Oh, my. The housekeeper had told her that their former mistress was away in Bath. Laurel had hoped to become settled before having to face the woman Jack said had banished her from the family.

Lady Portia was no ancient, probably only a shade over forty-five by the look of her, but her black hair was streaked with gray and her extremely fair complexion had gone rather pasty. Dark, piercing eyes only accented her paleness.

The extra two stone she carried on her rather short frame did not flatter. However, one could not fault her ensemble. Laurel doubted anyone had ever concocted a more elaborate one for mourning. Tiny tucks and black dyed lace trimmed every edge of the expensive bombazine.

Her dark, silver-threaded hair was curled in tight ringlets, caught up in a jet-studded bandeau. An attached black ostrich feather quivered with her every move.

Mr. Hobson cleared his throat. "Lady Portia, may I present…"

"I *know* who he is, Hobson! What are *you* doing here?" She narrowed her eyes at him.

"I…I was invited, ma'am. His lordship insisted that I—"

"Has you at his beck and call already, I see," she said to Jack.

Laurel beckoned the nearest footman and whispered, "Please bring another setting for her ladyship."

"Don't bother," the woman said, huffing as she waved a hand in dismissal. She glared at Jack. "So you are now Elderidge."

"I am." Jack left the table and approached the dragon. "And I am glad to meet you, ma'am. Let me assure you of your welcome here anytime you wish to visit your former home. It must have been so difficult for you, having to vacate after so many—"

"Save your breath. This old pile of stone is a boil on the backside of England and I hate it with a passion. You're welcome to it."

She turned to Laurel, who stood waiting for her turn at the woman's vitriol. All she received from the dowager was a puzzled look.

Perhaps no one had told the dowager whom Jack had married. Laurel squared her shoulders and lifted her chin. "I am Laurel, Countess of Elderidge."

The woman laughed, a bitter sound. "You have the attitude for it, I see. Well, my girl, you'll need it. Elderidge is of common stock and the Ton is not forgiving of that."

Laurel saw red, but she kept her anger in check and her voice cool and polite. "Elderidge is of the same family *you* married into, Lady Portia."

"Precisely my point." She turned to the solicitor. "So is Hobson here, but then I suppose he neglected to apprise you of that little-known fact, eh? Wrong side of the blanket, but still a Worth, if not so named. Blight on society, the lot of you!" She fairly sneered. "And here is the family by-blow at your table looking like a cream-fed cat." She trained a gimlet eye on Jack. "That certainly speaks to your regard for the title!"

"Enough, madam," Jack insisted with quiet authority. "If you have an ax to grind with me, I suggest we postpone it until tomorrow and keep it between the two of us."

She tried to stare him down and failed. Laurel was amazed at Jack's ability to intimidate with a mere expression. His sea captain's face, no doubt.

Finally the dowager blew out a noisy sigh and her wide shoulders slumped dramatically. "No axes, Elderidge." She dragged out a chair and with no grace at all, plopped down on it, propped her elbow on the table and rested her tightly coiffed head on her hand. "I have had the most *rotten* day of my life," she declared.

Laurel and Jack exchanged quizzing looks. It was Mr. Hobson who spoke, his voice soft with concern. "May I escort you home, Lady Portia? Was the journey from Bath so terrible?"

She nodded and rose again, almost absently, as she reached for his hand. "You're a good sort for a bastard, Hobs. Always thought so."

"Thank you. Come along now," he replied and gently helped her from her chair and guided her out of the dining room.

Laurel was shaking her head in disbelief as the door closed. Jack quirked his mouth to one side.

"Well, what do you make of *that?*" Laurel asked.

One of the footmen coughed.

"I think we should discuss it later," Jack said, turning his attention back to his roast of beef.

Laurel followed suit. She chewed thoughtfully, tasting nothing, wondering what would happen when the dowager found out that her stepdaughter was the one who now wore her title. Laurel's name obviously had not registered with the woman. If and when it did, they could probably expect another, even grander scene than the one just experienced.

When they had finished dessert, Laurel decided to employ the new rule she had learned and excuse herself even though there were only the two of them at table.

She had already departed earlier from the expected by ordering their three places set at one end of the table, hers to Jack's right and Mr. Hobson's to his left, for the sake of conversation and convenience. That departure from tradition had caused a small stir among the staff. What with the dowager's untoward visit, Laurel felt the need to apply at least a modicum of civility to what was left of the evening.

"I will leave you to your port," she declared as she laid down her serviette and prepared to rise. A footman rushed to the back of her chair to assist.

Jack stood and offered her a smile, though it looked somewhat forced, probably for the benefit of the three servants who hovered about waiting to clear. "My compliments. The meal was superb, my lady, as was *your* company."

"Thank you, Elderidge," she replied with a

wry twist of her lips. Then she raised an eyebrow in unspoken question she hoped he would understand.

He gave a slight nod and she watched his smile become real. Laurel's heart swelled with anticipation. Apparently they would never need words for this particular arrangement. Jack would come to her again tonight.

Jack stayed in the dining room for a quarter hour, sipping the port he detested, despite its quality. He almost wished he could abide smoking, if only to have something to do as he killed the appropriate amount of time.

He knew he ought to go outside and walk off some of the angry tension that contracted every muscle in his body. He had barely been able to sit still, much less eat anything after the dratted dowager had burst in and ruined the evening.

He had thought her to be in Bath and hoped she would remain there. She would know the terms of her husband's will, and Jack had feared that at any moment, she might blurt out the truth. Now he must devise some way to keep the two women apart.

Deception spread its tentacles like ivy on the facade of his life, creeping up to cover it completely. He felt smothered by it, wished he could rip it away. But then, his life might not have Laurel.

It would not do to go to her in his current frame of mind. On that thought, he pushed away from the table and strode out to the gardens.

How long would it take for Laurel to finish her evening ablutions and get rid of the maid? His strides ate up the graveled walkway through the well-tended roses, on past the edge of the hedges of the maze and out on to the green beyond.

Darkness enveloped him, so he broke into a run, trying to free himself of pent-up pressure. Finally, exhausted and sweating, he stopped, resting his hands on his knees and breathing hard.

Resigned to the fact that exercise had not helped much, he walked back to the house at a fast clip. Now he needed a bath. Problem on top of problems, he thought with a huff of frustration. And things had gone so well until midway through supper.

George waited for him at the foot of the stairs wearing a curious expression. "Are you unwell, sir?"

"No. Bring water for a bath and don't bother to have it heated," Jack said as he passed him.

When he reached his room, he was already tugging at his loosened neckcloth, anxious to strip off his damp clothes. He did so, donned his oldest banyan, then poured himself a brandy from the decanter on the table.

His door to the dressing room stood open, though the other to Laurel's room was closed. She would be waiting in there, wondering when he would come to her.

Nothing would help him more than to go now, sweep her onto the bed and bury himself in her welcoming body. There, he wondered if he would find the quiet lassitude that came after they made love. Was how she affected him a wondrous discovery he had never even hoped to make? Or had it only been that relief had followed release and lasted longer than usual, almost throughout the day, in fact? It seemed that her very presence at supper had renewed his ease within. Until the dowager showed up.

The liquor burned its way to his stomach and lay there, doing nothing to dispel his mood.

The dowager might, at any time, reveal her husband's bequest in front of Laurel as spitefully as she had the circumstance of Hobson's birth.

That strong possibility decided the issue for Jack. He must be the one to tell Laurel. If

Chapter Twelve

At last he had finished his bath. She had sat there on the bed listening to the commotion in the next room, hearing a door close as the servants departed and then the subtle splash as he washed. She imagined him naked, thinking of those strong sun-kissed hands of his soaping himself, perhaps thinking of her as he did so.

Who would have guessed that the mere sound of a man bathing could engender such feelings in a woman? She smoothed the soft fabric of her shift over her thighs and sighed with impatience. The subtle splashing had stopped. What *was* he doing?

The knock came at last, an almost tentative request. Laurel sighed. "Come in."

And there he stood, resplendent as always,

wearing a black robe that exposed his bare chest. His hair was damp, strands of it lying slick over his forehead as if he'd absently brushed it across his brow with his hand.

He seemed somehow vulnerable beneath the powerful shield of strength that surrounded him all the time. She had yet to see a weakness in Jack, nor did she now. What she detected was more of a yearning that peeked through. It touched her as surely as his hands had last evening.

Laurel opened her arms. The look of relief on his face as he crossed the room fueled her desire to hold him as nothing else ever would. He wanted this, wanted *her,* more than she had known. She needed no sweet words, no romantic verse or teasing entreaties. Only him.

He attempted gentleness when he embraced her, but Laurel felt it give way almost instantly. His mouth found hers and consumed with a fury. Her mind fogged with pleasure, feelings scattering thoughts like chaff in the wind. Hands, his and hers, claimed, stroked, clutched and soothed.

Growls, groans and sighs mingled as they rolled, pressed together, upon the pillowy coverlet. She tugged away the tie of his robe as he raked up her shift. His desperation seized her

or perhaps hers caused his own. One thrust
and he was home within her. "Yes!" she rasped
against his neck.

He began to move, slowly at first, a struggle for him, she knew. Deliberately, she rose
faster, increasing rhythm, altering his pace yet
begging for mastery. His body reacted almost
fiercely. Those long, strong fingers plowed
through her hair, holding her head immobile
for the wildest, wettest, longest kiss ever. Laurel returned it in kind, thoroughly emboldened.
Nothing forbidden, he had said.

She felt the building of pleasure with each
frantic thrust, knew as he grasped for the pin-
nacle, he swept her with him. Suddenly it was
all too great to bear and her body shuddered
with an explosion of pure heat, sparks showered behind her eyelids as she clenched them
tight. She cried out as he poured himself into
her with a soft roar.

Laurel could barely breathe the effort seemed
so great. He lay still for a long moment, then
braced himself on his elbows, his hands still
threaded in her hair. When she opened her eyes,
he was looking down at her with an expression of awe. Or, on closer inspection, perhaps
stunned regret.

She smiled to show him it was all right, his

abandoning of control. For a man who probably prided himself on his command of every situation, he might even feel embarrassed.

"That was *remarkable!*" she whispered.

He released the breath he'd been holding and looked to one side. "I want to say I'm sorry," he said on a sigh.

Laurel breathed a little laugh as she raised one hand to his clenched jaw, then trailed it down his neck to his chest. "But you won't say it and you shouldn't. I have never in my life felt so...*alive*. So free."

He withdrew slowly and moved to her side so that her head rested on his shoulder and his arm held her tight against him. No words were needed as far as she was concerned. Laurel felt so wonderful, she couldn't express it anyway. And he must be at a loss, as well.

They lay that way for a long time. Suddenly he asked, "Do you like this room?"

"I *love* this room," she replied lazily. "It is the most wonderful room in the entire world and I shall always love it."

"Let's go next door," he said. "You can love my room, too."

Laurel laughed and pushed to sit up. "All right. Too many ruffles for you? Is that why you were gone this morning when I awoke?"

"I never sleep more than four or five hours and I could never lie abed. Didn't want to wake you. Come on."

They got off her bed and he swooped her into his arms. He turned sideways to get through the dressing room doors and deposited her on his enormous four-poster. George must have turned down the bed for Jack before leaving, so she slid between the sheets.

"Are you cold?" he asked, following her under the covers, propping up on one elbow as he looked down at her. "Shall I warm you a little?"

She gave a salacious wiggle and grinned up at him. "Warm me a lot."

He began toying with her hair, winding it around his finger. "Do you have any inkling how you affect me, Laurel?"

"Hmm. Let me see… I make you wild?"

He winced. "Well, that, too, but only when you arouse me."

"How do I do that?" she asked, playing coy for the first time in her life.

"Without even trying," he admitted. "You might have noticed how difficult it is for me to contain my…need to move about. All of the time," he added and pulled a wry face. "I have to be forever *doing*."

She nodded and snuggled closer. "I understand."

"I wish to hell I did. The only thing good about it is that I get a great deal accomplished. But it's nice to just sit or stand, you know, at rest? Not rush about like a man on fire."

She traced a fingernail along his shoulder, admiring the line of his muscle. "I like the man on fire."

He issued a little grunt of satisfaction. "Well, you can always have *that* with a come-hither look. But you seem to give me something precious when we're together like this. Afterward, it's as if you lend me your stillness for a little while."

She slid her hand behind his neck and pulled him down for a kiss. "Then I take it back so you may borrow it again. Afterward."

The next morning, Laurel woke when Jack's clock chimed eight. Betty was humming softly in the dressing room, pouring water in the ewer.

When Laurel started to stretch, she realized Jack was still curled next to her, sound asleep. It was the first time she had ever seen him sleeping. For several minutes she simply watched him, noting how much younger he

looked, how boyish with his hair in total disarray and his cheek lying on one hand.

She wanted to kiss him awake, but decided
not. He was likely exhausted by last night, not
to mention all the cares he had borne since
inheriting. Carefully, she slipped out of bed
and snatched up his discarded banyan, an older
one that had seen much wear. She wrapped it
around her and returned to her room.

Betty was there now, laying out morning
clothes. Laurel laid a finger to her lips and
whispered, "His lordship's still asleep."

"Did you ask him?" Betty asked. "You know,
about me and George?"

"Not yet. As you know, we had that visitor
last evening at supper and later we…were busy.
I'll ask him today."

The morning progressed beautifully. Laurel
began to truly believe that life in the convent
had been a boon, preparing her rather well to
deal with her present circumstance. She continued to use her Mother Superior voice, which
was kind, yet firm, when dealing with servants
and staff.

She had always been one for making quick
decisions, sometimes to her detriment, but usually working better for her than dithering about

undecided. Her decision to come to England with Jack had been the best she had ever made.

She realized that her pretended self-confidence was becoming quite real.

Jack met her in the breakfast room for their midday meal. It was a well-lit, airy place, a third the size and much more intimate than the formal dining room.

"You are a veritable ray of sunshine," he said by way of greeting as he joined her at table. "Yellow becomes you."

Laurel preened, something she could not ever remember doing. "Flattery welcome, sir. You look well rested."

"For a slug-a-bed," he replied with a grin. "Never in memory have I slept so long. If I don't rush, I'll be late for my first local court session and I'm to preside. I also hope to meet with the vicar later to discuss the school."

"May I teach there?" she asked, gesturing for Thad, the footman, to begin serving them.

"The position is taken, and you, my girl, will be too busy with dancing lessons!" He winked. "I told Hobson to hire us a dancing master. I could use a few lessons myself. We can't risk any missteps when we return to Town next Season."

Laurel could hardly contain her happiness.

she could pretend confidence in herself so convincingly, he could just as well pretend to like being married. He had certainly empathized with George's possible evasion of that state quickly enough.

He looked at his watch. "I really must go. Have a good morning!" She watched him rise and accepted his perfunctory kiss as he excused himself to go down to the village.

Jack had endured a thoroughly exhausting morning. He dismounted and walked halfway home from the village, hoping he could recover some sense of well-being before reaching the manor. He hated to trouble Laurel with the problem of Rob Huntland, the farmer who had stolen one of their sheep, but she probably would guess something was wrong. Damn the man. Why hadn't he asked for the sheep instead of stealing the damned thing?

Dispensing justice had never been a thing Jack enjoyed, though he'd had to do it a few times aboard ship. At least then, it had been deserved. Perhaps it was warranted this time, as well, but the usual punishment did not seem to fit the crime. He knew he must set an example with Huntland or others would mark the light consequence and the flocks would soon disappear one by one.

He led his horse to the stables and left him with a groom. When he entered the house at the back, Betty was waiting. "Ma'am said watch for you and tell you there's a gentleman guest in the front parlor."

Jack handed her his hat. "Someone we know?"

"No, sir. A Captain Morleigh, I think he said."

A relation of Neville's then. Jack hurried in the event Laurel was entertaining the man alone. She would think nothing of doing that in her own home. However, it was a little-used area of the house and a complete stranger might get the wrong idea.

The minute he entered the parlor Laurel stood, greeting him with a happy smile. "You're here at last!" She held out her hand. "We have a guest! Neville's cousin, Captain Caine Morleigh."

"Captain," Jack said, nodding to the stalwart fellow. He was a large man with a definite military bearing. His scarred visage lent him a rather dangerous air.

However his ready smile reminded one of

Neville's. "Lord Elderidge," Morleigh said as he sketched a quick bow.

"Good of you to visit." Jack was not entirely sure why he had come. "How are Neville and Miranda? In good health I trust?"

"The best. I've been to London and am headed home. You weren't far off my path, so Neville suggested I stop by and see if I could be of any help to you."

"Yes, he mentioned that you might," Jack said as they took their seats.

The captain smiled and inclined his head. "I understand you were thrust into your position without any preparation, much as I was a while ago. He knows what I've been through due to that."

"You're heir to Hadley," Jack said.

Morleigh nodded. "No title as yet, but all of the duties, save sitting in the Lords." He wrinkled his nose. "Worst of the lot, I imagine."

Jack agreed. "I've just had a taste of enforcing laws this afternoon. If I serve in the House, I hope concocting them provides better flavor." He released a heavy sigh and shook his head.

"Who transgressed?" Laurel asked, sitting forward in her chair. "And what did you do?"

Jack pressed his lips together for a moment before replying, "Rob Huntland stole a ewe and slaughtered it. He was seen doing the deed. Caught red-handed, so there was no question of his guilt."

"So you'll have him hanged," Morleigh guessed.

"You would *hang* one of our people?" Laurel asked in a horrified whisper.

"It is a hanging offense, that's true, but I commuted it to transportation. There were circumstances and I chose to consider them."

"That's quite lenient," Morleigh declared. "The others might consider you soft and take advantage. Some would say you might let him stay and only take off a hand. You know, as a deterrent."

"No!" Laurel objected. "Not for a sheep!"

"He's probably right," Jack told her. "But I couldn't take the man's life, or even his hand, for attempting to save his wife's family from starvation. They're yeomen farmers who live adjacent to our lands. They were in a bad way."

"You let them have the carcass?" Laurel asked hopefully.

"Not directly," Jack admitted. "I ordered the sheriff to dispose of it as he saw fit."

Morleigh smiled and nodded. "And I suppose the sheriff is sympathetic to the offender's motive?"

"And to my conundrum. Do you suffer these problems, Captain?"

"On occasion, but I see you have little need of advice from me, not on governing in any event. However, if you have any questions on other topics, I'll be happy to answer if I'm able." He reached into his pocket and handed Jack a folded paper. "Here is my direction. Feel free to write to me if you like. We'll also see one another in London during the Season, I expect."

"Thank you. Things seem to be well in hand for the moment, but if need arises, I will gladly make use of your knowledge. For now, however, please stay and dine with us this evening and spend the night, if you've far to go."

"You're kind to offer, but I've already lingered awhile and should ride on. I confess an eagerness to be home after a week in the city. I miss my wife," he said with a self-conscious laugh. "Grace will be sorry she's missed meeting you both. Her condition prevented her traveling. I was forced to leave her home this trip."

"I hope it's not serious!" Laurel exclaimed.

He grinned. "Serious, but happily so. She's increasing."

"Oh, that's wonderful!" Laurel said with enthusiasm. "Please tell her we should love to meet her whenever it's convenient. And please wish her good health on our behalf."

"You're very kind and I will tell her," Morleigh said. "But for now, I must claim my horse from your comfortable stables and be on my way."

"I'll ring and have your mount brought round."

After Morleigh had taken his leave, Laurel turned to Jack. "He was good to come, wasn't he? A very likable sort." She took Jack's hand in hers. "Are you still troubled about the Huntland matter?"

Jack nodded. "Yes, though not so much as I was on the way home. Captain Morleigh seemed to think I handled things well enough."

"I wish you could have forgiven it and let him go. You couldn't do that, of course, and I understand why. It's only that I'm sure this Rob Huntland must be a good man at heart."

Jack shrugged. "People are seldom entirely good or bad, merely more one way than the other. There *are* those who are evil clear through, but I don't believe Huntland is one."

"I choose to see only the good in people for as long as they allow it," she replied.

"I know you do, my sweet. That particular attitude has been ingrained in you from infancy, so no one could ever fault you for it. But it can be a great disadvantage when it comes to judging people." He reached to trace her chin with one finger, marveling at the softness of her skin.

She clasped his hand to her chest and smiled. "Fortunately, I needn't be the one to judge people, and I certainly don't envy you the task."

He studied her clear brown eyes for a moment. "But you must learn to judge, Laurel. Everyone you meet, you should be aware of clues to their true character and act according to what you find." Jack glanced at the door. "That includes visitors. Have Echols direct them to a less-isolated part of the house in the future if I'm away."

"Does this have to do with Captain Morleigh?" she asked with a laugh of disbelief. "He's Neville's cousin, Jack! I had no cause to mistrust him."

"Nor to trust him, either," Jack argued. "Fortunately, he was as gentlemanly as you thought. I hope your luck always runs that true, but you mustn't count on it." He hated to impinge on her view of mankind, but he would hate it much worse if anyone ever tested it. "Evil is attracted by innocence such as yours. I only ask that you have a care."

"That's why you're so protective?" she asked, brushing closer, swaying her body against his. "I'm not all that innocent now."

Jack slid his arms around her and lifted her up for a kiss. "I see I must save you from yourself if you believe that. Maybe I'll debauch you further until you're as worldly-wise as I am." He wriggled his eyebrows and grinned as he smoothed his palms up and down her rib cage.

She gave him a playful shove. "I won't mind that, but you can't do that here in the parlor!"

"We could go upstairs," he suggested in his most conspiratorial tone, increasing his attentions and cupping her breasts.

"Jack! It's midafternoon!" But her admonishment lacked any sincerity and she offered no resistance at all.

"So that is a yes?" he said, laughing softly in her ear.

Supper was served late.

Chapter Thirteen

The next week established a pattern for them. The nights were heaven, dismissing all doubt concerning his preference for bachelorhood. Their daytime activities usually were separate and fraught with the adjustments of running the house and estate. Suppers were no longer stilted affairs, but congenial with conversations about their daily doings.

On that seventh night, Laurel broached the topic of their finances, a thing she had not dared to do since Jack found her examining the estate records. "Have you given any thought to investing more of the ready funds not needed for running the estate?" she asked. "I've been reading with interest of the progress in steam travel. We might profit quite well if it flourishes."

He looked up from his plate as if she had suggested a flight to the moon on a kite. "What do you know of the investments?"

She shrugged as she buttered a section of bread. "The Church invests. Sister Josephina was quite the businesswoman. Her father was a banker and she did work for him at home for several years before she was called to the Church. Since I had such an interest in the maths she taught, she told me all about the markets and how they work."

"Why?" He seemed nonplussed by the very idea. "It's not a suitable subject for women, who obviously have no control over money."

She laughed. "Don't be absurd! Some do, Jack. Well-informed widows, women who operate businesses. Your mother had charge of her funds after your father died, didn't she? Or did you handle her finances?"

"No, she never asked me to. Have you been delving into the estate's books again?" He looked upset to think that she had.

"Of course not. You asked me to leave that to you, so I have. I merely thought to suggest—"

"I'll have Hobson look into it." He shook a finger in her direction. "But you are to leave it alone. Manage the household accounts only."

"Yes, sir! As you wish, sir! I'll not strain

my little brain any further!" She tossed down her serviette.

He had the grace to look sheepish. "You needn't remind me how intelligent you are, Laurel, or take me to task for lording it over you. It's only that I would keep some duties for myself and our man of business if you don't mind."

"Or if I *do* mind! Well, as it happens, I don't mind at all. It's only that you think a woman too *stupid* to understand it!"

He was instantly contrite. "I do not think that, Laurel. Believe me, I never meant it to sound that way. But you have to admit, it's the way of the world and not likely to change."

"It should be changed! You know it should!" She crossed her arms over her chest and glared at him.

Jack nodded. "I expect you're right. Women should not be so…confined. Life's not fair and probably never will be, but society's ills are not all my doing. We go on as we are taught to go on and resist what is new. The nature of man, I suppose."

"The nature of man. I know." She swallowed her anger since it served no purpose and would only ruin the rest of her meal. It wasn't as if her dissatisfaction could alter the way things were, even in her own home. "I was simply looking for something else to do, that's all."

He brightened at that. "All right then. If you're bored, why not learn to ride? It's great exercise and fun, as well. I'll teach you myself if you like."

Laurel agreed, seeing that he needed to show her his expertise at something, since he was probably somewhat lacking in the knowledge of investments. Sometimes she forgot that her education surpassed his and he might feel the pinch of that.

"Thank you! I shall look forward to it," she said, injecting enthusiasm. She would not tell him that she was already quite accomplished in that skill, nor would she show it during lessons.

Perhaps a woman's real power lay in placating and persuasion rather than argument and anger. In any event, he looked quite satisfied with her answer and gave her the sweetest grin. She so loved to make him happy. That is, when she wasn't ready to give his head a resounding smack.

Only the tiniest bit of guilt over that thought prompted her to add, "You said I could learn to dance, too."

He beamed, as she knew he would. "Hobson's arranging for lessons. I'll send someone to see whether he's had any luck. You will love it, I promise. Meanwhile, I'll teach you to ride. First thing tomorrow if the weather holds."

Laurel saw that he wanted to make her happy, too. The wish was there in his eyes. If he had been a bit condescending this evening, she must accept that Jack was quite sensitive when it came to managing the assets. She really ought to leave that alone. Or at least not mention it to him in future.

The next morning dawned fair and it was already rather warm, but Jack had promised a lesson. She looked so smart in her new blue riding habit, he wanted to show her off. Perhaps they would ride to the village if she could manage her mount well enough to go so far.

"Are you afraid of horses?" he asked as he and Laurel walked arm in arm to the stables. She seemed more animated than usual, but he wasn't certain whether it was caused by anticipation.

"No, not at all. I've ridden a little before so I'm familiar with them."

"Where? At Orencio's?" He felt a sudden stab of jealousy that that rapacious Spaniard had taught her anything. "I can't imagine they taught you riding at the convent."

"I told you before, it was a convent *school*, Jack. For young ladies. We were expected to learn things one would need out in the world."

"But not music or dancing. You said you hadn't learned those, so I assumed—"

She laughed. "I didn't learn music simply because I have no ear for it, no talent whatsoever. As for dancing, granted, that was not among our lessons."

"So you were taught to ride in the walls of a convent? I do wonder how that was done."

"Well, we had two mounts, coach horses also used intermittently for plowing the vegetable garden. A sprightly pair for all that."

Jack huffed a laugh. "Plow horses?"

"Well, you are to teach me the finer points, aren't you?" she said, smiling up at him. "Then I shall be quite accomplished!"

The stable lad held the reins of their saddled mounts, a fine gelding for Jack and a docile mare for her. He helped her onto the block and watched as she mounted by herself. "Good show!" he commented.

"Thank you, sir." She arranged her knee over the horn of the sidesaddle and adjusted her skirts.

Jack handed her a small whip, then checked the length of her stirrup and instructed her how to place her foot for best balance. "There. Comfortable?"

"It'll do," she said, reaching down to give the mare's neck a pat.

Judging by Laurel's wily expression, he fully expected her to tear off down the lane at a gallop, but she did nothing of the sort. He mounted his horse and eased up beside her. "Where shall we go? To the meadow there?" he asked, pointing.

"I would like to see the lands, the village and perhaps meet some of the people hereabout," she declared.

"As their lady should," Jack agreed, smiling his approval. "That way, then. And have a care how you go," he warned. He feared she might prove overconfident and be thrown.

They rode down the lane at a walk and she managed very well. She listened to his every suggestion with rapt attention and minded to the letter. He should have known she wouldn't court danger in any way. "You are a natural, I think," he said. "Before long, you'll be a true horsewoman!"

She merely shrugged. So modest, he thought. Laurel might have spirit, but was a very practical sort, not at all headstrong. He congratulated himself yet again for having the good sense to marry her.

"My goodness," she said, surveying the fields and meadows as they rode. "Is all of this yours?"

"*Ours,* my dear," he replied, thinking this might be the perfect time to tell her the truth, that he had married her so that this could be hers, too. And that he had needed her inheritance to keep it all going as it should.

"Oh, look!" she exclaimed, interrupting his thoughts, pointing to the flocks scattered about the pasture like fluffy balls of cotton wool. "There are so many of them!"

"Not nearly enough," Jack admitted. "Some of the flocks were lost recently."

"Roughly half if the count was correct," she said offhandedly, still looking at the sheep. "So sad. And the crops suffered, as well. The farmers must have wondered if they, too, would succumb eventually."

"How do *you* know what was lost?" he demanded, though he suspected he already knew how.

She turned to look at him. "From the side notes in the ledger in the library, of course. Before you forbade me reading any more of it, of course."

Did he detect a note of annoyance in her reply?

He said nothing more. Now was not the time to make a confession about the inheritance. They rode on in silence for a while.

"That land over there beyond the hedge lies fallow," Laurel observed and pointed. "Is it for grazing?"

Jack smiled to show he approved her interest. "I wondered the same myself. Northram informed me that the fields are divided into three portions, two planted, one fallow, and they are alternated to conserve and replenish the soil." He was proud of the new knowledge he had acquired in the past few weeks. "I'm becoming quite the farmer."

"Plant turnips," Laurel said. "Those do more for the earth than doing nothing to it. "Also they would make good fodder to store for winter."

"You've studied books on farming, have you?" He couldn't imagine how she had learned such from what must have been a rather small vegetable garden that supplied the convent.

She nodded. "There are several good ones in the library and also almanacs and such that the old earl must have saved for reference. The turnips are a new idea here, but have been tested in other countries."

Jack sniffed impatiently and looked away. "So you've been plundering my library again." He knew from Hobson that she would learn nothing about her inheritance from the accounts ledger, but estate business was *his* business, not hers. How much clearer could he make that?

"I like to keep busy," she replied, sounding totally unrepentant. "And it might take all of us using everything we know or can learn if there's another growing season such as those that were had three and four years ago."

He hadn't the faintest idea what she was referring to, so he kept quiet to mask the fact.

"It was so cold the Thames froze completely over for two years running," she declared. "And snow stayed upon the hills until late summer." She paused for a few moments, as if waiting for him to comment. When he did not, she added. "People starved, Jack. Ours mustn't."

"It's good that you care about them, Laurel, but we do have the wherewithal to feed everyone should that happen again."

"Sufficient *funds,* you mean?"

"Precisely." This was skirting dangerous ground. He misliked the mention of money, knowing where it could lead, and he was not ready to tell her the truth just yet. Soon, though, he knew he must. Keeping it from her ate at him every day, but the sense of urgency had diminished somewhat. "Don't worry about it," he ordered. "We have plenty."

"Every well, however deep, has a bottom, Jack." She toyed idly with the reins as she looked out across the land. "Aside from that running dry, food might not be available for purchase. Shortage would be inevitable, what with the Corn Laws and restrictions on grain imports."

"Good God, woman, have you become the expert on affairs of state now?"

Jack quickly forced a laugh to soften the impulsive reproof. He had not meant to snap, but her industry shamed him. Instead of depending upon the manager to instruct him in the methods formerly used, he should have been in the library reading those books himself.

Laurel pushed her jaunty little top hat more firmly in place and urged her mare to a trot. "I hope we find something cold to drink in the village. It's quite warm today."

Ever the lady, Jack noted. She had ignored his scold and tactfully changed the topic of conversation. He wasn't certain he liked the roundabout way she had managed to make him more aware of his lordly responsibility.

And yet, he felt proud of her, too, that she had risked pricking his temper in order to share what she had learned. He hadn't specifically forbade her to use the library, only the accounts ledger, and she had at least minded that.

They went on to visit the village. Jack reined in at the Happy Ewe, the only local establishment that served anything to drink. The establishment served as a posting inn, a mail station and a place where local residents gathered for conversation and libation.

Perhaps it would not be considered proper in higher circles for an earl and countess to frequent such a place. However, this was their village, their people and he intended to set the rules.

He helped Laurel down and they entered the inn. "Good day, Master Wilson," he said, greeting the proprietor. "Have you two pints for a couple of weary riders?"

The scrawny fellow's mouth dropped open as his eyes flew wide in surprise. All conversation at the tables halted. Everyone hurriedly scraped back their chairs, staggered to their feet, bowed and curtsied.

Jack doffed his hat and dusted it on his leg.

"As you were, good neighbors. Lady Laurel and I don't mean to intrude, but we are quite thirsty."

The publican rushed to pull out chairs at the nearest vacant table. "Welcome, milord, milady! What will you have, sir? Wine?" He looked worried, probably about the quality of what he had available.

"Ale, if you please." He knew from earlier introductions by Northram that the rotund Mrs. Wilson, standing behind the counter watching, was the local alewife. "They do say we have the best in the county."

A hum of approval emanated from some of the patrons.

Laurel waited patiently for the moments it took for them to be served. Jack gave her a nod of encouragement when a pewter tankard was placed in front of her.

She lifted it without hesitation, took not a sip, but a couple of hefty swallows. Then she exhaled, daintily licked the foam off her upper lip, smiled and nodded her appreciation.

Jack had never liked her more. She had caught the mood of the public room quickly and did exactly the right thing. The local folk would love her.

When they took their leave, Jack could hear

the buzz of conversation behind them and knew they would be the topic for the day in Elderidge Close.

"Let's buy things," she suggested, when he would have mounted to go home again. "Else the other merchants might resent our giving custom only to the Wilsons."

Jack laughed. "We can't make a purchase in every shop, Laurel."

"Why not? There aren't so many and it needn't be much. As for the cost, we certainly enriched half of London whilst we were there and those weren't even our people."

She made excellent sense. "Why not, indeed? Where do we start then? You need thread and needles?"

"No," she said with a laugh. "But I can pretend I still sew. Come along!" She reached for his arm and they set off to shop. Jack hated shopping, but he loved seeing Laurel endear herself to everyone she met.

The day had gone so well, Jack thought about telling Laurel everything. She seemed so happy now, already well invested in the estate and content with him as a husband. Even so, he still worried about her potential reaction to it. He would wait a bit longer, just until he was certain she understood how he felt about her and their marriage now.

As the days passed, Laurel hoped life could go on forever the way things were, with no outside interference. The nights were even better than the days.

She hoped to conceive soon and produce the heir that would repay Jack for his generosity. Or perhaps a daughter first and then a son. She actively dreamed of becoming a mother now that she knew it was a strong possibility and not a forlorn hope.

The dance master arrived within the week and their afternoons changed in a delightful way. Mr. Riggole kept them laughing as he put them through the paces of the Grand March, country dances and the Waltz.

Laurel did love to dance and found she had a real aptitude for it. Jack proved exceptionally good right from the beginning, and she suspected he had never needed the lessons at all.

The way he held her as they swayed and turned in three-quarter time seemed so natural. He was a graceful man, though he fairly thrummed with contained and carefully controlled energy.

He excited her with a mere touch of his hand

as they came together in the statelier dances, the way his seductive gaze promised very close contact once he got her alone. Anticipation carried them both high until late evening when he finally followed through and lovemaking left them breathless.

Mornings, they spent riding out across the meadows, racing, laughing and loving the freedom and play both had been denied as children. Afternoons, they danced. Nights proved the best play of all when they made their own music.

She had never guessed that intimacy could run the gamut from deeply moving emotion to lighthearted teasing. Jack had truly opened her eyes. And her heart. She loved him without reservation.

The day their dance master declared them well taught and left for London, Laurel found herself at loose ends. Jack had gone into the village to attend the council. She missed him already, though he'd only been gone for an hour.

She decided she had neglected one obligation far too long. The dowager countess had not made another appearance since that fateful evening. Lady Portia was now their responsibility, even if she did not particularly like them. It was time to come to terms and reach an understanding. She changed into a walking dress and boots and rang for Betty.

"Go and request the carriage for me, would you?"

"Where are we going?" Betty asked. "We're not going away from here?" Betty must fear leaving George for even a day since he had not come up to scratch with a proposal yet.

"No, of course not. Whatever gave you that idea? I'm merely going to visit the dowager's house and you needn't come along. I thought I might as well make peace if the poor lady is to be living there the remainder of her life. She must be dreadfully lonely."

"She's off in the head," Betty said with a knowing nod.

Laurel thought so, too, given her actions that evening. All the more reason to see how she was getting on. "That's as may be, but I should make the effort to ease her mind now that she's had time to get used to our being here. Go along now."

A half hour later, Laurel arrived at the small stone two-story house, and the driver helped her alight from the open curricle. "I won't be long so you needn't unhitch," she told him.

"I figured," he replied with a twist of his lips. "Nobody stays long."

"She's had other visitors?" Laurel paused to ask.

"Some. His lordship come but never got past the door."

Laurel wondered why Jack hadn't mentioned the visit to her. Probably because it had come to nothing. She marched up to the solid oak portal and rapped the knocker.

A slovenly maid opened it. That face alone was enough to sour the dowager's mood. "I'm here to see Lady Portia." For good measure, she added, "And I shan't leave until I do see her."

The maid stepped aside so Laurel could enter. "This way," she muttered, not bothering to curtsy as was appropriate. Laurel sighed at how accustomed she had become to that gesture of courtesy from every female she encountered. *Haughty ways,* Jack's mother would say.

She entered a small parlor where Lady Portia was sitting with an embroidery hoop on her lap. The woman looked up. "Oh, it's you."

Laurel curtsied. "I've come to see how you are and if there's anything you need. Are you well?"

"Well enough for a charity case. And how are you? I see you've not stinted on your wardrobe. That's one of Madame Eveline's creations, is it not? She's overly fond of trim."

Laurel nodded. "You have a most discerning eye."

"You ought to be wearing black, seeing that your father's only been dead five months."

"So you know who I am."

"I'm not a victim of senility and I do read the London papers. The announcement appeared the day you arrived at Elderidge House."

Mr. Hobson's doing, Laurel guessed. She had not known about it.

The dowager poked the needle through the fabric, laid the hoop aside and clasped her hands in her lap. "I suppose you've come for the jewels. Well, you shall *not* have them. Elderidge gave them to me."

"Of course he did. I wouldn't dream of depriving you of gifts from your husband, Lady Portia. Please ease your mind about that."

The woman looked surprised. Then her face hardened. "You know I was the one who made him send you away?"

Laurel nodded. "You were very young and a new bride. How could you bear to raise the child of his first wife, one who was not received in any household of your peers? I quite understand why you did it and I hold no grudge. Besides, I had a very good life within the convent."

Lady Portia covered her eyes with one hand, shaking her head. "It was a dreadful thing to do. I knew it then. The guilt made me sick, but I couldn't bring myself to reverse matters. Every time he looked at you, he would have seen *her*." Her voice broke. "Please don't forgive me."

Laurel's heart went out to the poor woman. All these years she had carried a heavy heart and could not forgive herself. Laurel hurried to the divan and sat beside the older woman, placing her hand over Lady Portia's free one. "Listen to me, please. It was the best thing for me, all things considered, don't you see? I had a houseful of mothers to look after me, teach and guide me."

"Papist women! Unnatural in their ways!"

"They were not at all! They gave me kind attention always and I loved them." Laurel had to shake the woman out of these guilty doldrums. "Well, I loved them all but one. Sister Jean-Marie was a grouch of the worst order. Not a motherly sort at all. She rapped me with a ruler when I spoke out of turn. You remind me of her," Laurel declared with a wry laugh. "You won't rap me, will you, ma'am? Even should I be impertinent?"

Lady Portia sniffed and wiped away a tear. "I might, so you have a care!"

"Properly noted. I shall behave myself. Come now, ring for your maid. Let's have some tea and you can tell me all the scandal from Bath. I'll wager you know everyone there and all their secrets."

They got on rather well after that, and Laurel found the lady quite interesting. Only when it was time to leave did Laurel risk unpleasantness and ask about her father.

"Lady Portia, please answer me this for I really need to know. Did my father ever mention me, even in passing?"

The lady's lips firmed and she looked away before answering. "Not voluntarily. It was I who brought you up to him as he lay dying. I asked whether I should send for you."

"What did he say?" Laurel asked in a small voice.

"That he could not bear to see what he had wrought by indulging me. That you would hate him. He also revealed that he had done all he possibly could to earn your forgiveness after he was gone."

"What did he mean by that?"

Lady Portia turned away from Laurel and stared out the window at Elderidge House, just visible in the distance. "He told me then that he had willed his entire fortune to you. Not a farthing to the estate or to me, aside from my paltry dowry. I must have looked as shocked as I felt because he added that now I must rely upon your charity. It was a long-delayed punishment for what I had required of him and what I had denied him, you see."

Laurel could scarcely breathe. The silence was complete save for the ticking of the hall clock. The import of what Lady Portia revealed hit full force. If she had not been sitting down, it would have brought Laurel to her knees.

Jack had married her for the fortune. All that he told her, the necessity of their marriage to save her good name, the familial feelings that brought him to Spain, his wanting to return her to society as was her due, all of it. Lies.

Later, she could not even remember whether she had taken proper leave of Lady Portia. Even the ride back to the manor remained a blur in her mind. She ran up the stairs, took to her bed and wept until she thought she would die.

The dream was dead. Her hopes destroyed. Her marriage, a sham. He had lied and was lying still.

Chapter Fourteen

"What do you mean, she refuses to see me?"
Jack demanded when Betty gave him Laurel's
message. He had just come in from the village,
tired, dusty and smelling of horse. All the way
home, he had looked forward to soaking in a
bath and dressing for supper with Laurel. He
had news, damn it. "What's wrong with her?"

Betty made a face. "*Indisposed,* sir."

"Again?" he demanded. "So soon?"

She nodded and turned to leave.

"Wait a moment! This is not normal, is it?
Should she have the doctor?"

"No, sir. But it's best you leave her be for now."

"All right, if you're sure. Find George and
have him draw a bath for me." Jack exhaled
with frustration and stalked off to the library
to have a brandy.

Something niggled at his mind as he poured the liquor. The one-horse trap had been out of the carriage house when he rode back to the stables. No one was allowed to use that conveyance but himself or Laurel. She never had that he knew. Had she gone somewhere today?

He yanked the bell cord. Mrs. Mundy appeared. "Yes, sir?"

"Did Lady Laurel leave the house today?"

She shrugged. "Jem took her down to the dower house this afternoon."

He sighed. "Thank you, Mrs. Mundy."

"You're welcome, sir. Anything else?"

Jack shook his head. That was quite enough. He knew precisely what had happened. And there might be nothing under the sun that he could do to fix it. Why hadn't he told her of her inheritance himself? Everything had been going so well, he had put it off, waiting for exactly the right time.

Lady Portia knew of the will's terms, of course, surely having been present at the reading of it. And she had obviously mentioned it to Laurel. Whether out of spite or inadvertently, he couldn't guess, but it hardly mattered. The trouble was that Laurel knew now, and he had not been the one to tell her.

He felt the old compulsion to exhaust himself with activity return with a vengeance. Running, riding, even pacing would solve nothing. Instinctively, he knew that would only waste time.

What he needed to do was face this head-on, make Laurel believe how much he cared for her, how he had changed since making the fateful decision to marry her.

With that in mind, he hurried up the stairs, determined to make Laurel understand, to believe.

Jack didn't stop to knock when he reached Laurel's door. He opened it and marched in, prepared for her anger.

"What are you doing?" he demanded when he saw how she was dressed. The old gray frock she had worn when he first saw her looked so horribly out of place on her now. She was folding a nightrail and placing it in the carpetbag she had brought with her from Spain.

"I learned of my father's bequest."

"Portia told you. I should have told you myself. I would have eventually. That's why you're packing? Because you're angry with me, you're planning to live in London?"

"No. I'm returning to the convent," she said simply and continued packing. "I'll take the mail coach to London and Mr. Hobson will make arrangements."

"I forbid it!" Jack exclaimed. "You cannot go!"

She shook her head, not facing him. "You have what you wanted from me. Just as you planned, everything is yours now, by law."

"And so are *you*," he declared. "I won't let you go, Laurel. Not to Spain, not even to London." He approached and took her arm.

She snatched it from his grasp. "Don't touch me," she rasped through gritted teeth. When her eyes met his, they snapped with pure fury. They were also swollen and red from weeping.

He had made her cry. Jack's heart sank. "Laurel, you must know how I feel about you now. At first, I admit I needed what you could bring to the marriage. It was for convenience then—"

"*Your* convenience!" she snapped. "You lied, Jack. The marriage was not to save my reputation. It was not because of kinship or family loyalty. You wanted the money! I should have guessed when you put off the consummation for so long that you didn't want *me* in the bargain!"

"The fortune is still yours, too, Laurel. Anything you want, you may have. And now, with our marriage, the whole of the estate is yours, as well, and you have a *home*. You are my *wife*. And I did want you, desperately, even *before* I loved you!"

For a moment she looked as stunned as he was by his declaration. He realized immediately, it was true. He *did* love her. The words had slipped out, but they had been there in his heart, in his brain, for some time.

"I really mean it, Laurel. I wanted to tell you the truth, but we were getting on so well. You meant too much to me to risk losing you."

She put out a hand to hold him away from her and covered her face with the other. "Could... could you please leave me now?"

"You won't go to London, will you?" he asked. No, he actually pleaded, something he had never done before. "And surely not back to Spain! You couldn't join the order now, you know. That life was never for you anyway. You are meant to be a wife and mother," he said softly. "*My* wife. Mother of our children. Please reconsider and stay of your own accord. I don't want you to feel trapped here against your will."

She remained silent, her face covered, her breathing so shallow, he worried she would faint.

"I will go then, if you will stay," he said. "If that's what you want, I'll leave you alone, give you time, make myself scarce until you can think calmly and make sense of this."

She nodded once, her breath catching on a little sob.

Jack wanted to hold her so badly, he ached with the need. "Before I go, let me tell you this. Hobson put the idea in my head as a way to save the estate, keep our people employed, to bring you home where you belong and to the life you deserve. I had no other option but to consider it, with no funds of my own to run this place. And Elderidge House should have been your home all along. Now it is. I truly thought I was doing the right thing for both of us."

He paused. "Let me add that I did not agree to or decide on marriage to you until after we met. I liked you, admired your spirit, and you seemed quite willing to wed. Love grew, Laurel, and I worried all the while that the truth of why I married you so hastily, and that I used guile to do it, would send you running from me, just as it almost has."

Still, she said nothing, would not look at him.

Jack sighed and went back to the door. He

turned to her before he closed it. "I do love you, Laurel. And I need you."

He pulled the door shut and leaned against it in the corridor, wishing he had said more, wishing there were more to say. Finally, he pushed away and strode down the hall, the stairs and out into the dusky evening.

Laurel threw herself into a frenzy of spending for an entire month. In a way, it was to get back some of her own, but more so, to repay Jack for the lies and challenge his tolerance.

She did not leave the estate, but ordered by letter to Mr. Hobson that he send numerous tradesmen to her with samples and plans for refurbishing the entire house.

Her orders were immediately obeyed without equivocation. No one delayed to confirm them with her husband. She had secretly hoped Jack would object, but he gave her no satisfaction there. He allowed her every whim, regardless of the cost.

Then she stepped outside her venue and into his. At her behest, Mr. Northram, the estate manager, accompanied the stable master to London to purchase a new mare for her. She mistakenly thought Jack would challenge additions to his stables.

Apparently, her word was law, but Laurel did not mistake the reason for that odd state of affairs. Jack obviously had approved in advance that it should be so. Perhaps he really had meant what he'd said, that everything was to be hers, too. After that realization, all of the spending she had been doing gave her pause.

Laurel had not spoken to him for so long and he had made no overtures, no further attempts to reconcile. He slept in his room. She heard him in the dressing chamber, listened for his steps in the hallway each day as he came in quite late and went out very early.

However, each morning when she awoke, a vase of roses sat on her desk, a box of sweetmeats now and then and once a pretty pair of lovebirds in a cage.

She knew the gifts were from Jack and that he crept in after she was asleep and put them there. Betty swore she knew nothing about it and had naught to do with it. Though Laurel still didn't forgive him, she had to admit the peace offerings touched her heart. She missed him so dreadfully.

Perhaps it was true that love and hate were together the same side of the coin, and the opposite of both was indifference. One could not hate so devoutly if love was not involved somehow.

The house had been in grand upheaval for weeks with all the painting, stripping of old wallpaper, sanding and polishing. Old furniture was banished to the attics or parceled out to tenants while new arrived every day. Seamstresses squabbled over how to arrange the new draperies at the windows while workmen stumbled over servants.

True to his word, Jack stayed out of the way and out of her sight except at dawn, when she would see him from her window, riding out on the brown gelding that once had belonged to her father. He never looked up, never waved to her.

"Sir's back like he was," Betty commented one day as she fed the birds and Laurel stood watching for Jack to return from his ride.

"Like what?" she muttered, twisting her fingers in the curtain's fringe, her attention on the drive.

"Dashing about, doing this and that, working the daylights out of everyone who happens to cross his path and doing just as much or more himself. The man's a mean whirlwind. People avoid him like the devil."

"He's not *mean!*" Laurel exclaimed. Everything Jack was doing improved the estate considerably. She had seen with her own eyes how the homes and gardens of the tenants had acquired a shine of prosperity and how crops were flourishing. Even the cows looked fatter, the sheep fluffier. At least he was using her inheritance wisely and not for his own pleasurable pursuits. "You know very well he's not *mean!*"

"Mean to *you,* so you said."

"I never! He…he skirted the truth, made me think he really cared just to get my inheritance, that's all. Half the heiresses in England were probably married in the same manner for the same reason."

Betty nodded as she arranged Laurel's books on the new bookcase beside her escritoire. "Not just nobles. It's *men*…they're all the same. Take what they can get any way they can. Some even leave you hanging in the wind like so much tattered laundry."

Ah, this wasn't about *Sir* at all, or even men in general. "So George still hasn't mentioned marriage?"

"Not a word. If I had a dowry, maybe…"

Laurel smiled. Betty was bold as brass, hinting the way she did. Well, why not indulge her? Jack would certainly have something to say about *that!* "How much would it take to bring George up to scratch?"

Betty turned, eyes wide with surprise. Her mouth hung open.

"Fifty quid? A hundred?" More than the two servants would earn together in a year.

Betty recovered and shook her head, busying herself again with the books. "Bad of you to have me on so, ma'am."

"No such thing. I'll dower you a hundred. An early wedding present. Then if George declines to take the bait, some man surely will."

Betty sank onto the desk chair with a hand to her head. "My word, ma'am! That's too grand of you! What will Sir say?"

"We'll see, won't we! If *Sir* can marry for money, why shouldn't George?"

Betty frowned. "You think George won't have me without it?"

Laurel raised an eyebrow. "Would you have him *because* of it?"

Betty grinned. "Why not? I can make him love me like you did Sir." She ran the feather duster along the top of the bookcase and danced out of the room without another word.

Had she made Jack love her? Laurel wondered if it could be true. Was he lying again only to prevent the scandal of a permanent separation? Perhaps he had realized that she was necessary for him to get an heir. Though he had only mentioned having children the once, he must want at least one. As long as she lived, he would not be able to marry again and have a child.

That motive for his wanting her to stay did not seem right for Jack, though. He had shown no obsession with an heir. *She* was the one who hoped so much for a child. So far, she wasn't to have one and never would unless Jack returned to her bed. Was that reason enough to abandon her pride and forgive what he had done?

Laurel immediately recognized that as an excuse. She wanted to forgive him and to be honest with herself, Jack's reasons had been valid. The estate was hers, too, and only because he had wanted her to have that as well as the fortune. And she would never have accepted him if he had admitted in the beginning that he was marrying her for her money.

Laurel decided on the instant that it was time to end her childish attempts at retribution and set her marriage to rights. She might not like the way he had gone about securing her hand in marriage, but perhaps he had seen no viable alternative at the time.

At that moment, she spied him cantering

across the meadow toward the stables. Tentatively, she raised a hand and waved. He must have seen her because he reined in and stopped. For a long moment, he faced her way, then nudged his mount to a gallop.

Laurel knew he would return to the house and to his room to change from his riding clothes. She decided to be there when he came in.

Jack didn't know what to think of Laurel's gesture. It had only been a wave, maybe an impulse on her part, done without thinking. Or it could be a signal that she wished to talk. God, he hoped so.

He reached the stable yard within moments, dismounted and left the horse to a groom for tending. The ride had eased some of the pressure within, but not all. It never did, but it helped a little. Only Laurel could dismiss it entirely and give him the recent harmony of mind and body he had not known existed before.

If mere sex could grant that, he would have found out years ago. But he knew from his experience before meeting Laurel, that was not the answer. She had become the balm to his soul, the one person he had ever known who had that effect on him.

Bedding her was not all that he missed. The peace she granted and he craved didn't fully account for his sense of loss, either. He needed her by him, always. It was as simple as that.

He had begun to fear she would keep on the way she was doing for the rest of their lives. How many times had he kicked himself for offering to leave her alone for as long as she wanted? Maybe she still wanted that, but he was about to retract his offer and use that little wave of hers as his reason.

He hurried upstairs to change.

When he entered his room, she was standing there in the middle of it, hands clasped in front of her. He stopped, uncertain whether to approach, to speak, or wait for her to say something.

She settled it. "I have been thinking," she said, then cleared her throat and turned her gaze from his. "Perhaps you were justified, or at least believed you were." She paused. "And of late, I have behaved in a very childish manner, costing us greatly in every way."

He noted she did not ask his forgiveness. Imp. That made him smile. "So have I, Laurel. Shall we put all of this behind us? Perhaps start over as adults?"

She shrugged, obviously still a bit uncertain. "Perhaps we should."

He crossed the room and held out his arms. "Everything else in the house is brand-new. Let's make it complete with a new beginning."

She stepped into his embrace and he heard her sniffle. "It's all right, Laurel. *We* will be all right now, I promise. No more lies of omission, no deception of any sort."

For the longest time, he held her close, caressing her back, kissing the top of her head, breathing in her scent, just loving her quietly. Something melted within him, creating a softness he thought might stay forever.

"Folks will call me the Earl of Mush," he muttered into her curls.

She lifted her face. "What?"

He laughed and dropped a kiss on her nose. "I love you so much it turns my insides to porridge."

She sighed. "Well, I do like porridge."

Laurel congratulated herself hundreds of times within the next week. Jack had settled so delightfully in his role as earl and as husband. He swore she was responsible. Marriage to her had made him a different man, so he said, but she knew better.

He would react the same way he had the first day she met him if she were ever threatened by anyone. The firmness he employed when directing everyone to mind their duties still spoke of the ship's captain within him. All that had changed about him was the constancy of his overabundant energy. He slept very well and seemed able to relax at will.

One evening as they lay abed after loving, her head on his shoulder, fingers entwined, he mentioned it again, thanking her.

"What was your life like as a little boy?" she asked.

"Errands for Mum," he replied with a lazy smile. "I recall dashing up and down the street, in and out of shops for a loaf of bread, cord for wicks, this and that." He sighed. "That's how she kept me busy and out of mischief."

"Perhaps your hurrying then and the necessity you felt for helping her in your father's absence could have caused you to form habits early on," she suggested. "Those habits, combined with a young boy's natural excess of energy, might have set you on this course of perpetual motion."

"You really think so? What an odd idea, but it makes some sense."

She played with his fingers, tracing his nails.

"How was it after you went to sea? Your mother said once she could not imagine how you dealt with the inactivity aboard ship."

He laughed as he drew her hand to his lips and kissed it lightly. "Inactivity? You saw the crew and how busy they were when we sailed to England? Double it and you have the chores of a cabin lad."

"You had time for lessons," she reminded him.

"Taught on the fly for the most part." He brushed her hand against his cheek and let it rest there. "You could be right. Habits formed in my youth. Still, I cannot account for how something inside me slowly shifted as I came to know you. I pause more to think and plan than before. And now, this stillness…"

She hummed. "You make me out a placid cow."

"Taming the bull," he said, laughing suggestively as he tickled her bare ribs. "The snorting, pawing, *randy* bull…"

Laurel loved this side of him most of all, the playful silliness he let show when they were alone. She loved everything about him, really. Life could not be sweeter than it was at that moment and she savored every second.

She hoped it never ended, the happiness she

had discovered in her marriage of convenience that had turned into a love match. Laurel decided she must be vigilant against any threat that might destroy it.

Chapter Fifteen

~~~~~~~~~~~~~~~~

Company arrived the next afternoon. Jack had agreed it was time for them to begin entertaining on a small scale so that Laurel could practice her role as hostess. He suspected she wanted to show off her new gowns to other than himself, Hobson and the staff. He didn't blame her in the least, for she was like a beautiful butterfly just out of her cocoon, spreading her colorful wings.

He was as proud of her new assertiveness as he was of her appearance. Laurel was coming into her own and he felt a bit responsible for that. She felt confident, loved and appreciated, and that showed in her every expression.

The evening meal took on the air of a party and Laurel had carried everything off with expertise. Jack watched as she signaled the servants without anyone else noting it, directed conversation so that everyone was included and enjoyed herself in the bargain. He rarely relished meals with numerous courses that required lingering at table, but this night had proved different. He actually regretted it when supper was over and the women left the dining room.

Jack and the gentlemen soon finished their after-supper port and repaired to the parlor to join the ladies. They had invited his mother, stepfather, Miranda and Neville to stay the week. Laurel had insisted on inviting Lady Portia to supper and had sent a trap to fetch her, but she had not come.

"We plan to have a great harvest festival and we would love you all to come for it," Jack announced as they crossed the atrium.

"Ah, the country life! How do you stand the excitement of it all?" Neville asked, slapping Jack on the back.

"You should try it before you belittle it," Jack retorted.

"Oh, I have. We go often to my cousin Caine and his wife, Grace, at their country house. We're going there from here, in fact, to be there for the birth of their child. Could be weeks yet."

"Careful you don't get *too* countrified," Jack said, laughing.

"Not much chance of that. Even with these visits, rustication's still a real novelty for me. I've been a cit, traveler or foreigner all my life."

"So have I," Mr. Ives agreed. "Your mother and I will be here for your festival. I'll have someone tend the shop for a few days."

"That's good of you, sir. And, Neville, perhaps we could persuade Captain Morleigh and his wife to come for the celebration as well if she's able. We know so few people and should be cultivating new friends," Jack said as they entered the parlor.

"Ah, here are our lovelies, waiting for us to entertain them!" he said by way of greeting the women.

"I'll play first," Neville said, taking a seat at the pianoforte and executing a quick run up and down the keys.

"You'll play last, as well, unless Miranda or Mr. Ives know how," Jack said with a laugh.

He was thoroughly enjoying himself and saw that Laurel was in her element entertaining. How lovely she looked in a gown the shimmering, ever-changing color of the sun on the sea. The swell of her breasts above the nearly immodest cut of her bodice made him wish to abandon their guests and take her upstairs for a while. Her upswept hair gleamed like spun gold in the light of so many candles. Anticipation added to his pleasure in an evening that seemed absolutely perfect. This was how life should be.

The butler appeared in the doorway, only to be shoved aside by Lady Portia. "Never mind announcing me," she ordered, striding in as if she still ran the house.

Everyone stood. She marched straight over to the divan and plopped down with a sigh. "I ate at home."

Jack bit back a smile. "Lady Portia, may I present Lady Miranda and her husband, Mr. Morleigh." He indicated who was whom with a gesture of his hand. "And Mr. and Mrs. Ives, my mother and stepfather."

She merely nodded as they bowed and curtsied. "I'll have a brandy," she demanded.

Jack rolled his eyes and turned to the butler. The man bowed and went to fill the order.

When Jack looked back, the dowager was standing again, staring openmouthed at Laurel, who had turned aside to speak to his mother. Lady Portia's shocked gaze swiveled to him. She still gaped, her lower jaw moving as if she couldn't form words.

"Ma'am, are you all right?" he asked, worried that she was having a fit of some sort. He rushed over and took her arm. "Lady Portia?"

She blinked. "Who...who is she?"

"Who?" he asked. "My mother? Hester Ives."

Her head was shaking frantically as she grasped his arm. "This...this was wrong of you! Wrong!"

Jack looked helplessly at his wife and mother. What was he to do with a woman suddenly bereft of her senses?

"Take me home!" the dowager commanded, virtually dragging him with her as she headed for the door.

He shrugged and said over his shoulder. "I'll be back shortly."

"You hope," he heard Neville say in his usual dry tone.

Jack hoped so, too. Lady Portia had a death grip on his sleeve. "What's wrong? Are you ill?" He motioned for the footman to bring the trap around again.

She harrumphed. "I'm angry, that's what I am! It was bad of you, Elderidge! Very, *very* bad!"

He had no idea what she meant, or whether she even knew. He escorted her to the buggy and handed her up. "You take me! I have a few things to say to you, you jackanapes!"

Jack might have declined if he hadn't been so curious. And if he knew she was only angry and not gone completely mad. He climbed up and took the reins, slapping them lightly as he clicked his tongue. They were off down the moonlit, graveled drive to the dowager house.

"I'm sure I don't know what's upset you so, ma'am, but it can't be good for your heart. We'll send for your physician as soon as we get you home," he declared.

"Look at me!" She met his gaze and studied him for a moment in the flickering light of the carriage lamps. "You don't know?"

"Know *what?*" he insisted, his patience waned to nearly nothing.

She looked away and exhaled a gust of frustration. "Send for the midwife instead then," she suggested in a snide voice. "If you don't know what I'm speaking of…"

"I have no way to know if you won't tell me!"

"Was this ruse of yours to punish me further? Something you and Hobson arranged? Tell me the truth!"

"Ma'am, I'm at a loss here, and that's a fact.

You must explain yourself or let go this questioning."

She exhaled again in that noisy way she had. "We'll get the midwife to come then. You'll need her word because I know you won't accept mine."

"Midwife?" Was this some woman's malady that had driven her barmy of a sudden?

"She'll confirm what I tell you," the dowager declared emphatically.

"What will you tell me then that I won't credit?" Jack demanded, his patience at a definite end.

"That the woman you claim is my husband's daughter is no such thing! She is an *imposter!*"

Jack could only shake his head. This woman must glory in stirring up trouble. "Interesting that you chose tonight to inform me of it. Was that your sole purpose in joining our party or was it just an afterthought to spoil it once you got there?"

"No, I had no idea until I saw her back," she stated emphatically. "You will see what I mean. Find the midwife. She will tell you that the infant born to that lowborn hussy and my husband possessed a very large port-wine stain. I saw your wife's clear-skinned, unmarked back tonight for the first time since I met her. If you truly are in the dark about this, then she has fooled both of us, Elderidge."

"Birth spots fade," Jack declared.

"Not one that is raised and dark purple in color," she retorted. "No one knew of the devil's mark except my husband, the midwife, the child's nurse and myself."

Jack sensed a conspiracy against Laurel. "So you and this midwife have discussed the matter and decided to come forth with the news?"

"Of course not! I told you I only realized the deception tonight when your wife wore that revealing gown and had her back to me. As for discussing it, I have not seen the midwife for nineteen years, soon after the child was born. We can only hope the woman's still alive, lucid and residing where she did before."

"Nineteen years? My wife is nearly twenty-three!"

"Further proof," Lady Portia declared with a succinct nod.

"Where would we find this woman?" Jack asked, determined to put this lie to rest before he returned home.

"She used to live in the cottage just north of the vicarage. I have had no reason to keep up with the doings of the villagers. If she's no longer there, we shall ask the vicar."

Jack didn't reply. He simply drove past the dowager house, straight to the village of Elderidge Close. He thought perhaps the lady would protest, but she remained silent, lips prim and hands clasped in her lap.

"Say nothing," Jack ordered as he stopped in front of the midwife's house. He got down, rounded the trap and lifted Lady Portia from the seat.

Light emanated from the front window. Jack strode up the walkway and rapped on the door. "What is her name?" he asked Portia.

"I haven't the faintest idea, nor do I care," she replied.

A stout woman who looked to be around seventy years of age opened the door. "Who's needin'? she demanded.

"I am Elderidge," Jack stated. "May we come in?"

She backed into the room, a question in her rheumy blue eyes.

There was nowhere for all of them to sit, nor did he want to. This was best kept as brief and to the point as possible.

"Tell me of the child born to Lord Elderidge and his first wife," Jack demanded.

"I brought her, a healthy babe," the midwife said with a lift of her chin.

"When? Be exact, for I can easily disprove it if you lie."

"No call to lie about it, sir. It's in the church records." Gray head cocked to one side, she thought for a moment. "Back in ninety-nine, it was. November. My last birthin' of the century, as I recall."

"Describe the child. In detail if you please. Any unusual thing you remember."

"Was told not to," she replied. "Not ever. Gave my word and was paid."

"You will tell me now if you wish to remain in this village," Jack warned. Expulsion was the only thing he thought she might consider a threat.

She inhaled and crossed her flabby arms over her ample chest. "Well now, she had a head full of red hair like her ma."

"Other than that," Jack prompted.

The woman's lips quirked to one side. "Well, she were mighty large and well formed for only six months in the womb. A hefty one for certain."

"What *else?*" Jack demanded, giving her his most intimidating glare.

The midwife paused and frowned down at the floor as if coming to a hard decision. "She were marked if that's what you're wanting to know. A purple stain, large as the babe's hand."

"Where?" Jack asked, feeling ice pool in the pit of his stomach. Could this be true?

"Middle of the back, just below her neck. Shape of it a mite like a hand, it was." Now that she had given up what she'd sworn to keep secret, she became loquacious. "His lordship said none was to know of it. Shamed, he was, and rightly so!" She looked at Lady Portia. "You seen it, ma'am?"

Portia nodded.

Jack turned and left, unwilling to hear any more about this until he'd had time to think what the implications were.

They rode in silence to the dowager's house. He helped her down, escorted her to her door and pushed it open for her. She stood on the threshold, limned by the lamplight from within.

Jack asked, "How is it you saw the mark? You were not there for the birth, surely."

"No. Elderidge and I were married three months later. He expected me to bring her up, so he had to include me in their secret. He had kept the child hidden from view so she was never christened."

"Because of a birthmark no one could see if she were clothed?"

Portia shook her head. "Not entirely. Because his family and friends were appalled by his first marriage and avoiding him. Because he feared someone would remark on the size of a baby that was supposed to be premature, but was obviously full-term."

When Jack said nothing, she added, "The disfigurement bothered him the most, however. He felt it was the mark of sins he had committed with the mother." She had the grace to look ashamed. "I confess I used his superstitious nature to convince him to send her to the nuns and have nothing more to do with her."

"You had no compassion for that motherless child," he said, disgusted by her act of unkindness.

"Unforgivable, I know. But even as a babe, she was the image of her mother. I wanted, needed, Elderidge to forget them both. Of course I know now, and felt even then, how wrong it was to punish the child."

"The child had a name, Lady Portia. You cannot bring yourself to use it, can you?"

The woman dropped her chin to her chest. "No, Elderidge, the poor mite was given no name, not an official one that is. The nurse called her Pippin, I think. Everyone else simply referred to her as The Child when they spoke of her at all."

Jack stared at her for a long moment, wondering if her regret was sincere or only for his benefit. "I see. Not a word about this to anyone, do you hear?"

"Wait!" she said, grabbing his arm. "One thing you must tell me when you find out."

Jack waited for it, knowing it would be precisely what he was thinking himself.

She looked toward the mansion and back at Jack. "We must learn what happened to the child I had sent away, the real heiress to Elderidge's fortune."

He left her standing in the open doorway and walked woodenly back to the trap. How was he to return to the house and his guests and act normally? Who was he to turn to in order to find the truth? Hobson, of course. Hobson must have been a party to the deception, if indeed there had been a switch in children.

And there must have been. Laurel was not a nineteen-year-old girl. She said she was almost twenty-three. If the earl's child had died and the nuns had substituted another in order to keep receiving the support funds, surely they would have chosen one of the same age in the event someone should visit her in those first few years. Foundlings were not that hard to come by.

Jack suddenly recalled Laurel's recognizing a spar on board the ship and she had even provided a few details of what had happened when she had sailed before. He had dismissed that as a dream or her rich imagination as a child, just as he had her memory of her mother, who was supposed to have died in childbirth. What if she did remember those things?

Would she have said anything about either if she was a party to the deception? And obviously, there *was* some sort of deception.

It could be, as he first thought, that Lady Portia and the midwife were conspiring to cause trouble for Laurel. Could the dowager's hatred for her rival's child last so long or be that vitriolic?

No, he decided. The birthdate would be too easy to verify. Somewhere there was a nurse who would know the truth about the birthmark. The women could not maintain a lie like that and they would know it.

He could not confront Laurel with any of this until he found more answers.

Jack drove the trap to the stables and ordered one of the grooms to saddle his gelding. "Send someone up to the house to inform Lady Laurel and our guests that I was suddenly called away to London."

"You'll need an escort, milord. It's very late and highwaymen still roam," the groom advised.

"No, do as I say," Jack snapped. But he did go into the stables and retrieve the two pistols and bag of shot from beneath the seat of the carriage.

A quarter hour later he was well on his way, dread in his heart. He did not want to find that Laurel had deceived him in order to gain the wealth and title that another woman deserved. His only consoling thought was that perhaps she did not know what had transpired, that she had been used. But by whom and to what end? Most likely she and Hobson were in league. No one seemed to benefit by such a deception other than Laurel herself and the solicitor.

The ride was long and hard, broken only by two stops to rest the horse and refresh himself with a tankard of ale. He arrived in London, his initial anger dispersed by exhaustion and worry. A local inn stabled the gelding and Jack traveled on to Mayfair by hack.

The servants made no comment about his turning up in evening clothes just before dawn. He went immediately upstairs and changed into his old clothes, which he had left behind, then realized he had no idea where Hobson lived. It was a Sunday and he would not be coming to his office.

Jack rang for Echols and asked if he knew.

The butler smiled. "Of course. Mr. Hobson lives on Pembroke Street, number sixteen. Shall I send Will to bring him to you, sir?"

"No. I wish to go there. Find me a hack."

That proved swifter than Jack thought possible, given the early hour. A good thing, too, since he meant to surprise Hobson, possibly catch him before he fully woke.

He paid the hack to wait for him and marched up the walkway to the attractive two-story home. A rather grand abode for a mere solicitor, even if Hobson had enjoyed a rich, noble employer for the better part of his career.

Jack banged the knocker.

An elderly woman answered the door, her mobcap askew and her apron untied. She reached behind her to remedy that as she inquired, "Yes?"

"Earl of Elderidge to see Hobson," Jack announced.

She looked past him as if to find a nobleman.

"*I* am Elderidge. Get Hobson."

She rushed away, leaving the door open, so

Jack stepped inside and closed it. He waited for a few moments by the entrance, then ambled on into the wide hallway that divided the rooms of the lower floor.

Hobson had excellent taste, he noted. The furnishings had quality, as did the paintings on the walls. He glanced at a grouping of soft watercolors in simple frames, then moved on to a portrait of Hobson himself. It was a true, younger likeness of the portly little man, right down to the details of his fabulously groomed mustache and gold-rimmed spectacles.

He moved a few feet to examine the picture hanging next to it. The wife, he supposed. Jack's gaze immediately landed on the face of the woman. "My God!" he muttered.

It was Laurel! Or how Laurel might appear in ten years time. The woman was dressed in the billowing skirts, cinched waist and exaggerated hairstyle popular at the turn of the century. Laurel's mother, surely. And the hair was not red. It was that unusual shade of gold so familiar to him.

He heard Hobson approach, but still couldn't take his eyes off the portrait. "Laurel's yours," Jack said. No question in his mind.

The solicitor remained silent.

Jack turned and pinned him with an accusing glare. "What happened to the earl's child?"

Hobson sighed and ran a hand over his face. "She and the nurse died of a fever before reaching Spain."

"So you put your own in her place," Jack said.

Hobson nodded once. "Out of desperation."

Jack could imagine nothing that would warrant such a move other than unadulterated greed. "You and your daughter have conspired to trick me into marriage so that she could become a countess and inherit a fortune. It will not stand, Hobson. You know as well as I that fraud is grounds for annulment."

"You won't set Laurel aside," Hobson said. "The scandal would be horrific."

"For you and her, yes. For me? You must forget that I have not been one of the elite long enough to care a damn what the others think! I was a privateer, for God's sake. That didn't exactly set me up for the Ton's acceptance anyway! I could chuck it all and go to sea and consign the rest to hell!"

Hobson stepped back. "Please think about it, Elderidge. Remember the people who depend on you, who expect you to behave as earl on their behalf. Laurel is a good wife, isn't she?"

"She's a bloody *actress* is what she is! That sweet docile attitude, her ready forgiveness of how I persuaded her to marry me when we were virtually strangers to one another! I should have suspected she was not what she seemed!" He struck his forehead with the heel of his hand. "Fool!"

Hobson backed to the doorway of one of the rooms. "Come, sir, let me pour you a brandy. Let me explain."

Jack surely felt the need for liquor at the moment, but he was too angry to drink with the crook who had manipulated him so foully. "You have ruined my life, Hobson. I'll see you never work in England again. Maybe I'll bring charges and have you transported along with that lying spawn of yours!"

"Laurel knew nothing about it," Hobson said with a sigh. "The exchange was made when she was three years old, so how can you think she had a part in this?"

"You visited her. You took her gifts. Why should you not have told her? How could a man speak with his own child and not admit what she was to him? What he planned for her?"

"Please try to understand! I was a recent widower without the means to bring her up. The earl's infant, her nurse and several others died aboard ship before they reached Spain. Elderidge had ordered that I never speak of the child to him, ever, so when I was notified of their deaths, I couldn't tell him."

Jack turned on him. "You let that man believe his daughter was alive all those years? You sent his money to pay for the support of one that wasn't even his?"

Hobson nodded. "He did not deserve to know, and he owed me. Laurel is his niece, you know."

"But not his own get!"

"I thought if I sent Laurel in the dead child's place, my daughter would at least receive a good education and have women to care for her. She knows nothing of what I did."

Jack planted his fist in his hand, stinging the palm with the force of it. "No, I cannot believe all this took place without her knowing and conspiring. She fell into it with no persuasion at all on my part. She had the temerity to blame me for marrying her for money and used it as an excuse to spend like the bloody Regent!"

"It is all my doing, sir, I swear it. You know how trusting Laurel is, how easily led," Hobson reminded him.

Jack raised his chin and glared. "Then I shall lead her straight to the courts and trust she understands when I reveal her perfidy to the world, along with yours, Hobson."

"I beg you, be calm and listen," Hobson said.

Jack was having no more of Hobson's cajoling treachery. He felt betrayed, embarrassed by his naïveté and furious with himself for falling in love with a woman whose chief emotion was greed. Beautiful, smart, *biddable?* Why had he ever considered her perfect? She had made an utter fool of him, and he had let her, welcomed it with open arms.

"We are quit, Hobson. You are no longer employed by the house of Elderidge."

"Please reconsider," Hobson implored and grasped Jack's arm as he brushed past to leave.

Jack shook off his hand and glowered at the man. "Go immediately, today, and collect your daughter, Hobson. She had better not be in residence when I return tomorrow or I won't be able to answer for my actions."

Chapter Sixteen

Laurel worried about the reason for Jack's hasty departure for London. Estate business, she supposed, but who had come to notify him of it and when? And why had he not come inside to say a quick farewell and explain to their guests?

His parents had come all this way and had to return to Plymouth today to tend their shop. The Morleighs had also departed soon after breakfast, and Laurel had just finished the midday meal alone in the breakfast room.

"Mr. Hobson, ma'am," the butler announced.

Laurel rose as the solicitor entered. "What has happened?" she demanded when she saw Mr. Hobson's worried countenance. "Where is my husband?"

"Elderidge is in London," he replied, approaching to take her hand. "We must speak immediately, somewhere private," he declared. "The matter is urgent."

"In the library," Laurel replied, hurrying to lead the way. She turned as they entered and watched Hobson shut the door. "Has something happened to Jack?"

"He's all right. Please sit down," he said. "What I have to say will come as a shock."

Laurel sank to one of the armchairs facing the large mahogany desk. Hobson took the other, leaning forward with his elbows resting on his knees. "Laurel, my dear, I have committed a terrible act, though I did it in good faith. Elderidge is furious with me, and with you, I'm afraid. Though it is no fault of yours and all my doing entirely, I could not convince him you had no part in it."

Laurel frowned. "What have you done, sir?"

He sighed and looked down at the floor. "It is a long story, but we haven't the time for my excuses or lengthy explanations. Here is the gist of things. You are my daughter, Laurel. The earl's child died, and I took you to Spain in her place. Now Elderidge has found out and ordered me to remove you from here today."

"What?" Laurel's throat tightened. This

could not be! She jumped up from the chair and covered her face with her hands. "No! Not true!"

Hobson's hands gripped her shoulders from behind. "It *is* true, dearest. You are my daughter and I did it all for you. There was no going back once I set it in motion."

Laurel rounded on him, breaking his hold. "You could have! You could have told me!"

"Then you would not have stayed. You would not have the education I promised your mother." He stroked her hair. "So often I wished I could have you with me, to watch you grow into the beautiful woman you've become."

She turned away. "How could you have foisted me off on Jack, pretending I was someone I was not?"

"Wrong of me, I know. I only wanted the best for you! The earl cared nothing for his child. Nothing! But I loved you beyond all reason. When she lay dying, your sweet mother made me promise I would see you educated, give you the best care I could find. I had very little then to offer a child. The opportunity presented itself and I took advantage. Believe me, I wish I had foreseen what trouble it would cause, but at the time it seemed the perfect solution."

"And later, when you sent Jack to fetch me back? Did you never think how wrong it was to trick him into marriage with an *imposter?*"

Hobson hung his head. "I took nothing from him, Laurel. Without the real heiress alive, the fortune was slated to go to him as heir. He only thought it was yours for a brief span of time. With your marriage, he claimed what was rightfully his all along."

"You forced him to pretend, too, to cozen me into marriage in order to support this estate with money he thought was mine! I almost left him because of that!"

"Please forgive me. I never meant to hurt either of you." Hobson swallowed hard. "You love him, don't you?"

"Yes, and now you have destroyed whatever regard he had for me." Laurel could only think of Jack and how he must be feeling, especially if he thought she knew all about this and never told him. "He really said he would put me aside?" she asked in a heartsick whisper.

Hobson nodded. "I fear so, my dear. He would not listen to reason. But perhaps—"

"Reason? What reason is there about this? You deceived us both and now he hates me!" Now where would she go? What would she do?

"I truly am sorry everything has turned out this way."

"There is nothing we can do," she said. "Nothing."

"We must leave as soon as you can pack your things," Hobson said. "You will come home with me, of course, and we shall see what might be done to placate Elderidge after he has cooled his anger. Above all, we should try to convince him not to prosecute."

"Prosecute?" Jack would do that?

"For fraud," Hobson declared. "He could have us transported. He threatened as much."

"Oh, God." Laurel gasped. She tried to think what she must do now. She had to leave, no question about that, but she did not want to go with Hobson, the man who had ruined her life.

At the moment, she could not bring herself to think of him as her father. He had not seen fit to play that particular role in her life, and she refused to acknowledge him now because of it.

Laurel formed a decision on the instant. "Have you any funds about you now?" she asked.

He looked confused. "Why?"

"I need money. There is something I must do," she replied. When he hesitated, she raised an eyebrow. "I have cost *you* little enough until now, have I not?"

Hobson took a leather purse from his pocket and opened it. "How much do you need?" he asked.

"Fifty pounds should do," she answered without pause. "For those serving me under false pretense," she offered by way of explaining why she would need it.

He handed over the entire purse, his expression quizzical. "Seventy-five's there, I believe."

"Thank you," she said. "Please wait here."

Laurel took one long, last look at the man she had thought of as a friend all her life and said again, "Wait here."

She swept out of the library and rushed up the stairs. She rummaged in the back of her wardrobe for the keepsakes she had stashed there, the things kept to take out on occasion to remind her of her good fortune. She huffed at the very thought as she slammed the satchel onto the bed.

Quickly, she changed clothes, donning the wrinkled gray gown she had worn when Jack had rescued her from Orencio's. She kicked off her slippers and tugged on the worn half boots.

As an afterthought, she gripped the small rosary Hobson had given her at her confirmation, something to serve as a warning not to trust so willingly or take things or people at face value in future.

On impulse, she ran to the desk and scribbled a hasty missive to Jack, a brief apology for Hobson's actions and a curt plea for his forgiveness of her unintended role in the deception.

He would not forgive her, of course, but she could not leave without declaring her innocence even if he never believed in it.

She started to sign it, but realized she was not certain that the name she had always used really belonged to her. Laurel Worth, heiress to the Elderidge fortune, was dead. Hobson had not called her Laurel after informing her that he was her father and not the earl.

She certainly was not going back downstairs and asking the man what her real name might be. She scraped away the *L* and left a blotch of ink in its place.

Fine. She would choose another name.

Once done with the note, she propped it on her writing desk in plain view and hurried down the servants' stair to the back entrance. From there, she went directly to the stables and bridled the mare. A stable boy approached to saddle the mount, but she motioned him away.

She climbed to the mounting block and

straddled the mare bareback. "Tell his lordship he may collect the mare at the nearest posting inn. Tell no one this but his lordship after he arrives. Not Mr. Hobson or any of the servants. Understand?"

The boy nodded.

She kicked the mare into a gallop and set out across the field for the main road.

If she was to be transported, she would damn well transport herself. Hobson had disavowed her as an infant. Jack would never forgive her supposed deception, and he would annul their marriage. So be it and so much for love from any quarter. She was through with men.

Jack rode slowly, dreading his arrival at Elderidge House. Laurel would be gone and the place would never be the same without her.

He had spent the night in Town, wishing he could drink himself into oblivion, but knowing he must keep a clear head for the ride back to the country. There would be questions, perhaps silent ones due to his rank above those who would wonder at his wife's hasty departure.

All night he had lain awake, asking himself how Laurel could have dissembled so. Yet how could she not know how when her own father was so adept at it?

He almost convinced himself that she was also a victim of the ruse, but then recalled how quickly she had forgiven him for usurping what he thought was her fortune. And how readily she had accepted the idea that they had to marry before reaching England. Not a word of protest. Not an ounce of caution. Not a single misgiving at wedding a perfect stranger.

Well, perhaps not so perfect. Hadn't he fully intended to cajole her into marriage, thinking her to be the heiress? Maybe he ought to share some of the blame for making the confidence game so easy for the Hobsons.

It was still difficult for him to think of Laurel as a Hobson instead of a Worth. She was the old earl's niece, daughter of his half brother born on the wrong side of the blanket. Perhaps Hobson thought he would get back at least a portion of what his father left to the legitimate son.

Yet Hobson had never asked for anything. His only thought from the beginning of the entire farce had been to advance his daughter, to see that she married well and gained a place in society. Who, besides Jack himself, had been hurt by the old fellow's game?

Should he forgive Laurel for going along with her father's plan? Could he forgive that?

Well, he wanted to. He loved her, but was that enough? Could he ever trust her again?

What if she had not known? Could Hobson be telling the truth about that? Jack didn't think so, but admitted the slight possibility. If that were true, then Laurel had been hurt, as well. She might have loved him, too, and for her to be suddenly cast out and threatened must devastate her.

He had to know one way or the other, but how? If she were guilty, she would only lie about it. If she were innocent, would he know the truth by observing how she behaved? There was only one possible way to find out the truth. He would have to see her, question her, see how she responded and judge from that.

Jack turned his mount and headed back to Town. She would be at Hobson's now, for she had nowhere else to go.

"What do you mean, she's gone?" Jack demanded.

Hobson, red-eyed from weeping and jumpy as a cat, backed away from Jack's upraised fist. "She left me in the library, waiting for her to pack. After an hour or so, I sent someone to find her. Her maid gave me the note meant for you."

"Give it to me!" Jack demanded, holding out his hand.

Hobson did so and, after Jack finished reading the short message, he continued. "A gardener finally admitted seeing her ride away across the field. Astride a horse. With a travel bag."

"Was there no search?" Jack asked, too worried now to retain his fury. "Where could she have gone?"

Hobson wiped his eyes. "Of course I searched! Everyone did! She was nowhere in the village. Nowhere in the surrounding homes. No one had seen her there."

Jack thought. "She has to be in the area. She could not have gotten far with no funds."

"She had seventy-five pounds. I gave it to her, guilt money to pay her servants. She was furious at me when I told her the truth. I just wanted her to forgive me."

"Fool! She could buy passage with that much!" Jack hurried back to his horse. "She's going back to Spain. It's the only place she knows."

Hobson followed him out and grasped the stirrup. "Please let me come with you. This is all my fault. I told her you intended to prosecute us for fraud. I made her afraid." He had tears in his eyes as he looked up at Jack. "She was so angry with me. I fear I've lost my girl forever."

Jack looked down at the man and found it hard to hate him. It was so obvious he loved his daughter and worried about her.

Running made Laurel look guilty, but Jack thought she might have run anyway, out of fear or anger. Perhaps both. Or neither. He simply did not know, but he certainly intended to find out.

"Stay here, Hobson. She might calm down and reconsider, come to London and ask your direction. You are her father, after all."

"Not by her lights. But you *will* find her, won't you? You won't hold her responsible for what I've done? Please!"

Jack shook his head as he mounted his horse. "I'll bring her back."

Laurel looked out across the waves as the coast of England grew distant. She had boarded a packet in London under the name of Laura Smythe. It was bound for Calais, just across the English Channel. From there she intended to travel by coach down the coast to Bayonne. That was near enough to the Spanish border that residents would speak both languages.

While her Spanish was flawless, her French
would improve.

She planned to find employment as a governess or perhaps a private tutor. Her newly
composed letters of reference were false, of
necessity, but it was doubtful anyone would
check them. Circumstance had forced her to
the fraudulence, and she resented Jack's threat
that had made her into what he accused her of
being.

Why should she cavil at misrepresenting
herself now, since she had been misrepresented
all her life? And if she were checked upon and
called to account, she would simply disappear
and begin again.

Heartsore and cynical, Laurel suffered the
short voyage with staunch resolution. Never
again would she depend on anyone else for
her well-being. She would be a self-supporting
woman with no strings attached, no roots to
bind her anywhere.

Nothing to bind her other than the unre-
quited love she would always feel for her husband. No matter that their marriage would be
dissolved, declared invalid since she had wed
him under someone else's name, her love for
Jack was all too real and too deep to disregard.

She missed him already and knew she would

for the duration of her life. But she felt betrayed by him, too, and not a little angry. Why couldn't he have given her the benefit of the doubt or at least provided her the chance to argue her case to him personally before deciding to have her brought up on charges of fraud?

Jack certainly had faults she had never recognized before. She knew of his ready temper, but he had only exhibited that when he had good cause. Now she knew how judgmental he could be, how obviously vengeful. And, she now recalled, he had sometimes proved overbearing and not a little condescending. Especially about her accounting ability. He obviously resented that her education had been superior to his, though she had never given it much thought until now. Yes, he had his faults. She would dwell on those and perhaps learn to love him a little less.

As for Hobson, she had grown up with the fact that her father cared very little for her, whoever he might be. In her mind, he had been an unknown figure until Jack had told her she was daughter to an earl. That her father turned out to be only a solicitor made scant difference, all things considered.

She had consigned all the love she had stored away to her husband, and now found that she had misplaced it. Jack no longer loved her, but believed her a charlatan.

Laurel pushed away from the deck railing and marched to the other end of the ship to watch for the shoreline of France.

A new beginning was her only alternative. She refused to stay in England and be punished when she had done nothing wrong at all but trust too freely the men in her life.

When she arrived in Calais, there were also passengers disembarking from other ships. Laurel spied an older, well-dressed lady who appeared to be all alone on the dock and frustrated by the lack of anyone to assist her with her portmanteau.

The woman strode this way and that, circling her baggage as she hailed several men who passed her by without a word or notice. Obviously there were no gentlemen around who cared a whit about a female traveling alone.

Laurel shifted her own satchel and walked over to help. "Ma'am, may I offer a hand?"

"Thank God! Here," she said, shoving the heavy bag toward Laurel. "Let me carry the lighter one for you. I can do that much. Who are you, girl?"

"Laura Smythe," Laurel replied and forced a smile. She had chosen the commonplace name of *Smythe* and would use *Laura* because it was similar to what she had always been called. The diminutive woman looked pleasant enough, and vastly relieved to see a friendly face. She was fifty years old or thereabout, a pleasingly plump and grandmotherly sort. Laurel lifted the portmanteau with some effort. "May I know who you are, ma'am?"

"Cornelia Grierson is who. I'm for Paris, where my daughter's living. Wed a Frenchy, she did, but a nice-enough bloke for all that, though he's given me no grandchildren as yet. I have hopes, however. So I keep returning to Paris, expecting happy news. You?"

Laurel thought perhaps it would be easier to find work if she knew someone, especially someone who owed her a favor. She considered revising her plan. The older lady needed company, at least as far as her daughter's home.

"Paris also," Laurel declared. "Shall we travel together, ma'am?"

She could lose herself in Paris.

Chapter Seventeen

Mrs. Grierson talked nonstop as Laurel arranged their passage on a coach bound for Paris. The widow never slowed her biographical discourse even on the crowded journey, so that everyone squeezed into their coach knew her entire life's story by the time they reached their destination.

The Boulangerie Nicot on Rue Monge was a good-size, three-storied establishment. As they approached the entrance, Mrs. Grierson told Laurel that its two levels above the shop consisted of living quarters for the family, though at present there were only her daughter and son-in-law in residence.

"Generations of the Nicots owned the place long before the war," she said. "Severely regulated by the guilds then, don't you know! Had to emigrate when the rabble ruled Paris, but its back in the family now, free and clear!"

Laurel opened the door for her. "How fortunate he was able to recover—"

"Yes, yes! Ah, that enticing aroma!" Mrs. Grierson exclaimed, inhaling and closing her eyes to enjoy it as soon as they entered. "There is nothing like the glorious smell of Parisian bread!"

"Mama!" a sweet voice cried. A short, pretty brunette swept around the counter and embraced Mrs. Grierson. "You are back again! Louis, *Maman est ici!*"

Due to the woman's constant one-sided dialogue on the way to Paris, Laurel felt she already knew Mrs. Grierson's daughter and son-in-law almost as well as the occupants of her own home back in England. Well, what had been her home temporarily.

Fortunately, the *Maman* was made welcome and saw to it that Laurel received a proper reception, as well. Mrs. Grierson laughingly introduced Laurel as her *new little minder*.

They both were assigned their own rooms, which were quite charming, though modestly fitted out. Laurel could not help comparing the economical furnishings of the baker's home to the grandeur of Elderidge House.

She had not lived in that place quite long enough to lose her awe of its opulence, nor had she been away from the convent long enough to forget what true austerity was. At any rate, she felt quite comfortable in the Nicot home for the time being.

The young couple ran a bustling business that was surely proving profitable, judging by the number of customers. She admired their industry and liked them as people, too.

Margaret was as pretty as Louis was handsome and their natures seemed so in tune, she envied them for it. She also thought their kind tolerance of Mrs. Grierson's continual flow of advice and admonishments amazing.

The woman did remember to thank Laurel now and again for her company and help during their first two days there, though there was no mention of payment for those self-appointed duties. However, theirs was not an official connection.

Laurel knew she needed to travel on or find work. On the second morning, she came down to the shop to fetch Mrs. Grierson's breakfast. When she mentioned leaving Paris, Louis Nicot offered Laurel work in his kitchens.

"I must decline your kind offer, sir, as I have no experience in cookery and would do your business more harm than help," Laurel said. "However, might I impose on you to place an advert for me as a lady's companion? At my expense, of course," she added.

Her request had the desired result. "You wish to leave Maman Grierson?" he asked immediately. "Why?"

Laurel smiled sweetly. "I must earn my living, you see, and your mother-in-law is merely a new friend whom I was pleased to help along the way."

"We must come to some arrangement then," he offered eagerly. "That is, if you are willing to travel as her attendant. I think she might enjoy Italy next."

Laurel laughed, understanding perfectly. "As you thought she would enjoy England?"

"*Exactement!* Marguerite and I strongly encourage our dear Maman to become a woman of the world. What do you say, Mrs. Smythe?"

Laurel hesitated. "Has she had other companions? Surely you have not sent her off alone on her travels."

He frowned at that. "She was accompanied, of course. Unfortunately, she always returns here alone, except for this time. But you get on well with her, do you not?"

Laurel nodded. "Shall we discuss it with her then?"

He quickly summoned Mrs. Grierson for her approval, and the widow hired Laurel immediately, apparently delighted to extend their association indefinitely.

A trip to Italy seemed just the thing to provide needed distraction, so Laurel encouraged Nicot's idea when he presented it. So long as Mrs. Grierson was never encouraged to travel to England again, Laurel intended to remain in her employ and keep the man's garrulous mother-in-law out of his hair.

In fact, she was as eager to be away as Mrs. Grierson. The Nicots' constant expressions of their enchantment with each other, the frequent touching and private smiles, reminded Laurel too much of her own happy times with Jack. She sorely missed him and feared she always would.

Jack grew even more obsessed with finding Laurel. It had taken him two days to locate the mare she left behind at a posting station thirty miles away. That indicated Laurel had gone by mail coach. Crowded as those usually were with passengers, no driver he questioned recalled a small woman in a gray dress and bonnet.

Jack had gone so far as forgiving Hobson enough to enlist his help. After all, the man might know the way Laurel's mind worked better than anyone, having visited her in Spain when she was younger.

She was more familiar with Plymouth than any other place, so they had begun there. Jack questioned Hobson thoroughly about any interests she had expressed during those visits at the convent.

"She wanted to know everything about the world outside," Hobson said as they shared beer at a public establishment in Plymouth. "She asked about no place in particular that I can recall. You don't think she returned to Spain, after all?"

Jack beckoned the barmaid and ordered more beer, then realized he had more than enough if he was to keep his head clear. "I've pored over the passenger lists for every ship leaving port here. No Laurel Worth or Laurel Hobson was in evidence. Is there another name she might have used?"

Hobson pondered the question, then held

up a finger. "Did you take note of any similar names in case the spelling is wrong?"

"Of course, as well as any other names she might have borrowed from those people she's met since coming to England. What of her fellow students at the convent or maybe the nuns?"

"Can't recall any of them, it's been so long." Hobson sipped idly as he frowned in thought. "Perhaps she did not go by ship to Spain. She could have traveled overland to Wales or Scotland."

"No, I believe she would stick to things familiar to her." But had she? Jack thought for a moment. "Perhaps I've counted too heavily on that assumption." A sudden thought had him pounding his fist to his forehead. "Economy!" He grabbed Hobson's arm. "Laurel's zealous about frugality!"

He slapped his hand on the table. "She would not have wasted coin to come all the way to Plymouth when London was closer! She shipped out of *London!*" He jumped up, tossed some coppers on the table and left.

Hobson followed, bumping into Jack's back as he halted outside. "We'll hire horses," Jack announced. "A coach is too slow."

"The mail coach got us here fast enough.

Besides, I don't ride," Hobson admitted with a groan.

"Then go as you will." Jack left him there and headed for the nearest stable. Half an hour later, he was riding hard for the next posting inn on the way to London, intent on changing to a fresh mount every ten miles until he reached the London docks.

He had to find her, and he needed to do so quickly. Laurel hadn't enough experience out in the world to manage for long by herself. Urgency stole his appetite and all ability to rest along the way.

"I'm coming for you," he whispered into the wind as he rode. "Please keep safe."

The shipping offices had provided no hope thus far as he bribed the clerk in the last of them. Save for this small company's records, Jack had examined every list of passengers leaving London, names kept for the purpose of identifying those who might be lost if the ships did not make their next port.

He shuddered at the thought that Laurel might be lost at sea under another name and he might never know her fate. It was then his finger traced over the name Laura. He stopped, his breath caught in his throat. This was the closest thing to her name that he had found in all his searching. Laura...Smythe. A most common name, one she might have chosen for lack of any other, one that might not be easily traced.

"Here!" He motioned to the clerk. "Do you recall this person? A comely young woman, slender, dressed in gray?"

The old clerk adjusted his spectacles and peered down at the name above Jack's fingertip. "Mebbe," he grunted.

Jack reached into his pocket and plunked down a crown.

"Young, fair-haired," the clerk said immediately, pocketing the coin as he nodded. "Argued the cost was too dear. Said it weren't that far to Calais."

Jack grinned and tossed down another coin. "God bless your greedy hide, sir! Have you a vessel bound for France today?"

"The *Michaela Rose,* sails around two o'clock. Shall I book ye?"

"Aye, do it. Passage for two." He quickly paid the man and rushed to Mayfair.

He immediately went to Neville, thinking only briefly of how much he had always hated imposing on friends. Laurel had to be found and Neville knew France inside and out. Jack knew only the ports and those, none too well, having avoided them during the war.

His dislike of asking for help ceased to matter. He would move heaven and earth to find her, hopefully before she came to any harm.

Jack didn't even wait to be announced when the butler opened the Morleigh's door to him, but rushed past the servant and found Neville lounging in the library with a book and cigar. "Laurel's gone to France. Come and help me search? I am so damned worried, Neville."

"She's left you? I can't believe it!" Neville exclaimed. "I'll come, of course. You'd never get past the docks with your abominable French. Come explain what's happened whilst I pack a few things."

Jack followed Neville up the stairs, relating only the salient facts as they went. "She knows so little of the world outside. What if she falls in with the wrong sort? She hasn't much blunt and is dressed like a damned servant! Any man might think she's fair game, y'know?"

"Calm down," Neville advised. "Apoplexy won't help matters. Give me time to tell Miranda where we're going and why. Look in the wardrobe there and get one of my pistols and ammunition. Then go and collect as much coin as you can carry inconspicuously and I'll bring what I have on hand. We'll need it for bribes once we get there. What time do we sail?"

"Two o'clock." Infinitely glad to have something positive to do, Jack nodded. "Meet you at Gibb's landing?"

"In one hour," Neville agreed. Though the man moved methodically, seemingly without haste, Jack noted that he wasted not a motion. He envied Neville's ability to remain calm in a crisis, but then, it wasn't *Neville's* wife who was missing.

Two hours later, they were making their way down the Thames to the channel in a modest little trade vessel on which Jack had purchased passage to Calais.

"First, we'll question the coachmen. Every man, until we find the one she hired," Neville said, his gaze flitting over the other boats crowding the river.

"What if no one remembers her?" Jack asked, stating his worst fear, recalling his lack of success with the past coachmen. "What if we can't find her?"

Neville smiled and slapped him on the back. "Of course we'll find her, Jack! This will be nothing compared to tracking most of the fellows I've ferreted out."

"When you were a spy?"

"Intelligencer," Neville corrected absently. "We have her assumed name, excellent description, down to what she is wearing and carrying with her. We also know how much money she has, which will determine *how* she travels and how far she can go on it. With that much information, I could find damn near anybody."

Jack wished to God he shared Neville's confidence in his ability, but he dared not question it aloud.

Neville paced beside him as Jack tried to rid himself of the tightness in his muscles. "Surprises me you'd forgive her, Jack. Must be love," he said with a smirk.

"I don't care what she did. I just want her back. I do love her, which means I have to take her as she is, faults and all. Why didn't I see that before?"

"Excellent conclusion, however late in its arrival. I think you had the girl on a very high pedestal, a very difficult position for her to maintain," Neville observed.

"She forgave me for marrying her for the money I thought was hers. I can forgive her for this."

Neville issued a short laugh. "So you just tell her that she's let off the hook, and you think everything will be rosy from there on?" He shook his head.

"Why shouldn't it be?" Jack asked, stopping to face Neville with the question.

"You don't broach that topic at all with her. Never bring it up again unless you want another squabble."

Neville sighed and walked on as he continued speaking. "When you and she were newly married, you viewed Laurel as a little saint with no flaws."

"I did not!" Jack argued, then realized his friend was right. "Well, for the most part I suppose I did, but later there were things about her that I wished were different."

Neville smiled. "List them now, my friend, and never mention them again, especially not to *her*."

Jack nodded. "Well, she showed her intimidation when it didn't suit. Several times, when it wouldn't do at all. But we had that discussion and she saw the wisdom of bluffing it out." He pondered, finding it difficult to come up with many detractions. "Sometimes she presumed on duties that weren't hers. But she corrected herself when I insisted."

"Oh, my lord, Jack," Neville growled. "You must stop trying to *fix* her so you can keep holding her up to perfection. It's a wonder she didn't shoot you before she left!"

He pursed his lips and pinned Jack with a glinty-eyed glare as he elaborated. "In future you will see more of these little things that make you roll your eyes and groan. Trust me on this."

"Speaking from experience, are you?" Jack thought the baroness must be the standard of perfection in a wife. A little amused, he raised an eyebrow in question.

"Miranda is always late," Neville informed him. "Never been on time for anything in her *life*. Now, there were times in my work when a half second's delay could have meant the difference between life or death, so this made me cringe, as you might imagine."

"You brought her up short about that, I'm sure," Jack said with a nod.

"Ha. I wouldn't have done that on a dare," Neville said evenly. "You see, that lack of promptness is very much a part of who Miranda is, so I knew I simply had to adjust to it. Marriage is a continuous compromise of these little things. Think of your own faults that Laurel must tolerate. God knows you have those!"

"What faults?" Jack demanded.

"This bloody pacing of yours for one thing.

It's always driven *me* mad, so I can well envision what it must do to a wife who must accommodate to it all the time." He took a deep breath and glanced sidewise at Jack. "And there's that bloody temper of yours. That's what sent her running."

"Granted," Jack ground out through gritted teeth.

Neville went on. "You can also be overbearing and you have no sense of fashion whatsoever."

"Well, thank you, Mr. Brummel! So I'm not flawless," Jack grumbled. "Neither is she. Neither is anyone for that matter."

"My point precisely. But you want her back in any event. Selfish reasons, Jack? Sex? Household management? What?"

Jack heaved a sigh. "I don't think I can live without her. And she needs me. I just love her, damn it all."

"Well then, when you find her—"

"Don't try to change her," Jack interrupted, finishing the thought with a nod. "I've already decided that. Since I love her, perhaps her particular faults are part of the reason *why* I do. She would not be who she is without them."

"Good for you," Neville said. "If she proves

to be as deceptive as you thought at first, you have to understand *why* she deceived you and learn to read her intent in future."

"Lord, I need a drink," Jack muttered.

Neville laughed and slung an arm around Jack's shoulders. "They'll drive us to it, and that's a fact. C'mon, man, let's see what sort of wicked liquid they stow on this tub."

"Probably rum that'll have me casting up my liver."

Jack thought long and hard about their conversation as they crossed the channel. He vowed that Laurel would never hear a word of criticism out of his mouth, ever again, no matter what she did.

He and Neville shared a tot of rum and drank in silence for a while. The self-styled expert on marriage had had his say, leaving Jack convinced that his own thinking had been on the right path, if not quite there.

Neville had only clarified what Jack had already been thinking with regard to Laurel. He must love her just as she was and hope that she would return the favor.

Only then, aboard the small packet and facing into the strong sea breeze, did Jack pause to think how he might approach Laurel once he reached her. If he knew Laurel, she wouldn't fall into his arms, smiling thankfully because he had come after her.

When he considered how he had threatened her and Hobson, he could hardly blame her if she turned him away. She had changed her name, and that meant she did not want to be found.

The evening of the next day, Jack fully realized what a daunting task he would have had if he had come alone, the questioning at every place hiring out coaches and describing Laurel when his French was so lacking. Thank God, Neville had agreed to come and assist.

They had found no success as yet, but there were more coachmen—a great many more— to question tomorrow. Jack had great hopes of finding her here. They had taken a room for the night at one of the inns near the docks, a rough establishment, but reasonably clean. Neville had fallen asleep the moment he lay down, but Jack could not rest.

Oddly enough, he didn't feel the expected sting of resentment in having to ask for and accept the help of his friend for a second time. Perhaps he was mellowing a bit, learning to allow someone else to shoulder a part of his burdens. At least he was at last able to admit he couldn't do everything by himself.

One fault mitigated, he thought with a bitter smile. Maybe that was how it should be, altering his own flaws to make himself a better mate for Laurel might prompt her to do the same for him.

One thing he knew for certain. He could never give up until he found Laurel and she was safe in his arms. The emptiness he felt without her could not go on.

He really had ceased to care whether she had deceived him at first. She had not known him then, just as he had not known her. Both of them had been concerned only with bettering their own lives.

There would be no talk of forgiveness on his part. All he wanted was for her to come home, to be his wife again.

The very thought of returning to Elderidge House without her could not be entertained, even for a moment. She was his one source of joy and contentment, the anchor that held him steady in the unfamiliar sea of responsibility.

The old, too-familiar uneasiness with its plaguing constancy soon set him trodding back and forth upon the planks of the inn's floor, his insides screaming for action, his mind dragged down in the undertow of worry.

Chapter Eighteen

Laurel chafed at the delay in Mrs. Grierson's decision. She wished to heaven the woman would make up her mind. They had languished here in Cagnes-sur-Mer for four whole days. While the surroundings were unsurpassed in their beauty, Laurel felt on edge, trapped betwixt the too-luscious land and the Ligurian Sea.

The ancient port, so verdant and lovely at first with its swaying palm trees, rock-strewn shoreline and picturesque buildings, seemed cloying to her now. It reeked of holiday laziness, its languid horde of foreign inhabitants lacking any real sense of time or purpose.

Laurel craved action and diversion. She wondered at times if Jack's dislike of inertia had

transferred itself to her. She began to understand and appreciate his innate urge to tackle
any and every issue that presented itself simply to keep from standing still and stagnating.

Mrs. Grierson had promised to consider
what they would do next as she took her morning constitutional. She had insisted on going
out alone again. Laurel didn't worry about her
since there were so many families about, either
in residence or enjoying a holiday.

Now that Mrs. Grierson had returned from
her stroll in the sun, perhaps she would have an
answer at last as to when and how they would
leave France.

The lady made free with Laurel's room,
treating it as a part of her suite, coming and
going as she pleased. Laurel didn't mind, but
even if she had, it would have made little difference.

The accommodations were of fine quality in
the old mansion newly converted to an inn ca-
tering to well-to-do tourists. She learned there
were quite a few of those now that the war was
over and everyone felt free to travel. The Grand
Tour was no longer restricted to wealthy sci-
ons out to add exotic sights and culture to their
education.

Laurel felt an eagerness to get on with their

tour and experience new things and places. She hoped the busyness of it all would help to banish the hopelessness that overtook her whenever she thought of Jack.

Dreamy-eyed, pink-cheeked and windblown, Mrs. Grierson had swept in as usual without knocking. "I declare this is the most wonderful day, and it has only just begun!"

It was nearly noon. Laurel could not contain her impatience. "So what do you think? Do we go over the Alps, ma'am, or do we take ship for Livorno?"

"Neither for the nonce," her employer replied dreamily, tossing her reticule on Laurel's bed and flopping down beside it with a merry grin.

She was obviously delighted with her latest amble along the Promenade des Anglais, a favorite haunt for Englanders on holiday by the sea.

Mrs. Grierson seemed obsessed with that opulent trail of late, so much so that Laurel feared she would never agree to leave it behind. She suspected a certain gentleman was the main attraction for the widow Grierson.

"The ship would prove faster, and I'm not certain either of us would stand the journey well across the mountains," Laurel said. "Most do that for the adventure of it, I think. I understand it is arduous and most uncomfortable, especially for ladies."

Mrs. Grierson appeared too preoccupied to be listening to a word Laurel uttered. In fact, she was acting like a tabby with a secret source of cream.

Almost since the day of their arrival here, the woman had shed at least a decade of her age. It was as if she left all her cares in the coach that had brought them.

"I have the most remarkable news," she said to Laurel with a girlish laugh and a confiding tone. "You will never guess what has just happened! I must tell you or burst!"

Before Laurel could say anything to that, Mrs. Grierson rushed on. "Paolo has proposed! I am to be married!" She clasped her hands under her double chin. "Isn't it wonderful, Laura?"

Shock struck Laurel silent. *Married?* To the Italian gentleman whom they had only met the day they arrived? He, Mrs. Grierson and Laurel had dined together almost every meal since, but this was entirely too soon for any close attachment to have developed, especially an engagement.

Paolo Giordano seemed haughty to her, a man with the occasional sardonic smile and very little to say. Laurel thought he might consider his attitude that of a romantic. To her, he just seemed odd. A strange match that would be, given Mrs. Grierson's overly effusive nature.

However, he was not ugly, perhaps handsome by some lights, and at least a decade younger than Mrs. Grierson. Also his manner of dress and speech did indicate wealth and privilege. Laurel could not fault Mrs. Grierson for seizing the opportunity to make another marriage, especially when it seemed prompted more by affection than the man's worldly assets. Mrs. Grierson rarely gave a thought to money and so, should fare much better with a husband who had plenty of it.

Laurel's main qualm was that the two hardly knew one another. She supposed they must have made the most of their time walking out together each morning. Still, how much could one learn about another person in four days?

Then she remembered her own brief contact with Jack before their hasty marriage. Laurel figured she had no room to object on the grounds of their short acquaintance. They hardly needed her approval anyway, so any protestations she made would prove useless.

But more to the point, Laurel wondered what

this marriage would mean to her with regard to her employment as Cornelia Grierson's companion? A new bride would not need or want another woman's company.

Mrs. Grierson reached out for Laurel's hand as if she realized what troubled her. "You are not to fret for yourself, my dear. I shall write you the grandest letters of recommendation ever written, and I know at least three widows in London who will welcome your company. You may have your choice of them!"

Laurel found her voice and forced a smile. "Thank you, ma'am, and may I be the first to wish you happy."

She felt as if a ball of lead had settled in her stomach. Where was she to go now, and what should she do? Certainly not back to London, and she hadn't enough money left to settle herself anywhere. She had barely enough to continue on to Italy alone and would have none left to live on once she arrived.

Laurel really wished she had not bent to Mrs. Grierson's order that she purchase two new gowns and matching shoes for their journey before leaving Paris. She would need that money. Perhaps she could sell the clothes.

Mrs. Grierson slid off the bed and began to dither about the room. She lifted a fichu Laurel had carelessly tossed aside to be laundered. Then suddenly she turned. "Oh, in my excitement, I almost forgot to tell you! There was a gentleman asking after you as I came into the hotel."

"For me?" Laurel gasped.

"Um-hmm. Quite by chance, I overheard him speaking with the manager, Monsieur Beaumont, asking for Laura Smythe, so I interrupted them and said you would be down for the noon meal."

She lifted the small timepiece she wore on a chain. "Oh, my, we've only a quarter hour until it's served. Paolo is meeting us in the dining room." She plucked at the graying curls peeking from the edge of her bonnet. "I wish we had time to do something with my hair."

Laurel had frozen in place. No one knew her as Laura Smythe except Mrs. Grierson herself, the Nicots in Paris and Paolo Giordano. No one would be looking for her other than Jack.

"Wh...what did he look like?" she stammered. "The man who asked for me?"

Mrs. Grierson laughed. "Oh, a rough-looking sort, that one. Untidy, he was. Gruff, too. Someone's messenger, no doubt. Never fear, child. I shall be with you when you see what he wants."

She swept out of Laurel's room through the connecting door to her own.

Laurel felt sick. Jack must have hired someone to find her and fetch her back for trial. That was the only explanation. Now that she considered it, he would never come for her himself.

Besides, the description did not fit Jack at all. But he could look rough and untidy. And he certainly could be gruff. No, she decided, it would not be him.

"I want you to have this," Mrs. Grierson said as she glided back into Laurel's room. She quickly pinned a brooch of jet and pearls at the neck of Laurel's gown and stepped back. "Lovely!"

Laurel touched the pin. "I can't accept this, ma'am." But maybe she could. If she sold it, she might have enough money to...to what? Run? Where, then? If someone had detected her whereabouts here, he could likely find her anywhere she fled.

"Of course you can!" Mrs. Grierson exclaimed. "It's only a mourning brooch I had made after Clive died. I shan't wear it ever again, and it should continue to have good use. Besides, it looks very well with your new gown, though I wish you would wear a bit of color now and then. Or hasn't your mourning period passed?" She squinted at Laurel. "How long has it been, dear?"

"Long enough." Laurel sighed, wishing the grief would go away with time. She feared it never would. Something precious to her had died, though it was only Jack's love for her that had expired.

There was nothing for it but to go back to England and face what she must. Even transportation to New Wales would be preferable to running for the rest of her life, constantly looking over her shoulder for someone pursuing, wondering if Jack would ever give up and forget what he thought she had done to him. She would go back. At least she would see Jack again, for all the good that would do her.

Her erstwhile father would probably be glad of company in the penal colony, so she supposed she would have to forgive him for creating this horrid mess.

In truth, she wanted to forgive him. Laurel could not forget that Hobson had been the only one to visit her at the convent, to bring her gifts and show pride in her accomplishments. Somehow, he had assumed the place of father in her mind even then.

"Are you ready to go down, dear?" Mrs.

Grierson asked, tucking an errant strand of hair behind Laurel's ear in a motherly gesture.

"As ready as I shall ever be." She took a deep breath to fortify herself.

"Come now, don't frown so! And do pinch your cheeks to pinken them, won't you? You look pale as death. Always wished I were blond, though, despite the paleness. But you should think color, perhaps lips." She nattered on about a perfectly divine reddish lip balm she had heard about from some lady she had met. Meanwhile, Laurel girded herself for what was to come.

"Ah, there he is now! Look, Laurel, do you know him?"

Laurel exhaled slowly as she regarded the man standing at the foot of the stairs, waiting.

Until that moment, she had not realized how deeply she had wished him to be Jack, no matter the intent he might have for coming. But it was not him. Instead, this man did appear the rough and untidy sort that Mrs. Grierson had described.

Summoning all the courage she could muster, Laurel descended until she stood face-to-face with the stranger. "I believe you were looking for me," she stated.

"Mademoiselle Smythe? *Oui*. Monsieur

Nicot asked me to find you and deliver this on my way to Florence. I was delayed two days in Reims, so forgive me if it is urgent." He handed her a letter.

Laurel's legs nearly folded beneath her in relief. She accepted the missive with shaking hands and managed a word of thanks. The man nodded, turned and left immediately.

"Well, won't you open it?" Mrs. Grierson asked. "It's from my son-in-law so I should know its contents, shouldn't I? Perhaps it's news of my daughter! She could be increasing, in which event, we must return to Paris at once! Hurry, child, open it and see!"

Laurel had no reason to keep it private. She tore open the letter and unfolded it. It was an authorization to draw on funds from a bank in Florence where Nicot knew they were headed.

In an added note, Nicot stated that he had realized belatedly that his wife's *maman* would never remember to pay Laurel, so he had arranged her salary himself. He apologized for neglecting to reassure her before she departed from Paris.

Laurel refolded the paper and smiled at Mrs. Grierson. "He assures me you need not grant me any funds from your own purse, ma'am. My services will be paid for on his own account out of a Florence bank. He must have a very high regard for you to assume my salary, don't you think?"

Mrs. Grierson beamed. "Indeed! For a Frenchman, he is a priceless match for my Margaret! Always thought so. Now come... my fiancé will be waiting!"

Laurel laughed with relief as Mrs. Grierson rushed ahead into the dining room. Pausing just outside the open doorway, Laurel smoothed a hand over her stomach to quiet the burgeoning nausea she had felt since hearing that some man was asking for her.

Nothing but a messenger, a Frenchman, a traveler hired by Nicot. She closed her eyes for a few seconds to regain her composure before going in to eat.

"Laurel? Or is it Laura now?"

She opened her eyes and blinked twice. Right in front of her stood Jack.

Chapter Nineteen

Jack grasped Laurel's arms to keep her upright. He regretted surprising her so that she nearly fainted. Her eyes flew wide as her gaze locked with his.

"I've come for you," he said simply.

She didn't reply. He hated the fear and resignation he saw in her eyes, the surrender evident in her dejected sigh.

He lowered his mouth to hers and took it in a demanding kiss, hoping to stir her spirit to anger, at least. Anything was preferable to this attitude of defeat, even her fury. That, he could deal with.

Jack fully expected her to jerk away and deliver him a sharp slap as soon as she got over the shock of being kissed so soundly in a public place. Her mouth remained motionless, pliant under his as he plundered it like a rake of the worst order.

He was not prepared when her surprise dissolved, her hands slid around his waist and she responded with a passionate moan of welcome.

His head spun with relief and his body responded with sudden need of her. The kiss deepened; his hands and arms grasped her desperately of their own accord.

"Sir? Madame!" a starched voice intruded.

Jack broke away, realizing suddenly where they were and what he was doing. The manager, stiff as his starched collar, regarded them with a jaundiced eye. "Would you like a room, sir?" he asked in a sonorous voice. English. Cockney, with pretensions, Jack decided.

He glanced around and noted that he and Laurel were the focus of everyone in the atrium and those who could see them from their seats in the dining room. Shocked stares from all.

"A room would be most convenient," Jack replied as haughtily as he had been asked. "The best available, if you please."

"May I have your name for the book, sir?" the manager asked with a barely concealed sneer and a jaded look at Laurel that said he thought she was no better than she should be.

"Elderidge," Jack said with a lift of his chin as he slid his arm around Laurel's shoulder. "The Earl and Countess of Elderidge." He felt Laurel stand straighter, her shoulders squared beneath his one-armed embrace.

The manager gulped audibly, then recovered. "Of course, sir, if you will follow me?" Doubt apparent, the man bowed slightly as he passed by to lead them to the stairway.

Jack remained silent, as did Laurel, when they entered the suite that must have belonged to the master of the mansion when it had been designated as that.

He gave the man a coin and closed the door in his face. Then he turned to Laurel. "So, here we are." Jack was at a loss as to what he should do next. He could hardly resume that kiss, given the look of outrage on her face now. Fury, accomplished.

"That was uncalled-for!" she said, her voice low and fraught with wrath. "I have never been so embarrassed in all my life!"

"We certainly made an impression," he agreed as he began strolling about the room, examining the expensive accents of porcelain figures and gold leaf frames.

"You are wretched!" she exclaimed, folding

her arms tight across her chest and staring out the window.

"Sorely wretched with discontent," he admitted. "Nearly mad, in fact. That's why I've come." He lifted a little shepherdess from the table and smiled down at her. She reminded him of Laurel except for the chipped bonnet. He set it down and turned to her. "I can't live without you."

"Ha! You would have dragged me through the courts and had me sent half the world away!"

"Had you not the good sense to leave when you did, I might have done precisely that. My temper is abominable. But it is also short-lived, Laurel. I want you to come home."

"How did you find me?" she asked, rubbing her arms as if she were cold.

"Neville helped me track you to Paris. Once we learned your destination from the baker, I sent him home to Miranda and came on alone. You cannot begin to imagine how relieved I am."

She looked confused, upset, torn, too much like she had when she first saw him downstairs. Jack wanted her self-assured and in command of herself again, the Laurel he knew she could be. That was not trying to fix her, was it? Only snapping her out of one mood into another.

"So will you come home with me or are you afraid to risk my company?" he asked.

A fist pounded on the door. Jack cursed roundly at the interruption and went to open it, ready to give that pretentious manager a boot down the stairs.

"What?" he demanded as he flung open the door.

The fist hit him square in the nose, surprising Jack so that he lost balance, tipped backward and landed on the floor. When he looked up, he saw a total stranger rubbing his knuckles and glaring down at him with eyes as dark as hell itself. "Who the devil are *you?*"

"I am Paolo Giordano! This young woman is not to be dishonored. I offer her my protection." He beckoned to Laurel, his Italian accent softening from the former harshness he had used on Jack. "Come away with me now. This blackguard will plague you no more!"

Laurel had a hand over her mouth, and Jack could swear she was about to laugh. His temper flared, as much at her as her sworn protector. "She is my wife, you idiot!"

Giordano scoffed. However, he backed up a

step when Jack pushed up from the floor and stood.

Laurel hurried over and placed herself between them, facing Giordano. "He speaks the truth, sir. He is my husband. I beg you not to injure him further. Please go and assure your Mrs. Grierson I am in no peril. She must be worried after that scene below."

When the man hesitated, she reached for his hand and shook it firmly. "Thank you ever so much for thinking of my safety. Oh, and congratulations on your engagement."

He nodded once as he shot Jack a final, narrow-eyed look of warning.

Laurel closed the door and leaned back against it, looking up at him with barely concealed satisfaction. "Your nose is bleeding all over your neckcloth," she informed him.

He touched his nose and grimaced when his fingers came away red. "So it is. I've not been planted a facer like that since I turned twelve."

"I'm surprised you didn't return the favor."

"My temper does have limits. The man thought he was justified and protecting you. I could hardly blame him for that after the spectacle I made of us downstairs. So you know him well?"

"He's the fiancé of the woman to whom I am companion."

"To whom you *were* companion," he corrected, testing the bridge of his nose with thumb and forefinger to see if it was broken.

"I don't know what to make of this, Jack. Your coming for me, I mean. Do you still intend I should be punished in some way, or do you now believe me innocent?"

He unwound his neckcloth and began mopping blood from his nose with it. "I want you back is all. We'll begin again. No secrets, no hidden motives, no further talk of deception."

She quirked an eyebrow. "Your admitted deception regarding our marriage or what you believe was mine?"

"Either one. We *are* married, Laurel. For better or worse, remember?" He looked down at the linen he held, nearly soaked through with red. "Damn me, I'm bleeding to death, and you want to talk of placing blame?"

She shook her head and gave a sigh. "I won't go back with you. I cannot."

Jack stilled, ignoring the pain lancing through his nose. "Why not? I told you it doesn't matter anymore. I don't care!"

She looked sad. "But it does matter and I *do* care, you see. I refuse to live as your wife knowing you will never trust me, that you believe me capable of such avarice." She opened the door. "Go home, Jack."

And then she was gone, right out the door before he could move to stop her. Jack let her go, cursing under his breath when a fresh rivulet of blood splashed his shirtfront.

At least he knew where she was and whom she was with. He would follow her to the ends of the earth if need be, but he would never give her up.

He went to the washstand and poured water from the pitcher into the fancy basin. The bloodied nose was nothing. He deserved at least that much for embarrassing Laurel. There hadn't been more than a brief urge to retaliate, and even that died when he realized why the man had hit him.

The bloke had a mean punch, he thought as he dampened the cloth and set about making himself presentable.

Laurel had a protector for the nonce and the man was engaged to someone else. That was comforting. It would provide Jack time to persuade Laurel, to show her how much she meant to him. He sincerely hoped he wouldn't have to throw her over his shoulder and haul her back home by force.

Oddly enough, her refusal of his offer to reconcile had convinced him of her innocence as nothing else could have done. Her running away and changing her name should have been proof enough, but he had put that to her fear of punishment.

Now she knew he wouldn't do that to her, and still she refused. So the money and title were not what she had been after. She hadn't a greedy bone in her sweet little body or she would have leaped at the chance to go home with him.

How would he convince her that he now believed that only Hobson was to blame? Telling her outright wouldn't do. She'd think he was lying only to get her back.

He needed a plan.

"Paolo insists you stay and travel with us," Mrs. Grierson declared to Laurel after she learned what had happened above stairs. "I haven't dismissed you, dear. You are still in my employ and shall be until we find you another position! That husband of yours sounds like a perfectly horrid man!"

"No, he's not *horrid*," Laurel argued, "but I cannot go back to England with him. He believes I tricked him into our marriage for his wealth and a title."

The woman harrumphed. "What is so wrong with that?"

Giordano frowned at her.

Mrs. Grierson leaned toward him and covered his hand with hers. "Not to worry, my darling man, your fortune means nothing to me."

"She's right," Laurel added for good measure. "Money is the least of her concerns, trust me."

He inclined his head and smiled at Laurel. "Mrs. Grierson will need a chaperone until our marriage. You should not go back with him," Giordano said emphatically. "You will accompany us. It is settled."

"As far as Florence," Laurel agreed. "I'm certain I shall find something to do there."

"An excellent plan," Giordano said. "I will help you find a position, that I promise you." His dark gaze caught hers and held it, causing a shiver to ripple along her spine. Laurel felt uneasy.

"You must stay with me at least long enough for our wedding," Mrs. Grierson said, turning a sweet smile on her fiancé and giving his sleeve a fond pat.

Laurel didn't know if she could tolerate attending a wedding, seeing everyone else so happy when she felt so bereft.

She tried to continue hiding her feelings for their benefit, when she only wanted to retire and cry herself to sleep. It was hardly past midday, however. She had an entire afternoon to endure, knowing that Jack was somewhere on the premises.

She feared seeing him. If he insisted a bit more vehemently, or simply kissed her again, she might abandon her principles and go back to him. Doing that might satisfy her for a while, but in every look he gave her in future, she would be searching for his doubt. Once the newness of their physical joy passed, he might begin to hate her.

She knew only too well how closely love could be related to hate. Laurel had experienced Jack's hate, but only through Hobson's words, not face-to-face. That she could not bear to witness.

Laurel admitted that she loved him and knew that he probably loved her, too, but love alone was a fragile thing and not at all dependable. When not conjoined with trust, admiration and respect, it was little more than a powerful physical thing. That would not be enough to sustain a marriage.

"Oh, God," she murmured, covering her face with her hands, forgetting everything but her unhappiness. She wanted so much for things to be as they had been.

If only she could have remained that starry-eyed bride who saw no faults in him. If only Jack had never learned of her true identity and decided she was not to be trusted. She knew she would never be happy again.

Arms surrounded her but they were not Jack's. Too soft, too gentle, too redolent of rosewater.

"Oh, my dear child! That despicable man upset you so! Paolo, what must we do?" Cornelia Grierson leaned her face against the top of Laurel's head. "Poor girl, you need a mother."

"She needs a husband," a deep voice declared. Not Paolo.

Mrs. Grierson released her and Laurel uncovered her eyes. Jack stood there looking down at her. She knew he was going to do it. He would insist on her going back with him. Then he would kiss her senseless.

"No," she whispered. She rose from her chair, looking him directly in the eye. "I do not need you."

"I love you, Laurel," he said, hurt written all over his face.

She closed her eyes against the sight of his pain. "It is not enough."

He sighed. "What more do you want from me?"

"Go home, Jack," she said again.

"Not if you won't come with me. I'll have to stay with you."

That brought her up short. "You can't do that!"

He said nothing, but his stubborn expression spoke volumes.

"I'm not staying here," she said. "I'm going to Italy with Mrs. Grierson."

Jack shrugged. "I've never been to Italy. Not past the ports at any rate. I expect we'll love it."

Laurel threw up her hands and moved a few feet away from him, giving him her back. She was causing a scene in the dining room, but she didn't care. Let them look.

"This won't do, Jack! You can't simply follow me everywhere I go!" She rounded on him, shaking her fist. "I cannot be what everyone wants me to be, you hear?"

"Neither can I. Let's adjust our expectations a little and simply be who we are," he said. "After all, no one is perfect." She could tell he meant every word. "But you make me want to be, Laurel. You make me try for it." The sincerity was there in his eyes.

"Damn you, Jack! You are the most exasperating…"

"*Fool.* I know," he finished for her. "One of my greater defects, but I'm working on that."

"Stop putting words in my mouth!"

She moved farther away before he got close enough to kiss her. He meant to. She wanted him to. But if he did, she would be lost, thrust back into that role she could no longer fill.

After all, she saw him for what he was now—driven, obstinate, quick-tempered and far too used to having his own way. "You are not the man I thought you were," she accused.

"If you expected perfection, you should have taken vows at the convent, Laurel." He looked deadly serious.

"Leave her *alone,*" Giordano demanded. He was standing now, his hands fisted, his expression warning.

Laurel turned away and hurried out of the dining room and up the stairs to her room, not caring if a fight ensued. She did not want to be there to see it. She feared she might cheer on the Italian despite Jack's already injured nose.

She needed to think what to do next. She did not want to be Cornelia Grierson's companion, chaperone or anything of the like. And she certainly didn't want to return to the convent.

She knew in her heart she wanted to be Jack's wife, despite the problems between them. But she could not be as she had been before, weighing every word she spoke, doing his bidding about what duties to undertake, fitting her moods to jolly his at every turn. She threw herself facedown on her bed, too angry for tears.

Chapter Twenty

She was angry, yes, but Laurel knew she would get over it. For all his faults, he was Jack and she loved him. He was the one suggesting they begin again and be who they really were this time. But did he really mean that?

They would surely clash wills again, even more frequently, if she stopped acting the part of the ideal wife and countess. Could she count on him to tolerate her as she really was?

Mrs. Grierson entered her room without knocking. Laurel wished the woman to perdition. Why couldn't everyone just leave her alone?

"Perfectly played, my dear! I see you've mastered the art of managing your man! Good show. Would you like a tot of this brandy?"

Laurel heard the clink of glass and sat up. "*Managing?* What do you mean?"

"That little scene below certainly put him in his place. From now on, he'll step lightly around you, probably do anything you want. I predict you'll have flowers delivered before tomorrow," she prattled on. "A trite ploy, but ever their first gambit to mend a rift."

"Flowers?" Laurel scoffed. Then she recalled the bouquets that had appeared in her bedroom after she discovered his deception about their marriage. His first gambit. It had softened her, she remembered.

"Roses, perhaps, or something more exotic. He seems the sort to try for uniqueness." Mrs. Grierson grinned as she rolled the brandy around in the glass and offered it.

Laurel accepted the snifter and inhaled the mellow scent of the liquor before taking a sip. It burned. Warmed. Comforted. She took another.

"You shouldn't relent until he sends jewels," Mrs. Grierson advised.

"Jewels?"

"Oh, yes. I expect he will begin with something modest, since he won't want it to seem he's attempting to purchase your regard. Probably pearls." She pursed her lips and quirked them to one side for a moment as she swiveled her glass and watched the liquid coat the sides of it. "You should hold out for emeralds."

Laurel almost laughed. "I care nothing for jewels, and he knows it."

"Ooh, how mean on your part to tell him such a thing! Limits his ploys, you see. But you mark my words. He'll follow us to Italy. He won't give up. I know his sort." She pointed at Laurel with her brandy glass and offered a canny chuckle. "Determined as the devil himself!"

"How do you know his *sort?*" Laurel asked, knowing she might be sorry she did. But Mrs. Grierson had stirred her curiosity. This was certainly a Cornelia she had not seen before, and it offered Laurel a much needed diversion.

"I wasn't always this age, you know. Married at eighteen, a mother at nineteen, widowed at twenty. I've survived two husbands since." Her blue eyes danced with memories. Or perhaps anticipation. "Now I'm fifty-eight. Paolo will be my last. Being so much younger, he will surely outlive me."

"Do you truly love him?" Laurel asked. This attachment had taken hold so quickly, it seemed impossible, as did Giordano's attraction to the matronly Cornelia.

"I love his flattery and his interest in me.

What woman wouldn't? He's entirely too quiet, too proud and a bit stuffy. But that's common to his station, don't you think? He's from wealth, after all, so I doubt he can help it. Nothing wrong with his looks, though, you have to admit!"

"He looks very well," Laurel agreed. Giordano was definitely not ugly, though his appearance hardly appealed to *her*. She found his intensity…disturbing.

How could she ever have agreed to travel to Italy with a man she felt that way about? Hadn't Jack cautioned her several times about her overly trustful nature?

His saying so had angered her because she had thought it condescending to her and all women. All he had been trying to do then was warn *her* in particular, not insult her entire gender. Still, she had failed to consider then that it might be true. Life in the convent had sheltered her so, she had never learned to look for or expect any danger until it was nearly too late.

She had trusted Mr. Hobson, then Orencio and finally, Jack himself. Three mistakes out of three men surely proved him right about her.

She had been naive and in need of protection then, two things she must admit to herself and change immediately, for she had almost committed another mistake. Perhaps Mrs. Grierson was like her and should be more wary, too.

"We shouldn't go to Italy, either of us," Laurel declared.

"What? Why? Of course we must go. It's all arranged. Paolo is taking care of everything."

Mrs. Grierson laughed again and hopped onto the bed beside Laurel, her short legs dangling. "He's so sophisticated, isn't he! So very sure of himself. I like that in a man."

Perhaps a little too sophisticated and sure of himself, Laurel thought. However, if he were overly charming and ingratiating, she would mistrust him even more, she admitted. He had done everything right, nothing wrong and said precisely what was expected of him.

Perhaps that was it. His lack of any *apparent* shortcomings made him seem less human and, oddly, less trustworthy than a man who would exhibit some. It was as if he were hiding his true self behind that facade of perfection. She worried about Mrs. Grierson, but knew the woman wouldn't listen to her doubts.

Instead, Laurel tried another tactic to persuade her not to go off with a man she hardly knew. "Your daughter will miss you if you go to Italy to live, especially when she begins her family. Think how you would miss her. She's very fortunate to have you as a mother, Mrs. Grierson."

"Oh, call me *Cornelia,* please. This is a woman-to-woman discussion, not one of employer and employee or even mother to daughter, though I should like it if you were mine." She gave Laurel's hand a pat as it rested against the counterpane. "Margaret never listened to a word I said, probably because I talk too much."

Laurel declined to comment on that particular truth.

"Oh, yes, I'm well aware of it, always have been, but I can never seem to control it. I don't think Paolo cares a fig. Ofttimes, he actually seems to listen!"

Laurel laughed with her. Perhaps she didn't need Laurel's concern, after all, and she certainly wouldn't welcome it. Cornelia must know a great deal more about men than the average woman since she had dealt with so many husbands. The woman was certainly old enough to make decisions for herself.

Downing the remainder of her brandy in one swallow, Laurel coughed and laughed again. "You know, Cornelia, I feel *much* better."

"Brandy is magic!" The woman beamed and clinked her empty glass against Laurel's. "Now, here's what you should do…"

Laurel paid scant attention. Her mind was on Jack, wondering if Cornelia was right and he would follow them to Italy. Would her going, just to see if he would follow, be a fair test of his resolve to have her back? Was she ever to keep testing him?

Going seemed wrong to her, especially since she had already made up her mind. Every instinct within her sounded a warning not to go, and she would take heed this time.

Jack might have been a bit more politic when advising her to be more discerning about people and their intentions, but she couldn't deny that he had been right.

In that respect, she should have looked past his words and realized his deep concern for her welfare. He could seem domineering at times, but his heart was in the right place. Jack cared. He loved her. And he was as new to this marriage business as she was. They both had much to learn in dealing with each other.

Perhaps she ought to consider whether she could place enough trust in Jack now, instead of the other way round.

"I have decided. I will go back with my husband," she told Cornelia, interrupting the flow of advice with her pronouncement. "Tomorrow I shall tell him so."

"So soon?" The woman sighed.

"I want to. I will."

"Well, I suppose you must do as you think best."

"It will be the best for everyone involved, especially me," Laurel declared.

"In one way, I am happy you have made up your mind this soon," Cornelia admitted. "Paolo has been much distracted by all these hysterics. That man of yours might not survive any further fisticuffs."

Laurel nodded, suppressing a laugh, amazed at how her heart had lightened with her firm decision. "I wish you would come with us as far as Paris, ma'am. I have a feeling it would be better if you do."

"Oh, no thank you, dear. But I must go downstairs and tell Paolo immediately that you aren't coming along," Cornelia said, sliding off the bed and straightening her skirts. She set down the glass. "But I shan't breathe a word of it if your man's still within earshot. You should be the one to tell him." She grinned and pinched Laurel's cheek. "Besides, he should have at least one more sleepless night on your account, don't you think?"

It was wicked of her, perhaps, but Laurel thought so, too.

She fell asleep dreaming of their reunion and awoke with a hand clapped over her mouth and nose. A forearm across her chest held her flat.

"Make a sound and I'll kill you!" The gruff voice rasped in her ear. "I'll kill anyone you summon, too. Nod if you comprehend."

Laurel nodded, frantic to breathe. She recognized the accent. *Paolo Giordano.* When she glanced down, moonlight through the window glinted off the knife near her throat.

"Good." He lifted his arm from her chest, but kept the blade close to her neck. "Now you will rise and put on your shoes and cloak." Both lay upon the bed next to her. "I warn you again, do not alert anyone. The knife will silence you, and if the Englishman or Cornelia come in, I shall kill them."

She nodded again and he took away his hand from her face. "What do you want?" she gasped.

"Shhh. You will not be harmed if you do as I say."

As if she would believe that! But she did believe he would kill with no hesitation. What could she do? Perhaps if she offered no resistance, he would lower his guard and she could escape. Here in the hotel, there was no place to run without endangering the life of anyone they encountered.

She slipped into her half boots and donned her cloak, ever aware of the blade hovering near her neck.

"Now quietly walk in front of me," he demanded as he took hold of her upper arm. "The point is at your liver and that is a painful way to die."

They exited the hotel through the door to the gardens and Laurel knew she was doomed to go with him. His grip was punishing. Even if she could jerk free and run, he would catch her, kill her and get away before anyone could answer her scream. "Where are you taking me?" she whispered.

Less anxious now that they were outside and not likely to be overheard, Giordano answered in his usual oily tone. "Where you will bring me a fortune. Blond women as lovely as you are much in demand, a welcome addition to any harem."

Laurel shook her head in disbelief. "You never had any intention of going to Italy!"

He laughed softly. "Gullible females. How easy you are to collect."

"So I am not the only one," she surmised.

"Hardly, as you soon shall see. Move along. The tide waits for no one."

They were approaching the harbor's shore-line and she spied the small boat and another man waiting.

Oh, God, they were going out to a ship and were going to sail immediately. Jack would believe she had run away from him again and not even look for her this time. And even if he did, he would never find her.

Jack had devised no plan except to begin again with Laurel and do as he should have done at the outset. First thing tomorrow he would send flowers to her room. He thought that flowers had probably influenced her a little to forgive him before.

The clock chimed two and still he couldn't sleep. His whole face ached and he couldn't breathe through his nose. By morning, his eyes would be black. Perhaps he would play on Laurel's sympathy. He wasn't above using anything at this point to get her agreement to come home.

A staccato knock sounded on his door. He got up, pulled on his breeches and went to answer, hoping against hope that it was Laurel needing him in some way. Any way at all.

He no sooner had opened it a crack when Mrs. Grierson pushed past him and whirled around. "They are gone!"

"Who?" She was staring pointedly at his bare chest, so Jack grabbed his discarded shirt and pulled it on quickly.

"Your wife and my fiancé!" she declared, sweeping one arm wide. "They've run off together, into the night!"

"Don't be absurd! You're imagining things," Jack said. "If he's not in his room, that doesn't mean—"

"I *saw* them!" Mrs. Grierson insisted. "I thought I heard his footsteps in the hallway and feared he was going out to meet someone. I watched from my window to see where he was going and there were the two of them, headed through the garden! Together!"

She was frantically wringing the front of her nightdress as she released a loud sob. "You have to go after them!"

Jack wondered if the woman was one of those like the dowager, stirring up trouble for the sake of drama. "And you think he was with Laurel? It must have been some other woman. Did you actually see her?" He was not about to chase down the Italian and some lightskirt he was dallying with before wedding this older woman.

"I *know* it was Laurel! She's not in her room. Her half boots are missing and so is her cape. Oh, God, I would never have believed it of her...." She lapsed into tears and wailed.

Jack grasped her shoulders and shook her. "Listen to me! Laurel did not run off with him willingly. How long have they been gone?"

"I came to you straightaway. Moments... perhaps ten. Oh, I can't think!" She sobbed.

"Which ship were you to take to Italy?"

She shook her head violently. "I don't know!"

"Gather your wits, woman, *please!* Was anything said about it?"

Her weeping subsided to frequent sniffs. "He spoke of a ship but did not say its name, only that we would have a cozy cabin. And all the time he planned to—"

"*He* planned," Jack insisted. "Laurel might have run from me, but she would never betray you with him. He's kidnapped her."

"But why?"

"Ransom, maybe. Or maybe he's a slaver. No good purpose, that's certain. Which way were they going when you saw them?"

She pointed toward the harbor as she wiped her face of tears with her other hand. "You're probably right, damn his eyes. She'd not have gone of her own accord. Just yesterday she confided she was going home with you. I told Paolo of her decision last night."

"So he snatched her up because it would be his last chance at her. He must know I'll be after them," Jack said, hurriedly donning his boots without bothering with stockings.

"Oh, no, he won't think *that*," she argued, bitterness in her growl. "He called you a milquetoast and believes you incapable of fighting." She blinked up at him and sniffed. "Are you?"

"He'll soon find out, that I promise!" Jack yanked on his coat, stuck his pistol in the pocket and headed for the door.

"I'm coming with you!" Mrs. Grierson announced.

"No time for you to dress. Wait here."

She ignored that and trailed after him at a run, nightdress flapping and her slippers pattering away on the stairs behind him.

He figured she would give it up once they reached the gravel path, but heard her huffing just behind him. "Go back, ma'am," he called over his shoulder. "This could get ugly!"

"Uglier…the better," she retorted, short of breath. "He *used* me…to get to Laurel."

Jack went straight to the harbor. Rowboats bobbed against pilings at the pier and there were several ships anchored much farther out in the deeper water. The moon was high and full, casting a ghostly light over everything.

"Tide's coming in," he muttered, figuring he had only a few hours to determine which ship. He paused and squinted at their outlines, hoping to eliminate those too small to accommodate passengers.

Then he realized that the Italian might not risk taking Laurel to one that transported regular travelers, one where she might beg help and escape him. Damn the man, he could be carrying her to any vessel out there!

"Look!" Mrs. Grierson cried, pointing as she danced up and down at the edge of the water. "Just there, see?"

Jack followed her finger and saw the boat, a dinghy with three figures in it, one of them rowing against the force of the tide. Just then, one stood. He saw the flash of blue-white gown, the sweep of the cape as she swung it at the others. Then she jumped. Her action tipped the small craft over.

"Laurel!" he shouted.

Jack shucked off his coat, kicked off his boots, splashed into the surf and leaped into the nearest boat. He untied it from its mooring, grabbed the oars and began rowing for all he was worth, praying that Laurel knew how to swim.

The tide would bring her closer if she kept her head, rode the waves and didn't give up.

His muscles burned as he put all of his strength into the effort to reach her. Faster and faster, pulling against the rolling of the sea, he struggled past the breakers, searching frantically to locate her in the water.

He saw her then, riding the swells, arms pulling in unison, not flailing in panic. She kept her wits, thank God. He also spied a larger figure following only yards behind her.

"Here, Laurel! This way!" Jack called out. He fought hard with the oars, adjusting his direction as best he could without being swept backward.

In moments that seemed like hours, she was nearly even with his boat, but still too far away to reach, and he could not go sideways. Jack glanced back. They were near enough—he could swim her to shore. He dropped the oars, went over the side and swam.

Three more strokes and he would have her! Her scream ended abruptly as she was jerked under. Jack saw the man's head break the surface and he went for it. He grasped a handful of hair and yanked backward. With his other fist, he pounded once, smashing the nose. Hands came up to protect the face and Jack dived, knowing Laurel would be free.

A swell slammed her body into his and he grabbed her beneath the water. She began pummeling him ineffectually, but with all her might.

He grasped her waist and pushed her up to the surface so she could breathe, and she ceased fighting. Jack came up beside her. "It's me, Laurel!" he sputtered, knowing she had taken him for her attacker.

"Hold on," he ordered, dragging her arms around his neck, facing him. "The tide will take us in."

"Jack!" she screamed. "Behind you!"

Jack swerved to see the man behind him, one arm raised high, moonlight glinting on a silvery blade.

Jack deflected the blow, put a foot to the man's chest and shoved hard. When he turned to find Laurel, he heard a shot over the sound of the breaking waves. He knew it could not have come from the knife-wielder. Wet powder was useless. Anyone aiming from a boat in the rolling surf had precious little chance of hitting them anyway.

Jack turned his focus on Laurel so she wouldn't drown. They were near the shore, but not close enough. She reached for him and hung on.

His feet soon found purchase and he stood, gripping at the shifting sands with his toes, hauling Laurel up against his chest. He staggered through the shallows, laid her on the rock-strewn beach and collapsed beside her.

"There now..." he gasped, and coughed up the brine he had swallowed.

Laurel rolled close and buried her face in the clinging wet fabric of his shirt. "Take me... home," she groaned.

He sat up and dragged her onto his lap, hugging her tight and planting a kiss of promise on her tangled curls. "Immediately, if not sooner," he said.

"I'll wait for *him*. Make certain he is dead," Mrs. Grierson declared. She stood not a dozen feet away, holding Jack's pistol in both hands.

Jack smelled the gunpowder, acrid as it mingled with the cool salt air. The woman held herself stiff and still as a statue and looked much like one, motionless and blue-white in the moonlight. "You shot him."

"Yes." Nothing more.

Jack and Laurel sat there resting from their ordeal, holding and warming each other until he felt able to rise and pull Laurel to her feet.

"He meant to sell me," Laurel said. "Because I'm English. And fair. From what he said, I'm not the first."

"We'll tell the authorities. Perhaps the others can be rescued." He tightened his arms around her. "Try not to think about it."

"Why did he come after me?" she gasped.

"Because you would tell," Jack said simply. "If you were drowned, he could have claimed you went of your own accord. And no one would know of the others."

The rowboat he had appropriated earlier washed ashore with the incoming tide and brushed back and forth on the sand. Jack wondered how long it would take for the Italian to turn up. He would, because he'd never have made it out to the ships if that shot had missed him.

Jack looked up. Mrs. Grierson was waiting patiently, with one shot left in Neville's double-barreled pistol.

He heard a shrill whistle. Someone must have summoned the Watch. People would surround them soon and demand to know what had gone on. He hoped Mrs. Grierson's French was better than his. He did not want Laurel to have to relive the incident, even with words. He rubbed her back, trying to warm her.

"I worried you might not come for me," Laurel murmured against his chest as she returned his embrace.

"I will always come for you," he said, brushing a hand over her hair and cradling her head. "Always."

"He made me go with him. You believe me, don't you?"

"I never doubted it for a moment. You would never betray a friend. Or me."

"He said he would kill you if I screamed. If we had reached the ship, you would never have found me. He wasn't bound for Florence, as you might have thought."

"I know. Hush, love. Don't think about it anymore. It's over now and you're safe."

"I love you, Jack," she whispered, looking up at him. "I think I did from the very first day we met."

He smiled to himself as he stroked her cheek. No, maybe she had loved who she thought he was then. Now she knew him better, along with most of his frailties, and loved him anyway. "I know, my brave girl, and I love you, too."

Epilogue

Weeks later, Laurel basked in the warmth of home at last. She thought often of the poor infant who had died at sea, the one who might, had a fever not taken her, be living the life Laurel had now.

On Sunday they were to hold a service for her and place a small granite memorial beside the mother's grave. It would carry the name of Lady Pippin Worth, since *Pippin* was the only name they knew that anyone had troubled to give her.

Lady Portia had sold her jewels and was busy establishing an orphanage with the proceeds, in order to save other babies and assuage some of her guilt. Laurel's father was handling the purchase of property and business legalities for her.

Laurel looked forward to bringing everyone together for the harvest festival. There was much to celebrate, not least that the estate was returning to a profit after a few years stagnation and the old earl's death. Laurel kept a sharp eye on expenditures and investments with Jack's ever-reluctant blessing.

They were learning, understanding more each day, that they each possessed particular strengths the other must rely on and not covet. Though these sometimes coincided or overlapped, Jack was the strong one, the protector, judge and enforcer of laws within their domain. She offered patience, the voice of reason and— she laughed to think of it—financial advice and new ideas.

Midnight at Elderidge House was Laurel's favorite time of all. The servants were out of the way, their duties completed, and she and Jack enjoyed their time alone. The past two hours had proved particularly wonderful.

"You really are such a *man!*" She stretched her arms above her head and sighed dreamily as Jack traced a finger along her rib cage and smiled down at her compliment. That she sometimes uttered those same words as an accusation didn't signify to either of them at the moment.

When she lowered her arms, he leaned to nip her shoulder. "I love having the time to explore," he said against her skin. "Let's never travel again."

"Umm." Laurel smiled in agreement. They had gone overland from Cagnes-sur-Mer, back through Paris to the Nicots, and on to Calais. The journey home had afforded them precious little privacy, and that only available when they stopped for the night at wayside inns. Their two nights at the London house were little better, what with exhaustion from the trip and the rush of their second wedding.

Hurried couplings in unfamiliar beds were exciting, but definitely not as satisfactory as those of their first night home at Elderidge House.

"What do you think of Father's reaction to our Mrs. Grierson?" she asked, toying with a wave that curled over Jack's brow. She gave it a tug.

"Ouch!" He chuckled and grabbed her fingers. "Hobson's in for trouble on that front."

After a quick visit to the Nicots in Paris and ascertaining that no grandchildren were due in her near future, Cornelia Grierson had accepted Jack's invitation to come to England with them. She had been unusually quiet since shooting her fiancé and suffered a sadness they had constantly worked to draw out of her.

Only when they stopped in London to visit Laurel's father for her reconciliation with him, did Cornelia show any vestige of her former self.

She became even more vivacious at the private Catholic ceremony Jack had hastily arranged. He had insisted, so that no one would ever question whether he and Laurel were legally wed. Few women had ever felt as married as she did, especially this night.

"We should ask Hobson to come for a visit whilst she's here," Jack suggested. "I sensed a potential attachment there."

Laurel laughed out loud. "You'd want Cornelia for a mother-in-law? I cannot believe it!"

Jack propped up one elbow and looked down at her. "I quite like her when she's fixed somewhere betwixt magpie and mute."

"So do I, but she's seldom at that average, is she!"

"Not often." Jack nuzzled Laurel's ear. "But she's a fine shot. We could use her every year at the autumn hunt."

"Jack! You are the worst ever to say such a thing! Never remind her of that horrid event or she'll sink back into her doldrums."

"Sorry," he muttered, obviously neither sorry, nor intent on discussing their guest any longer.

Laurel loved to tease him by making him wait. It drove him wild, and she rather craved wild at the moment. She took his wandering hand and threaded her fingers firmly through his. "We must get planning on the harvest festival right away."

"In the morning," he murmured, seeking her lips with his.

She dodged his kiss. "Then there's Betty and George's wedding to discuss, as well."

"Be practical *tomorrow*," he ordered gruffly.

She held fast, laughing at him when he would have extracted his hand from hers to continue caressing. "Not to mention the—"

"Heir," he interrupted, murmuring into her neck between increasingly hot and insistent kisses. "If we must do estate business tonight, let's dwell on getting the *heir*."

She wondered what excuse he would use to insist on instant lovemaking once the heir was conceived. Not that it mattered in the least, since he didn't really need an excuse to seduce her.

Laurel gave up the game with pleasure, welcoming him into her without preamble, loving the impatience and boundless energy that was such a part of Jack. There would be a time for quiet control later in the night and she would love that, too.

She loved *him* and knew that he loved her, without any reservation. Nothing in the world mattered more than that.

* * * * *